Praise for COGHEART

"Vivid and gripping…a beautifully-drawn world and delicate detailing, as finely wrought as a watch's workings."
Kiran Millwood Hargrave, author of *The Girl of Ink and Stars*

"A gem of a book."
Katherine Woodfine, author of *The Mystery of The Clockwork Sparrow*

"A delightfully badly behaved heroine, enthralling mechanicals and a stormer of a plot."
Abi Elphinstone, author of *The Dreamsnatcher*

"A classic adventure in every way I love – machines, Victoriana and high, pulse-pounding thrills. It's got real heart too."
Rob Lloyd Jones, author of *Wild Boy*

"One of my favourite debuts of the year. Murder, mystery and mayhem in a thrilling Victorian adventure."
Fiona Noble, *The Bookseller*

"A magical and thrilling story. Prepare yourself for the adventure of a lifetime, a truly stunning debut."
Jo Clarke, *Book Lover Jo*

"WONDERFUL…a blend of Philip Pullman, Joan Aiken and Katherine Rundell. Don't miss!"
Amanda Craig

"Wonderfully gripping."
Charlotte Eyre, *The Bookseller*

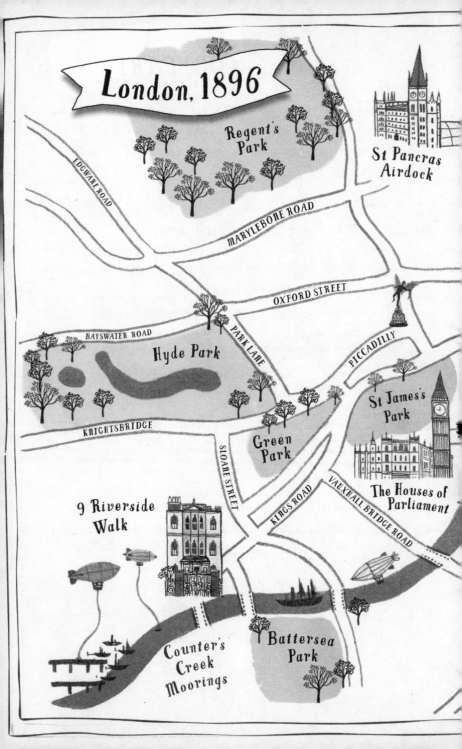

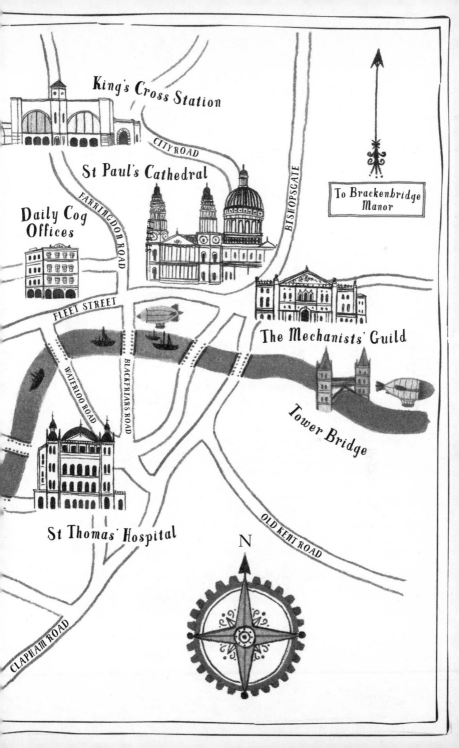

For Michael, with love.

First published in the UK in 2016 by Usborne Publishing Ltd., Usborne House,
83-85 Saffron Hill, London EC1N 8RT, England. www.usborne.com

Text © Peter Bunzl, 2016

Photo of Peter Bunzl © Thomas Butler

Cover and inside illustrations, including map by Becca Stadtlander ©
Usborne Publishing, 2016

Fir trees silhouettes © ok-sana / Thinkstock; Key © VasilyKovalek / Thinkstock; Brick wall ©
forrest9 / Thinkstock; Wind-up Key © jgroup / Thinkstock; Clock © Vasilius / Shutterstock; Hand
drawn border © Lena Pan / Shutterstock; Exposed clockwork © Jelena Aloskina / Shutterstock;
Metallic texture © mysondanube / Thinkstock; Plaque © Andrey_Kuzmin / Thinkstock; Burned
paper © bdspn / Thinkstock; Crumpled paper © muangsatun / Thinkstock; Newspaper © kraphix /
Thinkstock; Old paper © StudioM1 / Thinkstock; Coffee ring stains © Kumer / Thinkstock

A CIP catalogue record for this book is available from the British Library.

ISBN 9781474915007 03981/4

JFMAMJ ASOND/16

Printed in the UK.

COGHEART

PETER BUNZL

USBORNE

PROLOGUE

Malkin pressed his forepaws against the flight-deck window and peered out. The silver airship was still following; gaining on them. The purr of its propellers and the whoosh of its knife-sharp hull cutting through the air sent a shiver of terror through his clockwork innards.

The fox tore his eyes away and stared at his master. John's ship, *Dragonfly*, was fast but she had nothing in the way of firepower. The silver airship, by contrast, bristled with weapons. Sharp metal spikes stuck out from her hull, making her look like some sort of militarized porcupine.

Just then, *Dragonfly*'s rudder shifted, and she pitched

as John twisted the wheel into a one-eighty turn to swoop back past her pursuers.

The silver airship shrunk away, but within seconds she'd swung around to follow. She began closing in once more; her propellers chopping through the clouds, throwing dark shadows across their stern. When the two airships broke into a patch of blue, she fired.

A harpoon slashed across the sky and thudded into *Dragonfly*'s hull, the point piercing her port side.

Thud! Another harpoon speared into the stern.

Malkin let out a bark of alarm as a stench of burning gas filled the flight deck, and the needles in the rows of instrument panels flickered into the red danger zones. Over the whine of their stalling engines, the crackle of straining steel cables could be heard. The silver airship had begun to pull them in.

John locked *Dragonfly*'s wheel, and engaged her autopilot. He threw open the cockpit door and, with Malkin at his heels, dashed towards the engine room.

Pistons pumped, and crankshafts turned at full power, while the cabin juddered and shook. In the centre of the floor, a metal egg-shaped pod sat among a tangle of pipes.

John threw open its door. "No room for both of us," he said. "You go, Malkin."

The fox gave a whimper of disapproval. "No. It should be you, John. Humans over mechanicals. It's the law."

John shook his head. "I can't leave my ship; I need to try and guide her down safely – and you've no opposable thumbs!" He gave a half-hearted laugh and withdrew a battered envelope from his pocket. Crouching down, he stuffed it into a leather pouch around Malkin's neck. "This is for my Lily. See that she gets it."

"What's in there?"

John smiled. "Secrets. Tell her to keep them safe. She mustn't tell anyone about them, not ever. Can you remember that?"

"I think so." Malkin prodded the pouch, sniffing at it with his nose.

"Good," John said. "Make for Brackenbridge, that's where she'll be. If I get out of this alive, I'll come find her."

"Is there anything else?"

"And tell her I love her." John ruffled the mechanimal's ears one last time. "It's at least a day's journey from here, have you enough clicks?"

Malkin nodded.

"Take your winder anyway." John produced a tarnished key on a chain and hung it round the fox's neck, next to the pouch. "Though heaven knows who'll wind you if I'm not there."

"Thank you, John." Malkin stepped into the escape pod and curled up on the seat. "By all that ticks, I hope to see you again."

"And I you, old friend." John shut the door. With a clatter and hum the pod bay doors opened and in a jolt, the pod was free.

As John watched it through the open hatch, shrinking away in the sky, an image of his daughter, Lily, flashed into his mind. If only he could see her one last time. Tell her the truth about the past. He should've done it long ago, but he'd not been brave enough. Now Malkin would have to take care of things. Everything was in the letter.

Another harpoon smashed through *Dragonfly*'s hull, and whirring saw blades cut through the steel ribs, ripping cracks in the ship's tin chest. In a jagged screech, the cracks were wrenched into a doorway, and two silhouetted figures appeared. Their silver eyes glinted in the light. The thinner of the figures raised a stick with a skull handle, then John felt a blinding shaft of pain, and everything went black…

CHAPTER 1

Lily wrinkled her freckled nose as she trudged along at the back of the line of girls. With each step, her heart beat hard in her chest, and her green eyes flicked across the dog-eared pages of her beloved penny dreadful hidden inside her schoolbook.

She was enjoying a particularly gory scene in *Varney the Vampyre Versus The Air-Pirates*, where Varney had captured the heroine in the disused attic of an Italian boarding school and was preparing to feast on her blood.

Lily had her pencil poised to mark up the gruesomest passages of the magazine, so she could reread them later at her leisure. Another dubious volume, balanced on the crown of her head, wobbled with each step, but she didn't let it distract her from Varney.

"Heads up! Eyes straight!" With one copy of *The Oxford Guide to Perfect Poise* balanced on her head, Mrs McKracken, Lily's middle-aged deportment teacher, led the gaggle of girls in a circle around the Great Hall, her flat feet slapping across the polished wooden floor. The Kraken, Lily called her – though never to her face, that would be far too risky.

The Kraken was somewhat obsessed with posture. As for Lily, she barely gave it a second thought. In her opinion it was better to read books than balance them. That's what they were designed for, after all. And if you wanted to wear something on your head there was a perfectly good item designed for that too: it was called a hat.

Lily sneaked a brief glance at the other girls in her class. At the front of the line, Miss Lucretia Blackwell had her prim nose stuck in the air and three copies of *Sensible Etiquette for the Best Occasions* balanced on her perfectly coiffed hair.

Second came Miss Alice Harvey, who had seven copies of *Butterwick's Guide to Better Manners* balanced on her doughnut plait. With that monstrous hair-buncle, it was no surprise she never dropped a single copy.

Miss Gemma Ruddle was next. She had four precarious copies of *The Ladies' Manual of Politeness* balanced and would stop after each step and pretend to scratch her ear so she could adjust her leaning tower of literature.

Lily had long ago noticed the other girls never read in posture class. It seemed thinking and walking simultaneously was too difficult for them. She doubted a single important thought ever floated through their minds. If Spring-Heeled Jack, or Varney the Vampyre, or the air-pirates, or any of the other blackguards who roamed England, ever caught any of those girls in a dark alley they'd be dead for sure. Dead before they'd practised their conversational French, dead before they'd politely discussed the weather, or asked "Tea or coffee?"; in short, dead before their perfectly poised bodies struck the cobbles. And what use was deportment to one dead? No use. No use whatsoever.

"Stop," the Kraken yelled and one by one the girls stopped in a neat line behind her. All except Lily who, having failed to notice her untied shoelaces, tripped, stepped on Gemma's foot, and fell.

"Ouch!" Gemma staggered forward, clutching at Alice to try and keep her balance, but in vain; her four copies of *The Ladies' Manual of Politeness* slipped from her head.

"Careful!" Alice cried, dropping seven copies of *Butterwick's Guide to Better Manners*.

Thud-thud-thud-thud-thud-thud... Thud.

Lucretia wobbled from side to side, grasping at the top of her head, but she was too late. Three copies of *Sensible Etiquette for the Best Occasions* slipped from her brow and scattered at her feet in a *crash* of fluttering pages.

"Why don't you pay attention, you galumphing lump?" the Kraken shouted. "What've you got to say for yourself?"

Lily gazed up from the sea of fallen books. Was the woman talking to her? "Sorry?" she tried.

The Kraken huffed. "I said: *WHAT-HAVE-YOU-GOT-TO-SAY-FOR-YOURSELF?* Oh, never mind." She took *The Oxford Guide to Perfect Poise* from her head and threw it at Lily, who ducked as the heavy tome glanced past her ear.

"You've been reading. You're not allowed to read in my class—"

"I thought—"

"And no thinking either." The Kraken folded her arms across her chest. She'd turned a most putrid shade of puce; it perfectly matched her purple dress. Perhaps it was her tight corsets that made her face flush so?

The bell rang and the other girls scrabbled across the floor, grabbing their books and slamming them shut.

They piled the volumes on the Kraken's desk and lined up against the wall, waiting for the signal to leave.

"You may go," the Kraken said, waving them off with a hand, and the crocodile of young ladies filed out, whispering maliciously to one another. Lily dusted down her tights and stood to join them.

"Not you, Miss Grantham. I want words with you." The Kraken waddled towards her. "Why is it you think you can ignore my lessons in favour of these tall tales?" She plucked the schoolbook from Lily's hands and examined the gory magazine hidden inside its pages, paying particular attention to the image of a bloody corpse with bat wings.

"Where on earth did you get this balderdash?"

"Papa sent it in his last care package, Miss. He knows I like the penny dreadfuls."

"Does he indeed?" The Kraken looked unimpressed.

Lily continued. "He believes one should read a lot wider than deportment manuals if one plans to get an exceptional education. Don't you agree?"

The Kraken weighed the magazine in her hand. "No," she said. "I don't. Besides, this sort of bunkum is not approved of by the academy. It has no educational value."

"It teaches piracy and air combat."

"And what young lady needs to know that?" The

Kraken took a deep breath. "No. I'm afraid, Miss Grantham, I have to confiscate it. And if you've any similar stories, you'd better hand them over right away."

Lily shrugged. "I don't have a single other magazine of that kind."

"Nonsense. You've one there."

"I beg your pardon? Where?"

"The one you're hiding."

The Kraken craned her neck, trying to see what Lily had behind her back. Lily passed the magazine from her left hand to her right. "I don't know what you mean."

"Give it to me." The Kraken held out her shovel of a palm.

"Fine." Lily glowered, handing over *Spring-Heeled Jack and the Blackguards*.

"There. That wasn't so hard, was it?" The Kraken wedged both magazines under her sweaty armpit.

"No, Ma'am."

"Good." The Kraken handed Lily back her schoolbook. "Remember," she said, wagging a single finger, "if you've any more of these dreadful things you can be sure I'll find them. Now, run along, you don't want to be late for your next lesson. And straighten your pinny, it's wrinkled as an elephant's ear."

"Yes, Ma'am. Good afternoon, Ma'am." Lily brushed

at her creased pinny with ink-stained fingers and gave the Kraken a curtsy, but when the woman returned to her desk, Lily stuck her tongue out at her broad retreating backside. Then, with as much poise as she could muster, she flounced to the door and hurried off down the passage.

Miss Octavia Scrimshaw's Finishing Academy for Young Ladies was a cluster of wind-blown red-brick buildings that stood in a wild corner of England. The school was proud to proclaim its elegant reputation in the society papers under a scrolled coat of arms, but the truth was its reputation, like the buildings themselves, had steadily crumbled over the years and now was badly in need of repair.

Lily's father had chosen to send her to the school after she'd frustrated a number of governesses. His main criterion: it was out of the way and no one there would ask questions about her. He'd even given her a false surname: Grantham – a combination of G for Grace (from her mother), and Hartman – their real surname. He never explained why, or what he was trying to hide her from, but since the time of Mama's death he'd become preoccupied with keeping Lily's whereabouts a secret, even moving them from London to deep in the countryside. Lily suspected he was just a natural born worrier, though he still insisted she have the life of a normal well-bred Victorian young lady.

The trouble was, Lily reflected, as she sneaked up the last set of stairs to the girls' dormitory, she didn't want the life of a well-bred Victorian young lady, she wanted the life of an air-pirate.

Which was why, after her run-in with the Kraken, she decided to skip French conversation class and hide her remaining stash of penny dreadfuls before they were confiscated or worse, destroyed – like every other vaguely interesting or illicit thing in this institution.

The dormitory door was locked, but she knew how to deal with that. She took a hairpin from her bun of red hair, straightened it in her teeth, and popped it in the keyhole. Then she wiggled the pin about, while turning the doorknob. It was a trick she'd practised many times, first learned from *The Notorious Jack Door: Escapologist and Thief Extraordinaire* – the book, not the man himself. Although she wouldn't have minded having a few words with him about advanced lock-picking if they ever bumped into one another. Anyway, according to Jack, all you had to do was listen out for the—

Click!

There it was. Quietly, Lily pulled open the door and crept into the dormitory, her boots squeaking across the floorboards. Ticking radiators warmed the room, and Lily heard the voices of the other girls chanting French verbs in the downstairs classroom. A pale November sun hung above the opposite buildings, sneaking occasional beams of light in through the frost-covered windows to caress her face.

Lily stopped beside her bed and pulled her penny dreadfuls from the drawer of her side table; she was about to push them under her mattress when she heard a faint muffled sobbing.

She glanced about. It seemed the dorm wasn't empty after all. Through a thin dividing curtain at the end of the row of beds, Lily glimpsed the silhouette of a hunched figure sitting on the corner of a mattress. She walked over and peered round the edge of the drape to find Molly Tarnish, the mechanical maid, sitting softly crying to herself, her metal shoulders shaking beneath her starched white pinny. Beyond her, the door to the servants' staircase stood ajar.

Molly raised her head and snuffled away an oily tear. "Sorry, Miss. I didn't hear you come in. I should probably go."

"Oh, no need," Lily said. "I'm not supposed to be

here either." She pulled a grubby handkerchief from her sleeve and handed it to Molly, who blew her nose with a sound as loud as a steamhorn.

"Thank you," Molly mumbled, returning the hanky to Lily.

"Please, pay it no mind." Lily stuffed the damp rag, now covered in engine oil, back into her blouse sleeve. "But whatever's the matter?"

Molly held up a bright pink sheet from a pile behind her. "I put these in the washer with the school blazers and they all changed colour. Miss Scrimshaw's going to kill me when she finds out. She'll have me sent down the cog-and-bone merchants. Or worse, she'll strip me parts and melt me down like poor old Elsie." Molly burst into more inconsolable tears.

Lily patted her back. "Don't cry, Moll. We'll think of something. Maybe I could write to the school board on your behalf?"

Molly gave another choking sob. "Oh, please, Miss, don't get them involved, I beg you."

"Well, all right then." Lily examined the row of iron bedsteads, thinking. "I know," she said, "why don't we use your dyed sheets on the bottom of the beds, then we can use the old white ones as top sheets to hide them?"

Molly sniffed. "D'you really think so?"

"I don't see why not," Lily replied. "Come on." She unfolded a pink sheet and pulled the covers off the nearest bed. Molly watched her for a moment, then stood to help.

Working together, it didn't take them long to change the majority of the beds, and once the blankets were on you could hardly tell the bottom sheets had been dyed the wrong colour. They'd nearly finished, and were making up the last mattress at the top of the dormitory, when a noise made them both whirl round.

Alice Harvey was standing in the doorway with Lucretia Blackwell, their faces scrunched into sneers.

"Look, Miss Harvey," Lucretia said. "Lily's helping the help."

"What are you doing here?" Lily asked.

"Madame Laroux told us to bring you to class," Alice replied. "We're doing chapter twenty-two in *The Art of Making Polite Conversation* in French."

"I'm not coming," Lily told her. "I don't feel like it. Anyway, Madame wouldn't know polite conversation if it bit her on the behind." She threw a sideways glance at Molly, who bowed her head and stifled a wheezing laugh.

"How dare you!" Lucretia grabbed the last of the

sheets from Molly, and threw them on the floor. "Look what you've done, you stupid mech, you've dyed them pink!"

"I'm sorry, Miss," Molly mumbled back.

Lily balled her fists. "Why don't you leave her alone?" she said, stepping forward to shield Molly from the two girls.

"What business is it of yours?" Alice asked.

"She's a friend of mine."

"She? *SHE?*" Lucretia folded her arms across her chest and gave a disdainful laugh. "It's not alive, Lily. Mechs aren't living."

"Besides," Alice scuttled closer to Lucretia, "everyone knows mechs and humans can't be friends. Mechs have no feelings."

Lily sighed. It was exhausting dealing with such idiots. "Don't be ridiculous," she told them. "Of course they have feelings. They're no different to you or me."

Lucretia tutted at her. "Oh, Lily, Lily, how wrong you are. Let me show you." She whipped out a hand and struck Molly round the head.

Molly's eyes flared, but she didn't respond.

"You see?" Lucretia said. "It didn't even flinch."

Creakily, Molly rubbed her head. She bent down and gathered her dropped sheets and stepped to the servants' door. "Please, Misses, don't fight on my account. I am sorry, but I must go, I've work to do."

"Go then, mech," Lucretia spat. "Run along, before you're thrown on the scrap heap." She smiled triumphantly at Alice.

Lily had never wanted to hit anyone so much – she could barely stop herself. But she did, because she'd made a promise to Papa to behave, and behaving meant not causing trouble. Even so, as she ground her teeth and watched Molly hurry from the room, the anger ticked away inside her chest, threatening to explode.

Lucretia gave a haughty snigger, and Alice joined in.

Finally, Lily could take it no more – there was not causing trouble, and then there was standing up for what was right. Because mechanicals deserved to be treated like anyone else.

"Listen, you pair of simpering, fat-headed dolts," she said, "if you ever speak to Molly that way again I'll…I'll…"

"You'll what?" Alice sneered. "Don't *you* threaten me."

Lily bit her lip and thought better of her reply. Alice broke into a horsey smile. "See, you snotty little runt? You won't do anything – and that's the truth. Just because you're a mech-lover you think you can boss us around.

Well, you can't. Now, apologize immediately and we'll forget the whole thing."

Lily shook her head. "You'll never apologize to Molly, so I'm not apologizing to you."

"As you wish." Alice lunged at Lily, making a grab for her hair. Lily ducked away and the girl's hand scratched at her collar, pulling at her bun. She tried to push back, but Lucretia had joined in with her friend – she'd got a hold of Lily's other arm, and wouldn't let go.

Alice's long nails raked at Lily's scalp, scratching her ears. There was nothing for it, she would have to retaliate. She swung her balled fist at Alice's face.

Crack. Her knuckles made contact.

"I said I was sorry," Lily protested as the Kraken dragged her down the corridor, pulling her along by the scruff of her blouse. "Besides, she hit me first."

"Nonsense," the Kraken blustered. "Anyone can see she has the complexion of a bruised beetroot."

"Her face always looks a bit purply."

"What lies you tell, child."

They passed the main entrance, and Lily glanced at the Academy's motto carved in the granite lintel. *Vincit Omnia Veritas* – Truth Conquers All.

Not in this case, Lily reflected, as the Kraken manhandled her down a flight of stone steps, and out into the courtyard.

In the quad, girls in thick winter blousons and woollen hats and scarves strolled arm in arm, or perched birdlike on benches, their backs as straight as ironing boards. They whispered behind gloved hands as they watched the Kraken shove Lily down a narrow alley on the far side of the square.

Everyone knew where *that* led – past the row of tumbledown sheds and an outside latrine with flaky wood panelling, past a high wall fringed with crenellations of broken bottles, all the way to the coal bunker crouched in the far corner of the grounds, its doorway dark as a demon's mouth.

Rumour had it the bodies of the worst offending former residents were buried in that bunker, and when the coal ran dry their white bones would be revealed, poking from the dust.

"Please, Mrs McKracken," Lily cried, "don't put me in there, I'm afraid of the dark."

"Rubbish. The dark never hurt anyone." The Kraken unlocked the bunker and pushed Lily inside. "If you insist on behaving like a common chimney sweep, then you will have to live like one. Never speak back to those older and wiser than you. You'll stay in here until you learn the value of manners."

The Kraken's angry face disappeared with the slit of light as she slammed the door, and Lily heard the snap of the padlock and then her heavy footsteps lurching away across the yard.

Alone in the cold, dark bunker, fear pricked at Lily's heart. She felt around her, her hands brushing icy lumps of coal. Against the far wall, she found a wonky stool; she sat upon it, and it rocked back and forth precariously – one leg rotten. When she tried to put her feet on the crossbar, she discovered that was broken too, so she pulled her knees up onto the seat and hugged them to her. Their warmth, tight in her chest, felt mildly comforting.

Something crawled across her ankle and she brushed it away with the tip of her boot. Faint scuttlings echoed around the space and she tried not to think of all the horrible things it might be. Earwigs, spiders, mice, rats… But, as her eyes adjusted to the darkness, she saw something far worse: a dismembered arm, sticking out from beneath the pile of coal.

CHAPTER 2

Malkin ran for a long time; taking care to keep out of sight, he zigzagged between the trees in short bursts. He had to put as much distance between himself and the crash site as possible. He needed to get to Lily and give her John's last message, before his ticks ran out.

The sun had long gone and the air was thick with grey mist, its cold dew clinging to his fur in droplets. Bushes shook their damp leaves as he brushed past and, far above, the hulking engines of the silver airship chugged in unison, while its searchlight swept the forest looking for him.

He reached the trunk of an old oak and stopped under cover of its ivy-swollen canopy; his black eyes glinted in the haze, taking in the murky view. Ahead, the path was strewn with broken branches, and those spiky bushes whose burrs always caught in his tail fur. He twitched his nose in disgust. Perhaps he should turn back, go another way… But his senses told him the men were following, so he pressed on, treading carefully.

The ground was boggy and as he ran beads of mud squished between his claws and spattered the pouch round his neck. He was leaving paw prints that could easily be tracked – practically marking his route for them – he cursed the damp ground, the foul weather, the men, the airship, everything. He was a precision machine. Not built for this kind of adventure. The indignity of it: to be chased through the woods like a common scavenger!

More prickly bushes – they were everywhere.

He found a gap in the corner of a thicket and squeezed through.

A tunnel ran under dense vegetation for a few feet, then opened out into a narrow track, scattered with droppings. He stopped to sniff them – an old fox trail, but it had obviously not been used in a while.

He ran on, the undergrowth thickening around him once more. A solid arm of bramble blocked his path. He wiggled past it, and its fiendish barbs caught his leg – this was intolerable!

He scrambled onwards, glancing about. Now he was further into the woods the airship's searchlight was no longer visible and the hum of its engines had subsided. Far off, a distant owl let out a warning cry.

The harsh sounds of the men's voices and the barking of their wretched dog suddenly came close, echoing around him; then their lanterns appeared among the trees nearby, hovering like fat fireflies, and winking as they passed behind the trunks.

Malkin glanced briefly over his shoulder and counted the lamps. There were three in total. But there would be more men than that – one would be handling the dog, others weapons. They had descended from the airship like a swarm.

He skirted round a deep gully filled with rainwater; then a large millpond. The hulking silhouette of a derelict watermill sat on its far side.

He wished he could hurl himself in and paddle across, but he knew mechanimals and swallowing water should never mix. John had warned him: only a pint or two was enough to rust his insides.

John. He was gone now. Probably burned to death or worse inside *Dragonfly*'s tin belly. The thought of it made the cogs of Malkin's innards turn queasily.

On the far side of the pond he scrambled over a mossy

outcrop of boulders; tripped on a root, and tumbled forward, slamming into a pile of damp leaves.

He must concentrate. Time enough to think about John later.

He stood and shook off the leaf-dust, checked the pouch around his neck – it was still there, thank tock.

The dog barked closer. Mechanical barks, much deeper than his own.

Then the gruff voices of the men came through the winter air, from behind the pile of rocks.

"I think he went this way. Bracken's trampled."

"Here too. There's tracks by the water's edge."

"Keep looking. He's close by."

Malkin caught a glimpse of something – a fat black silhouette, with silver eyes, pointing towards him through the trees – and glanced around for somewhere to hide. He was in a hollow with only a few bare logs around. He had to keep moving.

He crawled forward, slinking across the clearing, keeping his belly low to the ground and checking for twigs which might snap under his weight.

He smelled them approaching, heard their feet climbing the boulders. Their clanking mech-dog barked ferociously and pulled forward, but the men kept him leashed. Lucky there was so much fog, or they would've let the dog run for sure.

"This way."

"I thought I heard him."

"He was here a moment ago."

Malkin scrambled over a bank, sliding behind a line of trees. As he darted across a gap between two bushes, he risked a glance back.

The mech-dog must have caught a brief flash of his white neck; it strained at the leash and bounded towards him, pulling its handler along behind.

Malkin picked up pace. He was at least thirty feet ahead of them now – or so he thought, through the fog. He needed to keep his distance.

He jumped a trickling stream and wove through a line of firs – let those stupid meatheads try and follow him here. Ahead, the gaps between the trees became wider, patches of grey mist separated the trunks and their number thinned; he glimpsed the last few firs standing alone in a sea of bracken, pushed up against a wooden fence that flowed into an adjoining field.

He crept out of the woods and waded through the tall ferns, arriving at a break in the fence. Tucking his tail in, he shimmied under a crossbar, and stepped out into an empty field.

It was colder out here, and the frosted topsoil meant his paws would leave no prints. He had to be careful on open ground, but the dense fog made for adequate hiding.

He stepped forward warily. In the distance, between the grey patches of air, he spotted the outline of a drystone wall and the hint of a cart track.

The voices were getting close again, but the field wasn't as big as he'd first thought and there was every chance he could reach the other side before they arrived. He took a diagonal path across its centre, running briskly.

Halfway across, the airship's searchlight blasted on above him, cutting the sky in two with a bright white column. Its engines pushed swathes of fog away, and suddenly he was exposed, his bright shape singing out against the landscape.

A crackle of gunfire.

Malkin glanced back.

"Stop there!" The silhouette with silver eyes emerged from the wood, and raised a steam-rifle.

Malkin froze, facing his enemy. His heart thrumming against his ribcage. Slowing time.

He stared, unblinking, at the mirrors in the dark face, trying to make out any flicker of expression in them.

The man let out a blast of breath. Malkin shuffled

backwards, slowly widening the distance between them. Was he really going to shoot?

The man squinted into his gunsight, taking aim, and brought his finger to the trigger. Malkin turned and ran, hoping the density of the fog would be enough to save him...

Crack!

A searing explosion pierced his shoulder.

The ground dipped under him. He rolled forward, somersaulting across the icy surface, spinning to a stop at the base of the field. The airship's searchlight flashed wildly around him, picking out circles of frost in the grass. A ghostly after-image of those mirrored eyes burned in his field of vision. He shook it away.

The men's long shadows chased across the open field towards him, lamplights floating before them.

"He's down!"

"I think you got him."

"I can't see where he's at. Where'd he go?"

Malkin staggered to his feet, shell-shocked, and limped towards the boundary wall. The dog, freed from its leash, barked and leaped after him; the men ran with it, firing wildly. The mirror-eyed shooter lagged behind, trying to reload his rifle, while others, without weapons, waved lanterns at the airship.

Malkin reached the wall, and slumped over it, tumbling onto the track beyond, loose stones scattering in his wake. He struggled to his feet and loped on.

Pain seared sharply through his shoulder. He rubbed his snout against it, feeling for an exit wound, but found none. The bullet must be lodged somewhere deep inside, like a stone in a paw. He heard the men's distant shouts – they hadn't given up. At least he still had his pouch. He couldn't let them have that.

The track branched in two and Malkin chose the left fork at random. He slowed, hobbling onwards, looking for an outhouse or barn where he could hide, but there was nothing. He was running out of tocks. Pretty soon he'd wind down – and if that happened in the open they'd be sure to catch him.

Suddenly, around the next corner, a cottage appeared; beyond it, dotted in the distance, were more. Brackenbridge village – he was nearly home. If he could just get to the other side safely…

He checked the pouch one last time for John's letter, and was relieved to find it still there. He'd made a promise to get it to Lily, for it contained great secrets. The last words of a father to his daughter was the sort of message one should deliver no matter the cost. And now his master was gone, Malkin was determined not to fail.

CHAPTER 3

Robert Townsend woke before the alarm sounded and lay listening in the dark. Something had disturbed his sleep – a noise outside. A distant but distinct *crack*. He glanced at the hands of the clock on the nightstand.

Twenty to six.

Crack. Crack. Crack.

There it was again. What on earth could it be?

Robert jumped out of bed and stepped across the cold boards to the window. Pulling back the curtain, he wiped the condensation from the glass with the sleeve of his nightshirt and peered out.

The village was empty. He scanned the nearby

countryside, searching for the source of the sound.

In the distance, behind a line of trees, a beam of light cut through the mist and came swooping across the fields – the arc lamp of an airship. A big one by the looks of it, and unusual for this time of the morning.

Robert knew every flight schedule by heart. Whenever he wasn't working he loved to visit the local airstation which served Brackenbridge and the surrounding area. He'd spot the zeps coming in along the airways, watch the fly boys in their goggles and leather helmets carrying their toolboxes, and the passengers dressed in smart travel clothes queuing on the gangways. One day, he vowed, he'd go up there with them, if he could only overcome his fear of heights.

This airship felt different. From its size and path, Robert had a feeling it was not a scheduled flight. When the mist separated, revealing the rest of the craft, he knew for sure he was right. He couldn't see its name or mark, but the ship had the look of a military model. Its silver reflective balloon seemed to suck in the moonlight, a harpoon gun stuck out from a hatch in its hull, and the front of its gondola was covered in metal spikes.

Suddenly the zep shut off its searchlight and changed course, climbing higher into the clouds. A popping sequence of musket flashes flared across a nearby field and Robert watched three flickering lamps emerge from the woods and float down the hillside. They gathered in the valley, and turned along the track towards the village.

Something was going on and he had to know what it was. He grabbed his trousers from where they hung on the end of the bedstead; jumped into them and snapped the braces on over his nightshirt.

As he struggled into his winter coat, he took one last look out the window. Lucky he did, or he would've missed the fox.

It tottered along the lane, throwing nervous glances over its shoulder. When it reached the green it stopped and swayed, glancing about, and its eyes alighted on the line of shops under Robert's window. Robert had the strangest feeling it was reading the sign for his da's shop, but that couldn't be, could it?

The fox nodded to itself and limped onwards. It passed the church and the walled graveyard beside the village green, then stumbled into Pincher's Alley – a scrubby track that ran behind a row of terraced airstation workers' cottages.

Robert waited for its shambling shape to emerge onto the bare field at the alley's far end, but it did not appear. It must've hidden down the lane somewhere, in one of the cottages' backyards. He decided to go look for it.

He threw on his socks and shoes and took the candle from his bedside, then he opened the door and crept along the hallway, treading softly so as not to wake his da in the next room.

At the base of the stairs he drew back the rag curtain and crept into the shop.

The familiar smell of beeswax furniture polish and the quiet ticking of the clocks made him linger as he crossed the floor. Each clock's shape and sound was so ingrained in him they felt as comforting as old friends. On nights when he couldn't sleep he often came down to watch the clocks and listen to their ticking; but not tonight. He put up a hand to silence the bell, opened the door, and stepped into the street.

A grey haze hung in the air, along with the pillowy silence of early morning. Far off, the barking of a dog echoed across the fields. He could've been the only human alive in the world.

First, he made his way over to the place where the fox had stopped and stared up at the shop. There, on the cold ground, among the patches of couch grass, he found a tiny cog.

It resembled those he was used to seeing in the carriage clocks his da let him repair, only this one was bent out of shape and covered in warm engine oil, viscous as drying blood. Robert knew it could mean only one thing: the fox was clockwork – a mechanimal.

He wiped the cog on his trousers and put it in his pocket, then he set off across the village, following the mech's route.

He passed the church and was about to turn off behind the airstation workers' cottages, down Pincher's Alley, when he heard footsteps in the lane behind.

He turned to see a large leashed dog, an unusual breed, like an Alsatian but bigger. As it came closer he saw its skin was covered in rivets. A mech-dog, then. It was followed by four men in long overcoats, carrying steam-rifles and lanterns – like those he'd seen from his window.

He shuffled aside to let them pass but they gathered round, letting their mech-dog sniff at him. When it got a good noseful of the oily mark on his trouser leg, it let out a low growl.

"Shut it!" one of the men told the mechanimal.

"Seen anything go past?" another asked Robert.

"Anything unusual?" added a third.

The fourth man didn't say anything, merely glared.

Robert decided not to answer their questions. He didn't like the look of them.

A big fellow with ginger mutton-chop sideburns

arrived, carrying a steam-rifle. His body looked lumpen, like a sack of rocks. He resembled a crusher, only without the policeman's helmet; above his upturned collar his cheeks were as red as bulging blood sausages.

But what made Robert gulp was the pair of silver mirrors sewn into the raw sockets of the man's eyes. Scars emanated from them, criss-crossing his cheeks, and running up under the brim of his hat.

"Who are you?" the man demanded, peering down a vein-blistered nose, until Robert's face appeared, reflected, in his mirrored eyes.

Robert's words dried in his throat. He took a deep breath. "I live here, Sir," he finally managed to wheeze.

"My colleagues asked if you'd seen anything unusual go past." The mutton-chopped man scratched at his eye socket, perilously close to his mirrored right eye.

"What kind of a thing?" Robert asked, his voice a strangled whisper.

"A fox." The mutton-chopped man pressed his thick lips together tightly. It seemed as if he was about to reveal something more, but then he decided against it. "Never mind." He jabbed a podgy finger at Robert. "Get back to your house."

"I saw your fox run that way," Robert blurted, pointing down the street that led out of town.

"You're certain?" The mutton-chopped man's mirrors betrayed nothing, but he didn't seem convinced. He glanced down at the dog straining on its leash; pulling towards the alley.

"Oh yes," Robert answered. "I watched it from my window."

"Which window?"

"One over there." He waved at the row of shops on the other side of the village, keeping it vague, in case the men were thinking of returning.

The mutton-chopped man nodded. "Thanks, lad. We'll be getting along, and you should too. A young boy like you oughtn't to be out on a cold November morning when there's danger about." He turned to go, and the others and the dog followed.

Robert dawdled on his way home, watching them, making sure they took the path he'd suggested. They hurried through the village, but when they reached the last house on the left they stopped, confused. The dog seemed to have lost the scent and wandered about aimlessly, trying to pick it up.

For a moment it seemed they would come back, but then the animal pulled them onwards. When they passed the last fence of the village, a black steam-wagon appeared at the edge of the woods, smoke puffing from its chimney stack. The mutton-chopped man pointed towards it, giving instructions, and the group split, the other four men making off down the road with their dog, while he walked back into town.

Robert decided to make himself scarce. He'd go look for the fox later when the mutton-chopped fellow was gone. Besides, he had chores to do before opening time. Better to get on.

As he trudged back to the clockmaker's shop, the low morning sun shone against its frontage, burning off the last of the mist and making the clocks in the window gleam.

Robert's family had owned Townsend's Horologist's for five generations. Its plain facade and classic sign did nothing to suggest the shrine of timepieces inside. Carriage clocks, pendulum clocks, cuckoo clocks and barometers covered every inch of wall, and at the back stood an old grandfather clock with a gold pendulum which had once belonged to Robert's grandfather. Front and centre was a panelled counter with a heavy silver till, behind which Robert spent most of his days.

When the sun shone, as it did this morning, the glass-covered clocks threw patterns of light around the walls, and every day, irrespective of weather, they filled the shop with their ticking, their different timbres giving the place a percussive music all of its own.

Robert's da, Thaddeus Townsend, moved in time to this beat while he worked. A short man with delicate features, his watery blue eyes were enlarged by the thick magnifying glasses he wore to adjust the timepieces.

People came to Thaddeus with all kinds of odd repairs. Not only watches and clocks, but other devices too: barometers, chronometers, musical snuff boxes, sometimes even simple mechanicals; and Thaddeus would take these things apart and attempt to fix them.

If a machine intrigued him, he often took on the work for cost. A skilled mechanist and engraver, and a dab hand at touching up miniatures, he enjoyed telling people how there was as much art in clockwork as in a beautiful sculpture or painting. His customers liked him because he cared. They came from all over the county to take advantage of his abilities and never paid what the labour was worth.

His da had so much talent, Robert wished he'd shut up shop and move them somewhere where people would pay fairly for their work. Or, he'd have dearly loved it if they could fix engines at the airstation, or restore old mechanimals, but Thaddeus preferred the quiet life of Townsend's Horologist's.

As things stood, Robert felt destined to be a clockmaker's apprentice for ever, which was a shame because he was simply no good at it.

A bumbler – all thumbs and fingers: that was how he thought of himself. He was thirteen now and, no matter how hard he worked, he could never manage the delicacy required for repairing the miniature mechanisms – or for dealing with the customers, come to that.

It hadn't always been so. As a child he'd been an enthusiastic pupil, nimble and quick, always wanting to learn things, but in recent years, he found he'd grown clumsy. Constantly misplacing tools, or dropping important cogs down the cracks in the floorboards.

This very morning, a mere hour after all the excitement with the men and the fox, he had broken a valuable carriage clock. Overwound it while he daydreamed about the mechanimal and the airship, and when he looked up he found the clock's teeth had sheered into the barrel mechanism.

"How many times do I have to tell you?" Thaddeus asked (for what at Robert's count was the hundred-and-thirteenth time). "It's seven-and-a-half turns – one wind is seven-and-a-half-turns." His da never usually raised his voice, but he did on this occasion. "Now I'll have to strip down the barrel and overhaul it. Why, the new parts alone will cost me more than my fee."

"I'm sorry," Robert mumbled, "I must've miscounted."

Thaddeus took off his glasses and pinched the bridge of his nose. "Few things in life are as fragile as clockwork, Robert. Learn to be more careful."

Robert sighed and Thaddeus squeezed his shoulder. "Never mind, we'll make a clockmaker of you yet. But perhaps you'd better work behind the counter today, for a while, until you get your confidence back."

Robert did as he was told, but a while turned into two long hours, then nearly three, and the whole time the fox and the airship and the mutton-chopped man with the mirrored eyeballs whirred around his mind like clockwork.

Finally, after work, when he had a few spare minutes to himself, Robert put on his thick coat and cap and scarf, and set out across the village.

He passed the walled graveyard and chapel and the terraced airstation cottages on their cobbled street, before arriving at Pincher's Alley once more.

He cut down along the scrubby track without a second thought. The rear windows of the cottages were dark. Robert glanced along the line of high back walls, looking for a place where he thought an injured fox might hide. Halfway up the lane, he noticed a gate ajar.

Behind the gate was an old wooden shed, whose roof poked up over the line of walls. In there would be just the spot for a frightened fox. Robert stepped through the gate and crossed the yard, squeezing past a pile of rusted farm equipment to approach the shed.

The lock had been broken off; recently, by the look of it, for the hasp hung loose by a couple of screws and the patch of wood above the doorknob was gnawed with toothmarks and freshly exposed. Robert opened the door and, taking care to cover his mouth against the dust, crept inside.

Oddments of wood leaned against walls covered in peeling paint. Piles of newspapers lined a row of shelves, and the floor was strewn with packing cases. On an old table in the centre of the space, bottles clustered in glassy gangs, and above them cobwebs thick as knitting hung like hammocks in the dark apex of the roof.

Robert looked around for the fox and saw its threadbare tail sticking out from behind a stack of boxes.

He stepped round an old steamer trunk and caught sight of the rest of the animal curled up on the corner of a faded water-stained mattress. It was a scruffy-looking beast with glassy eyes and careworn fur that looked like it was moulting in patches. A pouch, and the mechanimal's unique winding key were hung around its neck. Robert crept towards it, but it didn't move a twitch. It was frozen still. Unwound.

CHAPTER 4

The coal bunker was freezing. Lily rubbed her goosefleshed arms. Gradually, as her eyes adjusted further, she began to see more clearly. The space was not pitch black after all; in fact a dim light came in through a mesh-covered ceiling vent.

The arm, sticking out from the pile of coal, glinted in the soft glow. It was not human, as Lily had first supposed, but an old broken mech limb. It must've belonged to some poor servant who'd got the chop. How horrible!

Though it said one thing: no matter how bad life got, mechanicals had it worse. Lily stared at a cluster of dusty handprints on the concrete wall beside her: evidence of the bunker's past prisoners – miscreants all!

She'd never fit in at this hateful school. Whenever she did something exuberant she was punished for it. Admittedly punching Alice had been a step too far – the other girls were sure to have it in for her now. But she needn't worry, she only had to survive a few more weeks, and then, at the end of term, Papa would come to collect her.

Time drifted by, the light fading. Lily became vaguely aware of the crunch of footsteps coming closer. Yellow light slivered through the door slats, and when she heard a key turn in the lock she lifted her chin from her knees.

The door creaked open to reveal not the Kraken, whom she was expecting, but Gemma Ruddle – one of her annoying classmates – carrying a tallow candle.

Lily shaded her eyes and stared at Gemma, who giggled with embarrassment.

"Why, Lily, you look dirty as a duster."

"Is my punishment over?" Lily asked. Cold and grim, she was in no mood for such teasing.

"I don't know about that," Gemma said. "All I know is Miss Scrimshaw requests your presence in her study right away. I'm to take you to her."

"What does she want, I wonder?"

Gemma smirked. "Gracious, I've no idea. Would you like me to go back and ask her?" Then, without waiting for a reply, she trundled off down the narrow alley, back towards the school. Lily ducked through the doorway, pondering this worrying new revelation as she followed the candlelight and the smokey scent of burning pig fat that trailed behind Gemma.

They walked up the entrance steps and into the main corridor of the school, where Gemma blew out her candle, for the space was well lit with wall-mounted gas lamps.

Passing beneath one, Lily noticed her hands were flecked with coal dust; she looked around for a curtain or some chintzy upholstery to wipe them on, but there was nothing and Gemma kept marching on. In the end she decided to settle for the underside of her pinny and hoped Miss Scrimshaw would not inspect her appearance too closely, which was something the eagle-eyed headmistress was often wont to do.

"Here we are." Gemma ushered Lily to a bench outside Miss Scrimshaw's office. "You're to wait here until she calls you," she said primly, and before Lily could reply she sloped off, smirking.

Lily was about to sit down when she noticed the soles of her boots had left dusty marks along the hall carpet. She quickly scuffed them away with her toe, then took her seat and waited to be called.

Fifteen minutes passed with not a peep from the study. What was taking them so long? Were they trying to conceive of some terrible new chastisement? A cold thought struck her: maybe they were planning her murder, then they'd sell her organs to the bodysnatchers – just like the ones in her penny dreadfuls! Or perhaps they planned a fate worse than death? Perhaps she was to be finally expelled.

She edged towards the door and pressed her ear to the panelling, trying to hear what was being said inside. It was hard to make out because the thick oak surface muffled the sounds of the room.

"It's a terrible state of affairs, I must concur," Miss Scrimshaw was saying, "but the truth is I'll be glad to get her off our hands – she's been quite difficult of late."

"She's been difficult since she got here," the Kraken replied.

And then Lily heard another woman's voice – a sing-song foreign accent she couldn't quite place. "She always was an unruly child," the voice said. "Some might say understandably, considering her past. She's been hidden and forced to live a lie – her name, you understand. Professor Hartman's wishes, of course. I'm not so sure myself – there are always these excuses, *n'est-ce pas?* She's bound to be worse, *maintenant*, with this terrible new turn of events. So, I thought it best to take her out of the school, until things are settled."

What things? What turn of events? Who was this person who knew her real name? Lily pressed her ear harder against the wood, but the voices had dipped to a hushed tone.

She had to hear more; if only there was a glass or something to put against the panel. She took a step back and, glancing round the lobby, spotted a vase filled with dried flowers, which stood on a side table. That would do.

She tipped the flowers onto the table and was about to put the rim of the vase to the door, when, at that very moment, it opened and the Kraken appeared.

Her bulging eyes took in what Lily was up to. But, instead of telling her off, she merely took the vase and, offering the briefest of sympathetic smiles, ushered her into the headmistress's office, closing the door behind her.

Miss Scrimshaw was sitting at her mahogany desk consulting a letter. Her hair was scraped into its customary bell-jar shape and she wore a black dress with a dark blue ribboned collar. She glanced nervously at Lily, before her eyes darted away. "Miss Grantham – or Hartman, should I say. Thank you for coming. Kindly take a seat."

Lily walked across the expansive room towards the two high-backed chairs facing the desk. A woman in a voluminous black dress occupied one, her bony hands clasped in her lap. Though her face was obscured by the chair's headrest, her unctuous perfume filled the room with its sharp overripe scent. Lily knew at once who she was.

"Madame Verdigris, what are you doing here?"

Her father's housekeeper leaned forward and gave Lily a wan smile, half-hidden under a black gauze veil which covered her face. "*Bonjour, chérie.*"

"Madame Verdigris has some news about your father," said Miss Scrimshaw.

Straight away, Lily sensed it was something bad. So much black taffeta and poised concern: it was like the months in London, after Mama's death. Surely it couldn't be that, could it? Not Papa too? She felt bile rise in her throat, and dug her nails into her palms.

"What's happened?" she asked.

Madame Verdigris shook her head sadly. "*Ma petite*, I'm sorry to have to tell you this, but your father is missing. His airship crashed yesterday, flying home."

"Perhaps you'd better take a seat?" Miss Scrimshaw suggested, but Lily ignored her, gasping for breath.

"*C'est terrible*," Madame's melodious voice continued.

"The police, they have investigated the scene: but there was no body, only the remains of his ship. He has *disparu*, and we have now to presume he is...dead."

"Oh no..." Lily grasped for the chair, but it seemed to slide sideways. The women's concerned faces swept away in a blur and the floor lurched up to meet her.

Silence.

A square wooden box.

A flash of white melting snow.

The crack of breaking glass.

A sharp pungent smell, mixed with a brittle perfume.

Lily opened her eyes and the haze coagulated into Miss Scrimshaw's office. She must've fainted.

She was lying on the carpet, with Madame Verdigris kneeling over her, clutching a vial of smelling salts. She coughed and sat up, rubbing the sting from her eyes.

"*Bien, chérie*," Madame said. "Lucky, I had these." She wiped her hands on a lace handkerchief and stuffed the vial away in her clutch bag.

"Why you?" Lily asked woozily. They'd been halfway through some sort of conversation. "Why have you come?"

"We can discuss this on the journey."

"Journey? Where are we going?"

"Why, home to Brackenbridge, *bien sûr*," Madame said sniffily. She stood and brushed down the front of her dress.

"But I was to meet Papa," Lily said, "and Malkin." A sickening dizziness swirled around her once more, until she felt terribly confused. "Papa promised to take me flying…on *Dragonfly*." Tears came to her eyes, and she pulled the oily hanky from her cuff to wipe her face. "At the end of term, they're coming…he wants to fly me home."

"*Mais non*," Madame said, "obviously such things won't be happening. We are going home by public zep, *aujourd'hui* and we will have to hurry to catch the late one. And you will wait at the house with me until we receive news of your father, or until his body is discovered at the crash site."

"Good. That's settled then." Miss Scrimshaw took up the bell from her desk, and rang. Within moments the door opened and the Kraken appeared.

"Ah, Mrs McKracken," said the headmistress, "please could you ask Matron to help Lily and Madame Verdigris pack her things? I think her travelling trunks are in the storage room on the third floor."

Madame stood and adjusted the ruched sleeves of her dress. "*Ce n'est pas nécessaire*, Miss Scrimshaw. Lily has plenty of clothes at home, don't you, Lily? She can just take a case and what she's wearing." She glanced at Lily's dishevelled coal-covered dress. "Though perhaps something neat and black would not go amiss now, eh, *chérie?*"

As they left the room together Lily's mind was awash with fuzzy thoughts, but she couldn't help overhearing Madame tell the Kraken how, if the expense of forwarding Lily's things was too much, they should feel free to divide them up between the other girls.

"I'm not sure that they'd want that, Madame," the Kraken replied.

"Perhaps the poorhouse then," Madame muttered. "Or burn them."

And Lily had a sudden devastating inkling of what her new life without Papa would be like.

The landing lamps of the descending airships glinted off the glass panes of the airdock's vaulted roof. The building towered above the sprawling city of Manchester like a giant steel ribcage. In its frosty forecourt, lines of steam-wagons, and the occasional horse-drawn carriage, queued to drop passengers and cargo under the columned portico of the main entrance.

Attached to the side of the building was a zeppelin-shaped billboard, painted with the livery of The Royal Dirigible Company's fleet, and the slogan: *The Modern Dirigible – Travel that's lighter than air.*

As Madame Verdigris and Lily stepped down from the steam-wagon, Madame almost slipped on the frosty cobbles of the road. She clutched Lily's arm, her nails digging through the wool of the school coat. Lily waited, clutching her small case and shivering in the biting wind, while Madame smoothed out the silk of her black dress. Finally, when she was ready, she took Lily's hand once more and ushered her into the terminal.

Crossing the marble foyer, they passed rows of commuters waiting for their evening flights. The buzz of people was so overwhelming Lily thought she might faint once more. The space held too many memories. She'd stood on this spot with Papa countless times, seeing him off on his trips.

She glanced at the brass clock tower at the centre of the concourse, craning her neck to see its spire, which rose towards the lobby's ceiling. Here she had kissed Papa goodbye, and here he had left her with the Kraken and the other girls at the start of the autumn term. She gazed past the pinnacle of the clock to the extravagant fresco of a zeppelin stamped with Queen Victoria's crest:

Victoria Regina. It was surrounded by angels and cherubs and tiny clouds, scudding away across the cracked blue plaster. At the corners of the lobby, four oval gilt-framed portraits of the old Queen faced each other across the expanse of painted sky. Was Papa up there now, Lily wondered, lost somewhere in the wild blue yonder, with all the other disappeared aeronauts?

She stifled a sob and blew her nose with her oil-stained hanky.

Madame Verdigris was consulting the overhead chalkboard filled with flight numbers, her bag held tight to her chest. "*C'est ici – quai numéro un.*"

"I don't know if I can do this," Lily said. "Take a zep today, I mean." Her legs were buckling and her case felt heavy in her hand; she took a deep breath to steady herself.

"It will be fine," Madame said. "Commuter zeps are a most safe way to travel. Not like private airships." She pursed her lips together – she seemed to have realized she'd overstepped the mark with that one. "*Allez!*" she said finally, and took Lily's arm and marched her to the gate.

On the platform they joined a line of people queuing to board the tethered passenger zep. Behind it, Lily glimpsed a bloated dirigible waiting for its cargo.

"Welcome to the *Damselfly*, an LZ1 model zeppelin." A stocky mechanical porter in a blue uniform displaying the gold insignia of The Royal Dirigible Company jumped down from their zep's doorway.

Lily brightened at the sight of him. He had a funny-looking thick moustache, made from a tufty old clothes-brush, buckled under his polished nose, and when he ran down the gangway his leg-pistons clacked together and his long iron arms swung through the air. He reached the edge of the platform and, gathering the heavier trunks – two under each arm – carried them like they were the lightest parcels, and stowed them neatly in stacks in the hold of the airship. Then, collecting the ticket stubs, he chatted with the passengers in turn, as if each were a bosom pal who he hadn't seen in years.

When he finally arrived at the spot where they were standing, he gave a creaky little bow and tipped his hat to Madame, so that Lily saw the polished brass top of his bald head. "Ladies, might I see your tickets, please?"

"First class section," Madame Verdigris said, handing them over.

He checked the scrawl. "Miss Lily Grantham."

Lily nodded, looking down at the tickets in the mechanical's hands and spotting a gleaming brass plate on his forearm.

HARTMAN AND SILVERFISH Ltd.

First class Mechanicals and Mechanimals

"But, oh! You were made by my fa—"

Madame Verdigris pinched the top of Lily's arm, hard.

"By John Hartman, the famous inventor," the mechanical said proudly. "Are you any relation?"

"None whatsoever," Madame Verdigris replied, before Lily had even opened her mouth. "Perhaps you should get on with your job?"

He gave her a curt nod. "Of course, Madam. Very good. Hand luggage only? May I show you both to your seats?"

He took Lily's case and winked at her – or was it an error in his blinking?

"This way, please. Mind your step." The mechanical ushered them along the gangplank towards the *Damselfly*, and Lily glanced back one more time at the airstation.

As she did, she noticed a man clutching a lacquer

walking cane arrive and join the back of the queue of boarding passengers. His razor-thin figure was clothed in a dark wool suit and tall stovepipe hat, and he wore silver reflective O-shaped spectacles. Something about him seemed oddly familiar; he was, she thought, somehow connected to Papa – but she couldn't quite place him. She was still trying to put a name to his craggy face when she stepped into the corridor of the airship's gondola and he disappeared from sight.

In the compartment Madame installed herself by the window while Lily waited for the mechanical porter to stow her suitcase. When he'd finished, the mechanical man doffed his hat to her, and Lily shook his hand before he slid the compartment door shut and left.

Madame Verdigris settled back in her seat and tutted under her breath. "I don't know why you shake hands with them, Lily. You'll end up covered in engine oil, or worse."

"It's good manners," Lily said. "They only want to be treated like people."

"*Mon Dieu.* Where do you get these notions? Certainly not from that school of yours." Madame opened her carpet bag and took out some embroidery, a picture of Botticelli angels. In the confines of the cabin her perfume was almost unendurable. Lily reached for the window latch.

Madame put out a hand. *"Arrêtez-vous."*

"Why?"

"I cannot stand the sound of propellers and I hate to be battered by cold air when I travel. Not to mention the evil stink of smoke you'll let in."

Lily bristled. Why was Madame making such demands? And why had she asked Lily to deny she knew Papa – now, after everything?

"Why did you tell the porter I wasn't related to John Hartman?" she asked.

"Your father never liked revealing your identity."

"Does it matter now?"

"Do you want everyone knowing our business? Especially mechs, and especially now your father's gone."

Lily shook her head, but she felt a pang of pain in her chest. "I just don't see how it's your right to answer questions addressed to me," she said.

"Well, I do," Madame replied. "I'm your guardian, *maintenant*. Albeit temporarily. And until we find out what's been decided, I suggest we stick to the old rules. So please, sit back and try to keep quiet. We have a long journey ahead."

Lily did as she was told; though she would've preferred it to be someone more pleasant doing the telling.

She ignored the housekeeper and contented herself

with staring out the window at the view. *Damselfly*'s engines shuddered to life and it was winched by two large steam-wagons to the centre of the landing strip. They positioned it over a big X, directly under the take-off skylight, then the mooring ropes were unclipped, and the zep rose through the centre of the building, aided by gigantic wind pumps in the walls, pushing it upwards.

Lily watched through the compartment's porthole as the zep drifted past the metal struts that held up the glass-paned roof, and the roosting pigeons, who barely shifted as they floated by.

Last time she'd flown with Papa she'd been arriving here for the start of the autumn term. Then the evenings had been light and long, not dark and heavy as they were now.

Lily was flying without him and she felt danger at every turn. As the public zep swept into the starless sky, she wondered what had happened to Papa and Malkin. How, with such an unfeeling guardian as Madame watching over her, would she ever find out? Suddenly, she felt very alone and scared about her future…

CHAPTER 5

They'd not been travelling long when a knock at the corridor window made Lily glance up from her penny dreadful.

It was the thin fellow in the mirrored spectacles from the airstation platform, with a copy of *The Daily Cog* clasped under his arm. When he slid open the door and peered in, Lily gave a loud gasp, for the mirrors were not glasses as she'd supposed, but lenses sewn into the raw red sockets of his eyes. The man had no eyeballs!

He stared at the ticket in his black-gloved hand, then examined the brass numbers above the seats, his mirrors reflecting everything. "Excuse me, Madame,

Miss, I appear to be allocated this cabin. May I come in?"

Lily shook her head, but Madame Verdigris replied: "Certainly."

"Thank you, much obliged." The thin man settled himself in a spare seat and leaned his walking cane against the wall. Lily noticed its silver skull handle. He took off his hat and gloves, and placed them on his lap. "Sorry for the disturbance, ladies."

"Please, pay it no mind." Madame Verdigris returned to her embroidery, absently poking her needle through the eye of an appliquéd cherub.

The thin man unfolded his newspaper and smoothed the wrinkles from it. He opened it to arm's length and began to read the inside pages.

Lily could not stop staring at his face. Perhaps he'd been in an accident, for the rims of his eye sockets, around the mirrors, looked red with damage, and his cheeks were scarred with jagged marks. She decided he must be a hybrid – part human, part machine. She'd never seen one before – until now she'd never even been sure they existed. Underneath her revulsion she felt a little sorry for the man. It must be a difficult life to be singled out as different like that.

She was probably looking too much. She turned her

attention to the paper instead. It was the evening edition. Lily scanned the front page and gave a gasp. The lead article was about Papa's disappearance. She read the first two paragraphs.

⚙ DAILY COG ⚙

PROFESSOR HARTMAN MISSING PRESUMED DEAD

London, evening edition, 9th November, 1896   One penny

John Hartman, co-inventor of the modern mechanical, and infamous recluse, was travelling on board his private airship *Dragonfly* yesterday when she disappeared. The ship failed to land at its stated destination of Brackenbridge Airstation, and is thought to have combusted in a mid-air explosion. Authorities are currently searching the crash site in order to retrieve as much information as possible.

⚙

Prominent in the field of mechanical design, Professor Hartman co-owned the country's largest mechanical manufacturing business with his friend and colleague Professor Silverfish. But he forfeited his share of the business and vanished from public life seven years ago, when his wife was killed in a steam wagon crash. He leaves one surviving relative: a daughter, Lily, aged thirteen, whose current whereabouts are unknown. Our reporter, Anna Quinn, has attempted to contact the family

A lump welled in Lily's throat and she stopped reading. It was all true then: written there in black and white. She glanced at the thin man; his head lolled against the headrest, his chin tipped back. Was he watching her or sleeping? So hard to tell behind those lidless mirrored eyes.

She gave a cough, but he didn't move. Perhaps he really *was* asleep? He wasn't reading the paper any more – it drooped now in his hands. She stuck her tongue out at him and he flashed her a smile, sharp as a shark's.

"I must apologize again," he said, folding *The Daily Cog* and setting it aside. "I know how frustrating a stranger in one's cabin can be on long journeys."

Lily gave a timid nod, which he seemed to take as an invitation to continue.

"Odd they put us together, when the zep's so empty. Must be a mechanical error."

Madame Verdigris set aside her embroidery. "Was it the same mechanical porter who showed you aboard? I find these primitive mechanicals, with their synthesized emotions, most disagreeable, don't you? They make so many clerical mistakes. And with the back talk they give you, and all the winding… I'm often surprised they function at all."

"Quite true, Madame. You've hit the nail squarely on

the head there." The thin man smiled. "Or should I say, got to the heart of the matter?"

Madame Verdigris gave her tinkling cut-glass laugh – though Lily saw nothing funny about either of their remarks. It occurred to her that the thin man had twice addressed the housekeeper as Madame, not Madam, and she wondered how he knew the woman's preferred title.

The thin man leaned forward, his silver eyes flashing in the light. "Ladies, please allow me to introduce myself. My name is Mr Roach."

Madame Verdigris nodded to him. "*Bonsoir*, Mr Roach, I'm Madame Verdigris and this is my charge Miss Hartman."

"Ah, like the article?" Mr Roach asked, tapping the newspaper.

Madame Verdigris sombrely inclined her head in the affirmative.

Lily ground her teeth – hadn't the housekeeper just told her not to let people know who she was?

"You look upset, young lady," Mr Roach said, "and no wonder."

"I'm fine," she said.

"I've something here might cheer you up." Mr Roach put a hand in his pocket and pulled out a paper bag, which he held out to Lily. She peered inside. Striped gooey sweets were fused to the paper; they must've been in his pocket for weeks.

"No thank you, Sir."

"Go on, they're humbugs." He thrust the paper bag at her, but she shook her head. "What's the matter? You don't like humbugs? If I wasn't such a mild-mannered fellow, I might be offended. Perhaps you think I'd be better off eating carrots. Good for the old eyesight." He laughed and tapped the centre of one mirrored eye with a finger.

Lily felt a shiver rise up her back. "No," she said. "It's not that, only…" She studied his unreadable expression. She didn't even know how to put it politely; but she needn't have worried, Madame Verdigris stepped in on her behalf.

"I'm afraid, Sir, one rule of Miss Scrimshaw's Academy, where Miss Hartman is a pupil, is never to accept sweets from strangers."

"Sorry," Lily added.

Mr Roach frowned, the silver orbs of his eyes narrowing; he clutched the paper bag in a gaunt hand. "You could hardly call me a stranger, Miss Hartman – we've just introduced ourselves. I must say, I don't believe your rules apply in these circumstances. And one should never be without a humbug when one takes a long journey. I find they help with travel sickness on these commuter zeps."

Lily relented and took one, and Mr Roach gave a small victorious grin.

The humbug tasted delicious, but after a while her eyelids drooped and she felt rather tired.

She put her head against the frosty window, which thrummed and rattled with the zeppelin's engines, and watched her breath cloud the glass. Before she drifted off, she heard Madame Verdigris say: "I don't know why these zeps are so loud always. Where is the refinement one gets with an old-fashioned horse and carriage or a hot-air balloon?"

"Change is always monstrous at first," Mr Roach replied, "but people soon get used to it. You know I've the strongest feeling, Madame Hortense, there will be a lot of changes in your life these coming months, for better or worse, depending how you play your hand. I'll be watching closely to see how you handle things."

Lily tried to fathom the meaning of his words, but found them slippery and ungraspable, and they swam away from her like a shoal of silver fish, pulling her along into a fog of sleep.

When she came to, the zep was approaching a local airstation and Mr Roach was gone. She suddenly remembered he'd been far too familiar with Madame, his last words tinged with a threat of some kind.

"What happened to the fellow sitting opposite?" Lily asked, stifling a yawn.

"He left a few minutes ago to prepare for landing," Madame said. "He had an urgent appointment and wanted to disembark first."

"But how did he know your first name?"

"Pardon?" Madame seemed somewhat flustered. She tucked her needle into the edge of her embroidery and Lily noticed she'd filled in the cherub's eyes with silver circles of thread.

"I heard him use your first name," Lily repeated. "And he knew you were called Madame before you even gave your title."

"What an odd thing to say." The housekeeper let out a peal of laughter. "You must have dreamed it." She gathered her spools of threads and tucked them into her bag next to her needlework. "You were asleep for so long, Lily. In fact, you've tousled your hair. Perhaps you'd better tidy yourself before we arrive?"

Lily was tempted to pursue the subject further, but the airship had begun its descent towards the landing site, and soon the familiar shabby sign of Brackenbridge Airstation appeared, lighting up the cabin.

She struggled into her coat and scarf, and a few minutes later they disembarked onto the tiny local platform. A cold wind buffeted them as they descended the gangplank and took the wooden steps towards ground level.

Papa's mechanical driver, Captain Springer, was waiting to collect them at the entrance to the station, standing beside their steam-wagon. Lily recognized him at once from his bow legs and bent stance. As soon as Madame Verdigris had wound him up, he hobbled over and gave Lily a big creaky hug.

"By all that ticks," he cried, "it's good to see you, Lily!" Then he huffed and puffed on his wooden legs, his cogs clicking as he loaded her case into the cab and helped Madame to her seat.

Climbing in after them, Lily glanced back at the other departing passengers, all wrapped up against the cold. She searched among the faces for Mr Roach, but couldn't find him anywhere. He seemed to have melted into the night.

The journey to the house took less than half an hour, but Lily stayed awake the whole time, thinking about the silver-eyed man and how he connected to Madame.

Captain Springer pulled the steam-wagon onto the drive of Brackenbridge Manor and Lily and Madame stepped down onto the frosty path. As they walked towards the door, Lily glanced through the black skeletal trees of the garden, their branches like cracks in the sky, up to Papa's study window, where his lamp once burned late into the night while he worked on his projects.

She half expected to see the flicker of it now. But there was nothing. The window stayed dark.

An icy draught whisked across the grounds, throwing up the last few fallen leaves, and a flood of grief made Lily swallow hard. Batting away the dust and the cold sting, she followed Madame and Captain Springer towards the low-lit porch.

Madame took out a ring of keys, unlocked the front door, and ushered Lily inside. She nodded at Captain Springer to indicate he should stow the case in the vestibule beside the rack of Papa's old walking shoes. To see them made Lily's heart leap for a second. Their folded leather shapes and straggly laces, laid out beneath his everyday coat on its hook – it was almost as if he had just come in and left them there. But no, he would've taken his flying jacket and boots if he and Malkin had gone off in *Dragonfly*. These were just the things he left behind. The remnants of him.

Her heart cracked some more as she realized he was truly gone, and the thought cut deep. She took a breath and stepped through the glass door from the vestibule into the grand hall. She was still half-expecting the old cosy warmth of the house to greet her, but if anything it felt colder and darker in here than outside.

At the foot of the stairs Mrs Rust, the mechanical cook, awaited them. She must have stood there for the whole day for she'd wound down and was now frozen in an expectant pose, one hand resting on the curved bannister.

Lily walked towards her. Apart from Malkin, Mrs Rust had always been her favourite among Papa's mechanicals. But since Lily had seen her last, her old metal face had become more worn. Scores of worry lines crossed her rusty forehead and her nose bloomed with new chips of paint.

Madame Verdigris sent Captain Springer jittering across the tiled hall and off along the darkened servants' corridor, then she examined Mrs Rust. "*Mon Dieu*," she tutted. "These old models. It's stopped again." She strode around behind the mechanical woman. Pulling out her ring of keys once more, she searched through for Mrs Rust's unique winder and inserted it into the mechanical's neck, turning it viciously, until Lily heard the springs inside the iron lady begin to creak and groan.

When Madame finished the winding she stepped back and waited.

Mrs Rust's eyes sprung open. Her expression looked glazed for a moment, the way mechanicals' faces always did when you woke them, but then she blinked, caught sight of Lily, and let out a joyful cry.

"Cogs and chronometers! My tiger-Lil's back!" Mrs Rust scooped Lily into her arms, sweeping her feet off the floor. "How I've missed you, dear-heart."

"I've missed you too, Rusty." Lily kissed the mechanical's dented metal cheek, which was rouged with paint, and smelled slightly of lavender oil.

Mrs Rust put her down and took a good look at her, then her face became serious and she let out a long wheezing sigh. "Oh, Lily," she said. "I'm so sorry about your father. Poor John. By all that ticks, I don't know what we'll do without him."

Hearing Mrs Rust say Papa's name like that made Lily's heart flutter. "Me neither," she said wearily, and she leaned up to kiss her on the nose.

Madame Verdigris gave a discreet cough. "How have things been getting on here today, Mrs Rust? I trust you took care of everything before you wound down for the night."

"Yes, Ma'am. Sorry, Ma'am. I didn't realize I'd run out of clicks a'fore you arrived, but you took so long."

"*Malheureusement*, the zeppelin was delayed," Madame said. "Foul weather. Storm clouds on the line."

"Shame." Mrs Rust ruffled Lily's hair with a soft leathery hand. "I've made up the young lady's room, like you asked. Though I could've done with a little help." The mechanical cook gave the housekeeper a dark stare, but Madame didn't notice because she'd turned to Lily.

"Mrs Rust will help you settle in," she said. "*Mais*, quietly. You'll find things run differently round here with me at the helm. I'll accept none of the tearaway behaviour your father saw fit to tolerate, especially not in a *jeune fille rangée*." Madame tipped her head back to stare down her nose at Lily. "I shall want to see you in the drawing room straight after breakfast, when we shall discuss matters further."

Lily nodded meekly. She was too wrung out by the emotion of the day to find a suitable response.

"*Bon*," the housekeeper said. "Then I shall retire to bed. It's been a long trip."

She took the oil lamp from the hall table and swept

off up the stairs, leaving Lily and Mrs Rust alone in the glow of a single candle.

Mrs Rust picked it up and ushered Lily upstairs too. As they reached the first-floor landing, Lily heard Madame shut the door of the master bedroom, and saw the glint of her lantern through the gap beneath it.

"But that's Papa's room," she cried out.

"Smokestacks and sprockets!" Mrs Rust whispered. "Not any more. Soon as she heard he was gone this morning, Madame moved his things into the servant's box room at the back, and installed herself there before she came to get you. She even had Mr Wingnut set up your mama's old dressing table for her."

Lily felt ill all over again. Mama had been gone seven years, and Papa only a day, but already, Madame was acting like lady of the manor.

Mrs Rust opened the door to Lily's own room. At least in here, she was relieved to find everything was just as she'd left it. Her books still piled on their shelves and her notes and drawings pinned to the walls in fat bunches, hiding the yellow wallpaper.

She emptied her suitcase into the wardrobe, not bothering to unfold anything, while Mrs Rust busied herself filling the grate with kindling, her arms rattling like bicycle chains. "Madame's stopped me setting the fires this week while your papa's been away," she said, "but now you're home we'll soon have things running the way they're meant to. I'll make it cosy in no time, don't you worry." The old mechanical laid the last of the logs atop the kindling. "Oh, and you might be needing an extra layer. It's got pretty cold here these winter nights."

"Good idea." Lily took a blanket from the cupboard and shook it out over the bed, filling the room with a blizzard of dust.

"Clockwork and…" Mrs Rust let out a foghorn sneeze, "…cam-wheels!"

"Bless you," Lily said.

"Thank you, my tiger." The mechanical took an old scrap of sacking from her pocket and blew her nose into it. "A touch of pneumatic pneumonia. Can I give you a piece of advice? Don't tell Madame anything you don't have to. This past week while your father's been on his trip, she's been through his office with a fine-tooth comb."

"How dare she! What on earth is she looking for?"

Mrs Rust threw her arms in the air. "Crankshafts and carburettors, I wish I knew! Could be anything. She's a devious one, her. Got all kinds of wheels turning in her head and she was lording it up when we heard the news this morning. Put herself in charge, naturally!" Mrs Rust held the candle to the kindling and fanned the flames with her apron. Lily sat on the bed, watching her.

"Widgets and windscreen wipers," the old mechanical muttered at last, when the fire had caught. "You mustn't mind my blather. It's only the wittering of an old fussbudget. When you come down in the morning I shall make you a nice teacake with jam, just as you like it, and we can have a proper gossip."

"Thank you, Rusty, sorry we woke you so late. I hope you sleep well."

"You too, my tiger-Lil. You too." Mrs Rust placed the candle by her bedside and crept out. Lily pulled the blanket over her knees and sat listening to the old mechanical's creaking joints as she walked away along the passage.

Later, changing into her nightdress, Lily touched the long white scar on her chest. A cut made by a shard of windscreen glass during the accident. The mark had faded over the years, like the memory of Mama, but she still felt its sharp throb sometimes and now, with Papa gone too, those memories she'd tried so hard to forget were once again welling up inside – gnawing at her empty belly.

She brushed them away and pondered Mrs Rust's parting words. What was Madame after in Papa's things?

And what could she do about it? These new thoughts were not at all pleasant, and she was too hungry and exhausted to consider them. She hadn't eaten anything since breakfast. Strange to think that afternoon she'd still been at school.

She glanced at her bedside clock. One thirty. Beneath the hands, tiny ivory-inlaid sheep jumped over a stile. Papa had designed it for her and she found herself counting the creatures now, trying to ignore the whirr of her mind as she closed her eyes and drifted off into an uneasy sleep full of silver-eyed men and skull-topped canes.

CHAPTER 6

Robert pushed open the door to his da's workshop and laid the broken fox down on the workbench in the centre of the room. Rows of brass tools and clock faces glinted in the gaslight, throwing twitching shadows across the walls.

Robert examined the mechanimal's injury. Under the sackcloth outer covering, where the top of the fox's leg joined the metallic shoulder blade, the bulbs and hexagons of the connecting bolts were all broken, and the rest of the parts had fused together in a lump. He was about to get to work when he sensed someone in the room, and glanced round.

His da was standing in the doorway, arms folded

across his chest, a quizzical look on his face. "What've you got there, son?" Thaddeus asked.

"A mech-fox." Robert stood aside so his da could get a better view. "I found it hiding down the lane. Men chased it across the village. I think they shot it." He stopped there because he didn't know what else to say. None of it made sense. Why would anyone shoot a mechanimal?

"Let's have a look." Thaddeus stepped over and examined the mechanimal. He put on his glasses and peered closely at the shattered cogs visible under the torn sackcloth fur. "I've only ever seen such workings once before," he muttered. "From these tiny delicate parts, I'd say the master mechanist who put this creature together was Professor Hartman of Brackenbridge Manor."

"You mean that secretive fellow?" Robert asked, astounded. "The one who calls himself Grantham?"

"The very same," Thaddeus said. "Hartman's his real name – but I'm the only one in the village who knows that." He glanced at the fox. "Where did you say it was headed?"

"East," Robert said.

"Then that'll be it." Thaddeus massaged his temples. "What's this?" He had found something: a small leather pouch under the matted fur ruff of the mechanimal's neck.

Thaddeus opened the pouch and pulled out a bullet-singed envelope. On the front, in faded oil-spattered letters, was written one word: *Lily.* "Yes, of course," he said. "It must belong to the professor's daughter."

"He has a daughter?" Robert said.

Thaddeus nodded. "I think she's at boarding school now. And I've certainly never met her. When she's around, he likes to keep her shut away."

"Why?"

Thaddeus put the letter and pouch to one side on the bench. "Oh, I don't know, overprotective, I suppose. She lost her mother when she was quite young – before they moved to Brackenbridge, and then for a long time she was very ill. Maybe that's why he made her this pet?"

Robert could sympathize. He knew what it was like to grow up without a ma. Although he had a feeling Thaddeus meant Lily's mother was dead, not off somewhere else, like his own. He couldn't remember when he'd first decided to stop asking about his ma – probably when Da had refused to give a straight answer. Seemed every family had secrets of some kind, good or bad.

He glanced from the fox, to Lily's letter in his da's hand. "Should we open it, d'you think?"

Thaddeus shook his head. "One never opens other people's mail, Robert. But perhaps we can take it to her?"

"And we'll help the fox, won't we?" Robert said. "I'm afraid if we don't it might wind down for ever."

Thaddeus thought about this. "Men were chasing it you say? And John's airship is missing. It…crashed? I wonder if this is something we should get involved with…? It sounds dangerous."

Robert sat down on the stool beside his da. "It's something that needs fixing, and you always say, 'If something needs fixing…'"

"'…we should try our best to fix it, no matter the cost.' You're right, of course." Thaddeus gave his son a weary look. "Such terrible things happen in the world, don't they? Violence against mechs and humans. And sometimes it feels easier to give in, or not to get involved. But, I suppose without those evils there'd be no chance for us to do good, and doing good is what matters. Though it can sometimes be very frightening…" Thaddeus paused and tapped the workbench thoughtfully with his screwdriver. "No one conquers fear easily, Robert. It takes a brave heart to win great battles."

He peered at the fox. "Now, can we repair this, d'you think? Or has it ticked its last tock? Let's have a look…" He opened a drawer in the workbench and took out a roll of leather, which he unfurled to reveal neat lines of tools – rows of watchmakers' screwdrivers, needles and tweezers, each in their own individual leather pocket. From another drawer he produced various glass jars of tiny screws and cogs, which he arranged in a row behind the leather scroll of tools. At last he took his magnifying glasses from a hook on the wall and put them on, blinking his big blue eyes. With a pair of tweezers, he opened the bullet hole in the mechanimal's leg, prising apart the oil-encrusted sackcloth fur to examine its internal workings.

Robert stood on tiptoes and peered over his da's shoulder, trying to get a glimpse at the damage. Behind the shoulder blade, the bullet had smashed and distorted the animal's tight-knit internal clockwork. It had cut a path through splintered cams and springs, before embedding itself deep in a dented metal plate.

"This is a serious repair job," Thaddeus said.

"But you can fix it?" Robert asked.

The clockmaker nodded. "Yes, it'll take time, though. And I'll need your help. Go and get all the jars containing the copper cams and the watch springs; if there aren't enough, bring a few of the old clocks over, we can filch parts from them."

"Right you are." Robert set off to collect the bits and pieces they would need from around the workshop, while Thaddeus picked up his screwdrivers and set to work on the mech-fox.

It took them many hours to repair the damage the bullet had done to the mechanimal's shoulder. Robert helped remove the mangled cogs and logged them in the workbook, and when Thaddeus called for replacement parts, if they weren't in the selections he'd already brought, Robert would run and get them from the various jars and tins stacked on the shelves in the storeroom.

Sometimes the parts were more difficult to come by, and he had to search through the bench drawers for them. Once, when they needed a certain click-wheel, Thaddeus told him to go and check in the backs of all the timepieces in the shop itself, and not to return until he'd found one. But at other times Robert sat in the room helping his da.

Working together like this was one of the few opportunities he got to talk to him. Robert always enjoyed it, despite his dread of doing something clumsy, because he knew at moments like these he could ask his da difficult things.

"Isn't it funny," he mused, "how a mech cannot harm a human, and yet a human can harm a mech. How can that be?"

Thaddeus looked at him, his brows furrowed and his

big eyes blinked behind their magnifying lenses as he considered the question. "It's the first rule of mechanics, Robert: a mech cannot kill a human or seriously harm them."

"But how do they know that?"

"It's part of their design, built into their valves and circuits."

"And yet, we can kill them. Stop them from being." Robert carefully replaced a part inside the fox's leg. "What happens to a mechanical that doesn't tick any more, anyway?"

"I suppose they die," Thaddeus said. "If they can do such a thing."

"Or they disappear," Robert said. He held an oily cog in his hands, turning it over and over. The sharp teeth around its edge pricked at his fingers. "But what happens to them after that? D'you think they go to heaven? Do you think they have mechanical souls?"

Thaddeus thought about this as he replaced a spring around the fox's scapula. "I don't know," he said. "Common opinion is they don't." He paused. "I never told you this before, perhaps I should have mentioned it earlier, but, for a while, seven years ago, when he first moved here, I used to go to Brackenbridge Manor to wind the clocks for Professor Hartman. When he learned that I repaired timepieces as well, he'd occasionally ask for help fixing one of his mechs. Though I never saw this one."

Robert's eyes widened. He hadn't realized his da had worked on proper mechs before. It was yet another thing that had been kept from him.

"All of John's mechs were so delicately made," Thaddeus continued, "and when they were working, something about them seemed different, more...alive."

"How so?"

"They're not like the regular models. They have quirks, can think for themselves. If that doesn't make them living things, I don't know what does."

"But why aren't there more of those ones about?" Robert persisted, pressing the teeth of the cog against his palm.

"Perhaps John made them specially," Thaddeus said. "Certainly the mass-produced mechs never have that amount of personality. It takes skill to make such things. I think he only let me help him with his repairs because he saw a kindred spirit – that and the fact he didn't like sending his mechs away to be fixed, said it destroyed their personalities." Thaddeus took a break from repairing the fox's leg, and packed his pipe with fresh tobacco from a pouch in his pocket. Then he lit it and took a few long puffs.

"What are they like then, his other mechanicals?" Robert asked. He couldn't imagine having such a life of privilege: to have so many mech-servants around you, even to have a mechanimal pet, like the fox.

Thaddeus blew out a ring of smoke. "One of the mechs up at Brackenbridge, Mrs Rust, the cook, used to sing as she worked. Songs she'd made up. And I suppose one might say if she created such wonderful things then she possessed a soul. But still, when she broke down and John and I repaired her insides, I could never see where her spark of life came from."

"The thing is," Robert said, "if you opened up a human, I don't expect you'd find evidence of a soul either, or what's unique about them, come to that."

Thaddeus shrugged. "I don't know enough about these things to tell you. But one thing I do know is this… feelings and intuition, love and compassion, those are the things make a soul, not blood and bones or machine parts." He ruffled his son's hair with a calloused hand. "The soul's a matter of the heart, Robert, and the heart's a mystery even the greatest scientists don't understand."

Robert nodded, but he wasn't sure he understood either. He watched Thaddeus put his pipe to one side and return to his screwdrivers, digging away at the cogs inside the mechanical fox. It truly was a remarkable device. Robert remembered it moving down the street, just like it had a fox's soul. Perhaps his da was right. The truth was there was less difference between humans and mechanicals that anyone would like to admit.

At three a.m. Thaddeus finally laid down his tools and announced they were done; taking a needle and thread, he stitched the fox's loose sack-fur back together until the machinery in the leg was entirely hidden. Robert piled felt blankets onto the workbench and they laid the mechanimal down on its side among them.

After all this, Thaddeus took the unique winder from where it hung about the fox's neck, placed it in the keyhole and made ten sharp turns. Then they stepped back, and waited to see if it would wake…

The fox juddered and Robert held his breath. He could hear the springs and cogs turning, ticking inside it, but the mechanimal didn't move, or open its eyes.

"Perhaps," Thaddeus said, "the new parts need time to bed in."

"And perhaps we can try winding it again tomorrow?" Robert added.

Thaddeus put a hand on his shoulder. "After your chores, please. It will still be here then. If it works it works; and if it doesn't it doesn't. We've done as much as we can for tonight, and sometimes that's all one can do."

They took up the lamp and left the room, both so tired that they forgot about the letter, left under the pile of tools on the workbench.

CHAPTER 7

The morning after she'd arrived home, Lily woke to find the snow was falling thick and fast. She put on her winter coat to take a walk in the grounds. Two strange steam-wagons were parked in the driveway: one a Rolls-Royce Phantom with a mechanical chauffeur and numberplate S1LVERF1SH, the other a small squat vehicle with a black chimney stack barely bigger than a top hat. Neither looked to have anything to do with Papa.

Among the distant trees, she caught sight of two standing figures. She recognized them at once as Papa's other mechanicals: Mr Wingnut and Miss Tock. Frozen like statues, rakes in their hands and a wheelbarrow at their side, they were gradually being covered in snow. Why on earth were they out in this weather? And run down too – surely they'd corrode? She hurried to the back door and tumbled into the kitchen, searching for Mrs Rust.

An iron range warmed the room with the scent of freshly baking biscuits, and the mechanical cook hummed softly to herself, clattering about whipping eggs in a bowl with her whisk arm-attachment. Her selection of replaceable hands gleamed on their hooks along the dresser – spatulas, sieves, saucepans, spoons and fish slices – each one well-used, and sparkling.

"Why are Mr Wingnut and Miss Tock unwound in the garden?"

"You're up early," Mrs Rust said, ignoring the question.

"I didn't sleep very well, so I decided to take a walk." Lily clapped her gloved hands together to banish the cold. "Tell me."

Mrs Rust looked sad. "Madame sent them to clear up leaves yesterday and when they froze halfway through the job, she refused to wind them. Said it wasn't her business to follow round useless mechs making sure they worked. She only wound me to cook, and Captain Springer to take her and collect her from the station. Before that she had him locked in the cellar."

Lily's eyes brimmed with tears. "Can't we help them?" she asked.

"I don't think so, dear." The old mechanical shook her head. "Madame took all our winding keys as soon as your papa was gone."

"It's only been a day, he could still come back, make things better. Couldn't he?" Her head ached from thinking about it.

"Perhaps that's our job." Mrs Rust took a wheezing breath. "I know sometimes life can be painful, my tiger. But, remember, if you can't change what's happened today, you must bide your time, until you're strong enough to fight tomorrow." She set her bowl aside and held out a rack of biscuits. "Here, have an almond thin. I made them special, to put warmth in your belly."

"Thank you." Lily took one in her gloved hand and bit into it. The biscuit tasted delicious, but…oh, it was hot! She sucked air in through her teeth, waving a hand in front of her face.

"Steam and steel!" Mrs Rust clucked. "I didn't realize they was still piping – comes of having heatproof fingers! But, give it time, dear, and the hurt'll fade. I'd say the same to you about your papa if you'd let me." She set the rack of biscuits aside. "We'd best save the rest of these for after breakfast."

"Yes," Lily said, "we'd best." She slumped in a chair by the fire and put her feet on the fender, warming her boots. She tried not to dwell on the fates of the other mechs, or Malkin, or Papa – it was hard not to do, but something about this room made her feel safe from the bad in the world. Perhaps it was Mrs Rust herself? She was so warm-hearted and understood everything Lily was going through. Not like Madame. If you had to guess which of the two had feelings, Lily knew who she'd choose.

Mrs Rust swapped her whisk hand for a spatula from the dresser, clicking it into place. "Stopwatches and spinning tops!" she cried. "I plum clean forgot – Madame Verdigris wants to see you in the drawing room straight after breakfast."

Lily gulped. It was as if she'd been summoned just for thinking ill of Madame. "I wonder what she wants?" she asked.

Mrs Rust gave a jittery shrug. "By all that ticks, I've no idea. She's got some lawyer and another fella with her – I think it's disgusting. Your father's barely been missing a day. The way she carries on you'd suppose they already *knew* he was dead rather than..." She tailed off. "Steam engines and stovepipes, I'm sorry... I didn't mean to..."

"That's okay, Rusty." Lily picked at a fingernail and

took a breath, holding in another sharp wave of sorrow. "Why don't you tell me what else has been going on?"

The old mechanical took the kettle from the stove and poured a spurt of water into the pot to warm it. "I'm all zeroes and ones today," she lamented, spooning in the tea, before filling the pot to the brim with water.

"Since Madame's been in charge she's been snuffling in everyone's business. Thinks your father had valuables hidden in the house." Mrs Rust laid some teacakes on the stove top, pressing them down with her spatula hand. "Even interviewed Captain Springer, Miss Tock, and Mr Wingnut yesterday morning. I could've told her they don't know anything. That's why she's let them wind down."

"But *you* do know something?" Lily said.

"Cam-springs and cold cream! I couldn't rightly say." Mrs Rust gave her a darting nervous look as she scraped up the teacakes and buttered the browned underside of each. "There were so many things your father was working on, but I doubt any of them was valuable enough for him to be disappeared for." She placed the plate of teacakes in front of Lily. "Eat up, my tiger. You don't want to face *her upstairs* on an empty stomach."

Lily took the top off the marmalade jar and spooned some onto the warm bread. She felt lucky to be so doted on, considering the way everyone else here had been treated. If Papa was around he'd put a stop to it, but he wasn't, and it seemed his secrets were the reason everything had gone wrong in the first place.

When she arrived in the drawing room half an hour later, Lily found Madame already present, along with Mr Sunder, a grey lawyer from the firm Rent and Sunder. Also present was a barrel of a man, who perched on the edge of his chair with his hat on his knees. His handsome square-jawed face looked thinner and more lined than when she had last seen it, but it lit up immediately at the sight of her. "Lily," he cried, "there you are."

"Professor Silverfish!" Lily broke into a broad smile.

"Yes, it's me." Her godfather stood and gave her an enormous bear hug. "You've grown so tall. Have you still got those tin-toys I bought you?"

She shook her head. "They broke, I'm afraid."

"How?"

"I took them apart to see how they worked."

Professor Silverfish laughed. "A girl after my own heart." He drew back and winced, and Lily heard a ticking coming from his chest. "Speaking of hearts," the professor said, "I'm afraid I've been most unwell, Lily."

Carefully, he undid the buttons of his jacket, revealing a lumpy metal device buckled on over his shirt. Tubes from the device ran in and out of his chest.

"It's all right," he reassured her, when he saw her look of horror. "It's perfectly harmless. A clockwork prototype, a hybrid heart, nothing more. It keeps me from going completely kaput." Professor Silverfish ran a hand through his spray of white hair. "Of course it takes a lot of winding, like one of the mechanicals, what! And it means, in many ways, I am invalided. I cannot function as I used to. But still, I try my best. And I've come to see you, Lily, in your hour of need."

"Papa never told me you were so ill," Lily said. "I just thought you'd gone away."

Professor Silverfish's face fell. "Yes, I missed your father in recent years, missed everyone. But I had to visit warmer climes, for my health. For this—" He tapped the contraption on his chest. "I only wish I could've been here for you, with everything that's happened…your mother's death…and now John's disappearance… I hear you've been taken out of school." He trailed off.

Lily took a deep breath. She was glad he'd stopped talking; the things he was saying and the horrible device only made her feel worse.

Professor Silverfish seemed to sense her discomfort.

"I'm sorry," he said. He buttoned his jacket, muffling the loud tick of the device, and took a deep breath, before sitting back down with a wince.

Madame Verdigris, who had been conversing quietly with Mr Sunder, gave a discreet cough. *"Bien,"* she said, "if we might get the proceedings under way."

"Of course." Professor Silverfish nodded. "Lily, why don't you take a seat?"

Lily sunk into Papa's old leather armchair in the centre of the room, and watched Mr Sunder sit down opposite her on the sofa. He produced a sheaf of documents from a folder in his lap and, shuffling them together, placed them on the table in front of him.

"Miss Hartman, since your father went missing yesterday, certain protocols have been taken into consideration... He did leave a letter with us...concerning your welfare...if anything was to happen to him... I am going to read it to you now."

Mr Sunder took out a pair of pince-nez and polished them with a spotted handkerchief. Lily waited for the worst, but only the soft tick of Professor Silverfish's heart machine and Madame's shallow steady breathing filled the silence. Finally, Mr Sunder perched his spectacles on his beaky nose and began to read.

"I, John Hartman...being of sound mind and body,

do hereby set down my wishes regarding the future care of my daughter, Lily Grace Hartman…"

His cold words, echoing round the room, sounded most unlike Papa. Lily glanced tearfully at the professor, and then at Madame Verdigris, lingering in the bay window; her hawklike profile, black as a cameo, was framed by the lines of the sash. Madame turned and spoke impatiently to the lawyer. "We know this, skip to the important bit."

"Perhaps the young lady would like to…"

"I said skip to the details."

"Right." Mr Sunder gave an embarrassed cough. "The terms… All patents, devices and properties are to be held in trust for Lily, who will come into ownership on her eighteenth birthday… Mr Hartman has stipulated that until then Madame Verdigris is to be appointed guardian…and, er, trustee of the patents…to be informally advised by myself…and the girl's godfather." He nodded to Professor Silverfish.

"What about Mrs Rust?" Lily asked. "I thought Papa would've appointed her my guardian?"

"Lily is right," Professor Silverfish said. "And what of the other mechanicals who work for John – Captain Springer, Miss Tock and Mr Wingnut – he must have made some provision for them also?"

Mr Sunder shuffled through the few short pages, his lips moving as he read the words. Finally he turned them over as if he expected to find something on their blank side. "I'm afraid not, Sir, Miss…" Beneath his spectacles, his eyes darted nervously to Madame. "It would seem there are no clauses relating to mechanimals in this, er… document."

Professor Silverfish leaned forward in his chair. "Do you not think that odd, Sir?"

"Not in my experience," Mr Sunder replied.

"Well," said Professor Silverfish, "I do."

"I do too," Lily said. "Papa loved his mechanicals as much as he loved me and Mama. They're practically a part of our family. Mrs Rust especially. After Mama, she was the one who took care of me. I would've expected him at least to have thought about her."

"When death is preying on their mind, people do not always behave as they did in life, Miss Hartman," the lawyer said.

Lily's heart kicked in her chest. "Then you *do* think my papa is dead?"

"Not at all." Mr Sunder gulped. "I'm merely hypothesizing… I mean, until he's found…or until he is pronounced, er… That's to say…" He shuffled his papers in his hands nervously. "Anyway, Miss Hartman, if you knew anything about legal matters—"

"And being *une enfant*," Madame cut in, "we wouldn't expect you to."

"Yes, quite," Mr Sunder continued, "then you'd know mechanicals don't have the same rights as we humans do..." He looked to Madame once more for help. "For example, mechanicals are not allowed to own things, or to be in charge of a steam vehicle, or an airship, or indeed a child. Things a responsible adult might undertake are forbidden to them on the grounds they lack intelligence, selfhood, et cetera, et cetera..."

"Which is why your father picked me as your guardian," Madame Verdigris added.

"Is this true?" Lily asked the professor.

"I'm afraid so," he said. "I never considered the legal side of things."

"*Bien*. Enough of this." Madame placed her hands on the headrest of Lily's chair. "Let Mr Sunder finish, he's a very busy man. Mr Sunder, tell Lily about the other matter we discussed..."

"Yes, Ma'am, but it's rather delicate, if I might speak to the adults alone first?"

Lily gave a pleading look to the professor. "I think," he said, "if it relates to Lily's rights she should be present. We must respect—"

"D'accord." The housekeeper cut him off. "You may speak in front of the child, Mr Sunder. I suppose the professor is right, there should be no secrets between us." She grasped Lily's shoulder and gave it a painful squeeze.

"As you wish." Mr Sunder smoothed the tuft of greasy hair atop his head, playing for time. "Ladies, Professor Silverfish, thanks to Professor Hartman's...projects, the estate has accrued considerable debts over the years. More than his patents and holdings are worth."

"What do you mean exactly?" Professor Silverfish asked.

"I mean the money is insufficient to pay either for Lily's keep, or to stay in this house."

"You see?" Madame said to Lily. "It is as I feared."

Professor Silverfish shook his head. "I don't understand. None of this seems possible. Surely John would've sold his patents? If things were so bad, he'd have done everything in his power to make sure Lily was provided for."

"Perhaps he was less circumspect than you imagine, Sir." Mr Sunder took his glasses from his nose and polished them again vigorously with his handkerchief.

"What would you advise us to do?" Madame asked.

Mr Sunder glanced between Lily and Madame, his gaze lingering on Madame. "My advice to you, Miss

Hartman...to your guardian...is to sell everything of value...mechanicals, devices, and then, possibly, even the building itself."

"You can't," Lily said. "They're Papa's things. Our things."

"It seems we've no choice," Madame Verdigris told her grimly.

Lily couldn't believe it. There was always a choice, wasn't there? Isn't that what people said? If only she could persuade them...

But then she saw the professor's resigned expression, and the lawyer's solemn face. She turned and caught the brief smug smile on Madame's lips, and was shocked to realize that this horrible woman was now in charge of her life.

Afterwards, while Madame showed Mr Sunder to the door, Lily took Professor Silverfish aside.

"Please don't leave me alone with her," she begged.

The professor's face dropped. "I'm sorry, Lily. There's nothing I can do. It's your father's decree and, for the moment, I don't think it would be wise to go against it, despite the fact I don't feel Madame Verdigris is entirely trustworthy."

Lily shook her head. "She isn't," she said. "Mrs Rust's told me things about her – how she deliberately ran down the mechanicals yesterday, and she's gone through Papa's papers while he's been away."

"Really?" Professor Silverfish looked shocked. "Well, that doesn't sound like something she should be doing."

"No," Lily agreed. She took the professor's coat down from the hatstand and helped him as he wheezily struggled into it, then she buttoned the front closed over his bulky mechanical heart.

Professor Silverfish put on his top hat, tapping the rim until it sat comfortably on his head. "If you like," he said finally, "I can arrange to have John's things stored at the Mechanists' Guild. I'm sure it's something he would've wanted – to help other researchers making new machines. But, only if you're happy with such a decision, Lily?"

"I'm happy with it," Lily said. They had reached the front door, and she stared at Madame's poker-straight back. The woman was standing on the driveway, waving to the lawyer as he puttered away in his little grey steam-wagon.

"Good." The professor ruffled Lily's hair and stepped out into the cold. "I want you to do one more thing for me. I want you to keep an eye on your guardian and report back on her movements." He took a card from his pocket and placed it in Lily's hand, closing her fingers around it.

With the compliments of

PROFESSOR SILVERFISH

Makers of first class
MECHANICALS AND MECHANIMALS

9 Riverside Walk, Chelsea

"This is my new London address, you can write or telegraph any time to tell me how you're getting on. And if there's anything else, anything you need..." He gave an embarrassed cough. "I'm so sorry we've been out of touch for so long, Lily. I'd only recently returned to England when I heard the terrible news, and I felt it was imperative I come visit you."

"I'm very glad you did." She gave him one more hug. "I do wish you and Papa hadn't lost contact."

"Well, it was understandable really. Towards the end of his time in London, we had a falling-out."

"About what?"

"Oh, the business mostly. And, because I was sick, I missed your mother's funeral, for which I don't think he ever forgave me." Professor Silverfish gave a start when he saw Madame Verdigris approaching up the steps of the porch. "But now is no time to talk about that. Next time you're in London you must visit me and I'll tell you about it." He folded his arms over the ticking machine on his chest. "Right, I'm afraid I have to go – there are things I need to do for my health. I do hope they find your father, Lily. If you need advice, or you have any further trouble with her," he nodded at Madame, "then you must contact me right away."

"Thank you, I shall. And I shall keep this safe." Lily slipped the card into her pocket.

"See you do." The professor bent down and kissed her on the top of the head, before striding away from the manor. As he passed Madame he didn't even tip his hat.

"What was that all about?" she asked, but Lily brushed her aside and ran to the edge of the porch. She watched her godfather get into his Rolls-Royce Phantom steam-wagon. Her last hope was leaving without her. When he was seated comfortably, the professor looked back and gave her a brief wave goodbye, then he signalled to his mechanical chauffeur and they drove off down the drive, making tracks in the deepening snow.

CHAPTER 8

That afternoon in the village, everything was quiet. Snow had been falling all day, and thick drifts of it muffled the streets. Robert only had one visitor at Townsend's: Mrs Chivers, an old woman from the village with selective deafness, who'd traipsed through the knee-deep powder in her winter woollens carrying her mechanical canary and its tiny unique winding key. It had stopped working and no longer chirped. Robert examined it, and she pouted and scrunched up her wrinkled face like a paper bag when he explained that it would be a couple of days before he or his da could make the repairs because parts were not arriving owing to the bad weather.

Later, while Thaddeus busied himself in the workshop, Robert got on with the accounts. Adding the lines of numbers in the book required every ounce of his concentration, and the hours drifted past in a sea of ticks, until, before he knew it, the November light was fading.

When the row of clocks in their cases chimed out four, he closed the ledger and reached out for the oil lamp on the edge of the counter. Removing the glass chimney, he struck a match and held it to the wick, then replaced the glass and watched the flame's amber tones fill the room, scattering shadows between the clock faces.

A movement caught his eye. A thin, odd-looking man, his eyes hidden by the brim of his stovepipe hat, stood silhouetted in the doorway. The chime of the clocks must've masked his entrance, for Robert had not heard the bell and he could've sworn the fellow hadn't been there a moment before.

The thin man thrust his lacquered cane into the umbrella stand and let go of its silver skull handle.

Outside the shop, the large mutton-chopped gent from the morning before limped into view. Robert watched him stop and lean his wide, wool-coated back against the etched glass window. Presently, he lit a fat cigar and gazed off down the street.

The thin man was hunched forward, examining the

clocks in the shop's display cabinet. He cleared his throat, took off his gloves and, with their fingertips, brushed the melting snow from the front of his long coat. "Good evening, Master Townsend, quite the place you have here."

"We're proud of it, Sir."

"Indeed you should be." The man tipped back his stovepipe hat and the shadows lifted from his face. "My name is Mr Roach." Robert gave a gasp, for his eyes were mirrored just like the mutton-chopped man's.

Mr Roach laughed. "What's wrong, boy? Have you never seen a hybrid before?"

"Nnnn…no. I mean…only your colleague outside." Robert shook his head and involuntarily put a hand up to touch his own cheek. "What…what happened to you?"

"Nosy, aren't you?" Mr Roach's lidless eyes didn't blink. The two silver lenses trapped the room in their surface. Unflinching. "My colleague and I were blinded in combat. Our master repaired us."

"Oh." Robert felt hairs rise on the back of his neck.

Mr Roach leered at him. "If you think we look bad, you should've seen the enemy combatant."

"W-why…what happened to him?"

"Let's just say he lost his head."

Robert gulped, and Mr Roach laughed.

"Of course we wouldn't even be fighting wars if mechs could do the job, but they're far too stupid."

Robert's blood boiled at such a lie – he knew mechs *couldn't* kill humans, it had nothing to do with them being stupid.

"And now I must speak with your master, the clockmaker," Mr Roach was saying.

Robert realized his mouth had fallen open, and snapped it shut. "I'm afraid Da's busy. Were you looking for something in particular?" He had a horrible notion he knew exactly what the man was nosing for.

"So the clockmaker's your father?" Mr Roach's mirrored eyes gleamed. "Surely you have some idea of our *foxing* problem?" He gestured with his black gloves, indicating the mutton-chopped fellow outside. "You met my colleague, Mr Mould, on the street yesterday morning and were kind enough to give him some information about the mechanimal we're looking for. Only your information proved to be false. Now we're wondering if you know something more."

"Are you from the police?"

"Exactly so, boy." Mr Roach gave a parrying smile, though his eyes remained cold. "A very secret police. Mr Mould thinks you might be able to assist us further in our inquiries if we take you in for interrogation."

Robert swallowed a prickly dryness at the back of his throat. "I'm afraid I can't help you. I told your colleague everything I saw."

"Perhaps you did, or perhaps you didn't." The corners of Mr Roach's lips twisted into the slightest of smirks. "We might never know unless we apply a little pressure." He picked up Mrs Chivers's mechanical canary from the counter and tapped its face with his long bony finger.

"Mr Mould has a most singular way of dealing with those who refuse to cooperate with our enquiries. He has methods for making them sing." Mr Roach pushed the face of the canary onto the sharp corner of the display table.

CRAACK went the clockwork canary.

And Mr Roach pushed harder until the thing's face dented into an irreparable splintered mess. Then he placed the broken mechanimal on the counter in front of Robert.

"Well, I must be going, Master Townsend. No doubt we will see each other again before long." Mr Roach pulled his cane from the umbrella stand and his eyes flashed white as he opened the door.

The bell jingled cheerfully as he left.

Robert let out a sigh of relief for, as soon as he'd gone, it felt as if the air returned to the shop. He picked up the broken clockwork bird and watched as the pair crunched away through the drifts, and disappeared at the dark end of the street.

Thaddeus was incensed when he found the destroyed mechanimal; he gave another long lecture on caring for customers' property, until Robert mumbled an excuse and said that he'd dropped the thing. He didn't want to worry his da unduly, and he was afraid if he told the truth, Thaddeus might get rid of the mech-fox before they'd even got it working again.

For the rest of the afternoon he pretended nothing out of the ordinary had happened. Besides, Roach and Mould could still be watching the shop. Quietly, he got on with his work, tidying up the mess, but the whole time he was thinking about the mechanical fox – it must've been truly valuable if those men were making such violent threats to get hold of it.

When he finally finished his chores, he could barely contain his sense of inquisitive excitement as he took the lamp back to the workshop to check on whether the mechanimal had awoken.

It lay in exactly the same spot as last night – frozen on the felt blanket in the centre of the workbench. Robert wound it once more with the key, and waited, but again nothing happened.

He peered closely at the keyhole on the fox's neck, and saw straight away what the problem was: the mechanism inside was minutely misaligned. He took down a screwdriver from his da's selection and, putting it into the keyhole, pushed until he felt the click of the mechanism slotting into place. Then he replaced the key, wound the mechanimal yet again and waited.

After a while there was a low sound and a series of clanks and crunchings reverberated around the fox's insides. The mechanimal's ribcage began to judder; a shiver ran along its spine, and its body began to slowly shake and tick.

Soon the ticking grew louder and more regular:

TICK...

TICK...

TICK...

TICK...

TICK...

TICK...

And, with a crackling creak, the fox awoke, its entire frame stiffening into an alert pose. Robert stepped back as its face bristled and blinked, and it shook the stillness from the rest of its body.

Its eyes darted round the room and, when it saw him, it arched its back and let out a low warning growl – a deep mechanical sound which made his knees quake.

Robert flashed the fox a grin but it glared back at him, unblinking; then it gnawed angrily at its repaired leg and gave a yelp of pain.

"I know. It hurts," Robert said. "It'll take time to feel better. A few days, while you get used to the new parts."

The mechanimal growled and bared its white teeth at him. "Of course it hurts, you insolent meat-puppet. It hurts like a steel-toothed ratchet-claw!" Its glassy black eyes seemed to stare right through him. "Who are you?" it demanded. "What d'you want? Where the clank did you find me?"

"Don't be scared," Robert told it. "I only want to help." He held out his empty palm and stepped towards the fox.

Its growl deepened.

"Shush," Robert said, and he reached out to the mechanimal.

Lightning fast, the fox snapped at his fingers.

Robert stepped back, tripped over a battered trunk and landed seat first on the floor, banging his head on the leg of the workbench. There was a long silence during which he took off his cap and rubbed his head. He stared sheepishly at the mech. "You could've killed me with those sharp teeth, you know."

"I did warn you, monkey boy. Now, if you don't tell me who you are in the next tick-tocking minute, I shall bite you for real."

"I thought you couldn't hurt humans."

"In your case, I think I might be able to make an exception."

"You're bluffing."

"Try me and find out."

Robert straightened his jacket. "No thanks," he said. "I don't want any more trouble. My name's Robert. Robert Townsend."

"Then this is the clockmaker's shop?" the fox asked. "And you are…the clockmaker?" He gave Robert a disapproving stare. "You look far too stringy to be the clockmaker."

"I'm his apprentice."

"Oh, I see. I suppose you would be. You're only a pup, after all, and a mangy-looking one at that."

"Who are you calling mangy?" Robert said. "You're the one who looks like you've been dragged through a hedge backwards."

"I'm on a mission," the fox snapped. "There are

those who wish me harm. Are they still sniffing about, the meatheads who were chasing me?"

"I don't know," Robert said. "I caught a couple of 'em skulking round the lanes yesterday morning – the fat silver-eyed one with ginger mutton-chops and some others. You ought to be thanking me. I sent them off in the wrong direction when their dog was on your tail. Then, today, one came in the shop to talk to me. Another mirror-eyed man, thin, with a scarred face – Mr Roach, he said his name was. Very creepy." He paused for breath. "What do they want you for anyway?"

"Talk a lot, don't you?" the fox said. "Bit of a barking blabbermouth. Ask a lot of questions."

"Sometimes," Robert mumbled.

The fox ignored him and lapsed into silent contemplation. At last, it spoke. "You're not going to tell anyone about me?"

"No."

"Then I apologize. I'm usually better mannered, but this injury's given me the jitters. My name's Malkin, by the way."

"Pleased to make your acquaintance, Malkin," Robert said.

"And I yours." Malkin gave a slight nod of his head, which Robert assumed was meant to stand in for a bow, and winced. "Most people don't believe mechanimals feel pain," he said.

"But you do, don't you?" Robert asked.

"Of the more extreme kind, yes." The fox gnawed at its injury once more. "My leg aches like it's been put through a bandsaw and that's a new sensation for me."

"We fixed it for you, my da and I. Though it'll take time before it's fully healed."

"Thank you. But this puts me in an awkward situation. You see, I've a message to deliver, and time is ticking by." The fox felt with his nose around the ruff of his neck and looked up sharply. "Wait – what the tock! Where's my letter?"

"Oh crikey," Robert muttered. "I forgot." He searched round the workbench, under the tools and screwdrivers, until he found the envelope and pouch. "I can put it back. But I wouldn't walk anywhere for a few days, if I were you. Maybe I could take the letter, if you'd like?"

Malkin considered this. "No, I don't think so," he said huffily. "I promised to deliver it myself. But perhaps you could bring Lily here, from Brackenbridge Manor? You must go straight away. It's of the utmost importance."

Robert shrugged. "I don't know. That's a long walk and it's already dark. I don't want to risk it tonight, in case those men are still about, but I can go tomorrow for you, if you like. After I've finished my chores."

Malkin sniffed. "I suppose that's acceptable," he said. "I only hope it's not too late." Then he thought of something else. "Oh, but perhaps you can give Lily the other message when you fetch her? You're to tell her: *The secret's in the safe…*" He looked confused. "Wait – is it: *The secret's safe,* or *the secret's in the safe?*"

"Well, which?" Robert asked.

Malkin's ears drooped, and a look of worry crossed his face. "Do you know," he said, "with all that's happened, I'm not entirely sure."

CHAPTER 9

At dusk, Lily walked along the dark landing. She'd been summoned again to see Madame and was dawdling nervously, stopping outside each room on her way, and touching each locked door with her hand.

Here was the library, with books piled outside because there was no space on the shelves within. Here, Papa's study, with the buzzer beside it, and the spyhole so he could see who was coming and going. Then his workroom – the big metal door had the words *Do Not Disturb* painted on the surface beneath a lightning bolt. Finally, his bedroom: the master suite. Since he'd gone Madame had certainly wasted no time taking it over.

Lily knocked on the door and, without waiting for a reply, entered.

The green velvet curtains were partly drawn across the far window to keep out the cold and on the bedside table a small gas lamp glowed with a flattering light. Madame Verdigris perched primly at Mama's dressing table, applying lotions to her face. The odour of her perfume, mixed with the dusty scent of dried flowers which filled every vase in the room, made Lily feel vaguely sick.

She went and stood by the window, glancing out into the night. In the garden, under the skeletal trees, the falling snow had almost covered Miss Tock and Mr Wingnut. Just like Papa himself, his machines were gradually disappearing. Soon they'd be invisible, hidden under the frosty white surface, like secrets. If she could only find their keys she might be able to help them. "Why've you let those mechanicals wind down?" she asked.

Madame glanced up from the mirror, her face almost hidden beneath a mask of cold cream. "Is that what the rusty rebel in the kitchen's been telling you, *ma chérie*?"

"I noticed it for myself."

"Of course you did."

Madame plucked a rogue hair from a mole on her

chin, and winced. Then she applied some paste from Mama's shellac case over the spot. Lily felt sick. Papa had kept those things in Mama's memory, but they'd not been used since she died. Not until now. "You've been through their possessions," she muttered.

Madame dabbed rosewater onto her chin with a bony finger. "Whatever Mrs Rust's said, Lily, there's something I want you to bear in mind: all mechanicals are liars. Never take the word of a common mech over a human being."

Tears pricked Lily's eyes. She kicked at the carpet. "Mrs Rust is not a common mech. She's been with us always. She understands. She's looked after me every day since Mama's death. And she'll look after me until my papa returns, just like the others."

"Your father will not return. I am in charge *maintenant*."

"No." Lily shook her head. The belief had been growing in her heart that somewhere her papa was alive. "He'll return, I know it. And Mrs Rust has more love in her little metal finger than you have in your entire bony body. So don't *ever* tell me to take your word over hers again."

"Have you quite finished? *Asseyez-vous*. Sit down with me." Madame patted the velvet seat beside her.

Lily sniffed and blew her nose on her sleeve. "I'm perfectly fine here, thank you." She folded her arms across her chest.

"As you prefer." Madame took up a washcloth and began wiping the ghostly white cream from her face. "But I wish you wouldn't question my decisions. You know, I was the one who suggested your father send you to Miss Scrimshaw's Academy. I thought it would do you good, though, frankly, I see scant evidence of that." With a last flick of the washcloth, she cleaned a hint of kohl from her eyebrows. Lily noticed that they were plucked unevenly, and their opposing angles made her look like she wore two expressions at once. "You could at least try to behave in a way that would make your father proud." Madame stood and indicated the seat in front of the mirror. "Now, *s'il vous plaît*, let me tidy you up."

Lily lingered by the window, then did as she was told.

"I have been considering our situation." Madame picked up Mama's old silver-backed hairbrush from the nightstand and began brushing Lily's hair, tugging at the tangles. Lily winced and gritted her teeth as Madame hacked at a particularly trying knot with the hairbrush.

"You are no longer a young lady of means," Madame said. "Plus, we've no money to speak of. If we remain

123

here we'd be obliged to sell Mrs Rust and the other mechanicals."

"Please," Lily sobbed. "You can't."

"They barely function. They're all wound down. The other day Mrs Rust poured engine oil in my soup instead of cream. Anyone would think she wanted to poison me." Madame took some hairpins from a glass pot and pricked at Lily's head with them. "No, once mechanicals get like that, one is constantly buying upgrades, and, *malheureusement*, Lily, we can't afford the parts."

Lily shook her hand away. "I don't care," she said. "Mrs Rust is staying. They all are."

"*Désolée*, but we have no choice." The housekeeper stuck in another hairpin, scraping it against Lily's scalp. "Unless you know of something of superior value? An invention of your papa's we might sell? A perpetual motion machine, for example?" Her piercing eyes watched Lily in the mirror, and she gave a vicious tug on a strand of unruly hair.

"I don't know what you mean," Lily said. "I don't know what that is." The woman had too many questions – it felt as if she was poking around her insides. Lily tried to blink back her tears, but they rolled down her cheeks.

"Don't get upset, *ma chérie*," Madame cooed. "If we want to save Mrs Rust and the house then we need to discuss these things like adults. There. *C'est fini.*" She inserted a last hairpin and stood back to take a look at her creation. "*C'est magnifique,* don't you think?"

Lily regarded her tower of pinned hair in the mirror; it looked not unlike the terrible hair-monstrosities the girls in her class were so fond of. "It's a mess," she said. "Like everything else."

That night Lily dreamed of a clear sky and shimmering stars reflected on the ocean. It was summer and she was running along the beach; trying to catch Papa and Mama, who walked ahead. When she stumbled, Mama stopped and bent down to take her tiny hand and help her up. Then the three of them walked on together.

Papa carried his walking cane, and used it to point out landmarks: rows of iron ships and tall spider platforms out to sea collecting gas and oil for industry that Lily didn't understand.

They weaved their way along the tideline of the bay, while Lily ran in and out of the shallows, letting the seawater rush cold across her feet, and jumping away from the breakers.

Mama found something. A stone in the sand. She picked it up.

"This is for you," she said, giving it to Lily.

Lily took the stone and studied it. It was heavy and the underside felt lumpy in her palm.

"What is it?" she asked.

Mama reached out and turned the stone over in her hand, revealing a bright golden fossil at its centre, like the curving shell of a snail. "An ammonite," she said.

"How did it get there?"

Papa crowded in beside Mama, peering over her shoulder. "Billions of years ago, when it died," he said, "it sank into the mud, and was buried. Then minerals seeped in slowly, replacing the organic matter, until it was petrified. It's the pyrite that gives it that gold colour – fool's gold."

Lily looked at the fossil. "So it's been hidden inside the stone for ever, until we found it?"

"Yes," said Mama. "The secret's at the heart of it."

She put a hand to Lily's face.

Suddenly, the three of them were in a carriage, in the dark cobbled streets of London, driving home surrounded by falling snow. The sounds of the city were muffled. But Lily knew at once what day this was: it was the day of the accident.

She sat on the back seat of the steam-hansom, wedged between Mama and Papa. The metal chimney chuffed and sputtered and the wooden wheels creaked and turned as the mechanical cabbie in the exterior driver's compartment steered them home.

They had been out to dinner. Mama had on her taffeta red dress with the beautiful lapels and her long dark hair hung loose about her shoulders, her warm hand clasping Lily's leg. Papa wore his tall top hat that grazed the roof of the carriage; his suit tails, which made him look like a penguin, were folded under his legs.

Lily still held the stone Mama had given her in her hand, as if she had jumped from one moment to the next. She glanced at the beautiful golden ammonite buried at the heart of the rock. When she flipped the stone between her fingers it looked as if the fossil disappeared and reappeared. "The secret's at the heart of it," she whispered.

Her parents were talking together over her head. Soft words, gliding back and forth, accompanied by warm laughter.

Lily glanced down. On the floor of the carriage, between Papa's feet, was a darkly varnished rosewood box with polished brass corners. Odd – she'd had this dream many times, and yet she had never noticed it before. "What's inside?" she asked Papa.

"My invention," Papa said. "We have to keep it safe

and hidden. It's a secret, like your fossil." He nodded at the stone in her hand.

"Why?" Lily asked. She suddenly knew she'd had this conversation before. The box, the words, everything, it all seemed strangely familiar, like it was part of a memory rather than a dream.

Papa opened his mouth to reply, but no more words came, and Lily saw through the windscreen the other steam-wagon careering towards them. The other driver's flashing silver eyes in the moonlight. The sweep of his headlamps across their windscreen, the screaming skid as its wheels crunched across the icy cobbled road.

Then Lily felt the impact. A deafening explosion tore the night in two as the steam-wagon smashed into the side of their carriage.

The golden fossil in its stone flew from her hand, fracturing the windscreen into a spider's web, and Lily and Mama went flying after it. Smashing through glass and gaslights, streaking reflections and snowflakes. And Lily fell into a white drift of blankness; her head filling with a fuzz of bright blinking patterns…

CHAPTER 10

Lily opened her eyes. Her mouth was dry and her body soaked in sweat. Her heart beat erratically, her pulse thudding through her. She took several deep breaths, holding in the air, then let it out slowly. She wouldn't sleep now, that was for sure.

The hands on her bedside clock said it was nearly three. She stood unsteadily and stared out the window. Behind the curtains, snow was falling in thick flakes; it was almost as if she was still in her nightmare. She shuddered at the thought of Mama's words, spoken months before the accident:

The secret's at the heart of it.

Why had she remembered that phrase? Was it to do

with the fossil? She wasn't even sure where it was any more. And had Mama really said it? Or was it remembered from somewhere else? Then there was the new part of the dream; Papa's invention in the box.

We have to keep it safe and hidden, he'd told her.

The box *was* a memory – she was sure of that. Another fragment from the accident she'd tried to blank out. But she couldn't because it was part of the puzzle of all this.

It had to be in his study. She would find it.

Lily sat up, lit the candle by her bedside, then pulled on her slippers.

The door to Papa's study would not open. Madame must've locked it. Lily didn't bother with a hairpin, she knew where to find the spare key. She found a nearby chair to stand on and ran her fingers along the top of the door frame until she felt the key cold against her hand. Then she took it down and put the bit in the lock.

The study was filled from floor to ceiling with shelves of dusty boxes and books. Blueprints and plans lay strewn across the desk blotter, files and folders were stacked on the occasional table, and balled papers were scattered about the rest of the room.

Papa was always neat and tidy. Someone had obviously been through his things, and Lily had a strong suspicion who.

She caught a distinct whiff of Madame's perfume. Mrs Rust was right: the housekeeper had been prying here. But if she hadn't found anything, how was Lily to know where to start?

Angrily, she kicked over the waste-paper basket and a crumpled telegram toppled out. She picked it up and smoothed it flat across the blotter on the desk, so she could read what it said.

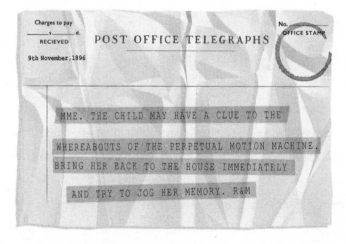

Charges to pay
____s.____d.
RECIEVED
9th November, 1896

POST OFFICE TELEGRAPHS

No.____
OFFICE STAMP

MME. THE CHILD MAY HAVE A CLUE TO THE WHEREABOUTS OF THE PERPETUAL MOTION MACHINE. BRING HER BACK TO THE HOUSE IMMEDIATELY AND TRY TO JOG HER MEMORY. R&M

The perpetual motion machine – wasn't that the thing Madame had mentioned to her this very afternoon? Maybe that's what Papa's secret invention was? The thing in the box? If so, Lily hoped the housekeeper wouldn't find it. She had the distinct impression she herself was meant to make the discovery, otherwise why would she have remembered it in her dream?

She pulled a few random books from the shelves and flipped through their pages, hoping to find inspiration, but nothing jumped out at her. Then she examined the blueprints on Papa's desk, but they weren't of interest either.

Finally, she stepped over to the fireplace, where Mama's ashes sat in an urn on the mantel. Lily traced the engraved words on its surface with her finger.

Grace Rose Hartman, 1847 – 1889
Wife, mother and heart of our lives.

She so dearly wanted to remember Mama. She closed her eyes and tried to summon her to mind, her smell, her voice, her laughter. But seven years had passed and she'd become a fuzzy face, lost in the recesses of time. The only thing Lily had left of her was the snatched picture in her dreams, that and the youthful portrait above the mantel.

The portrait was painted before Lily was born but Mama's soft brown eyes and loving smile felt familiar. Lily missed the warmth of that smile, and the safety of those arms. Life had been so cold without them, like a part of her had gone missing. And now perhaps Papa was gone too.

Lily held her breath…

What was it her parents had said to her in her memory, in her dream?

The secret's at the heart of it. We have to keep it safe and hidden.

The safe! Lily dragged the chair over from behind the desk. She pushed Mama's ashes carefully along the mantel until they were clear of the picture, then she reached up and, clutching the side of the frame, pulled it towards her. The picture swung out from the wall, hinged on one side. And there, behind it, was the safe.

Something told Lily that Madame had already looked here: the number lock seemed to have been scratched at with a nail file.

But Madame probably knew nothing about safes. Not as much as Lily and The Notorious Jack Door, anyhow, and Lily had the double advantage of knowing more special Hartman family dates than Madame, so she was sure she'd be able to guess the combination.

She started with her own birthday, twisting the lock around and stopping the numbers one by one under the arrow until the tumblers inside clicked.

That didn't work, but she wasn't surprised; Madame would've tried her birthday, and Papa's too, perhaps even Mama's, or Malkin's, because Lily found none of those worked either.

Then she had a horrible thought. She reached up to the safe lock and dialled in another number – the date of Mama's death. The date of the accident.

The safe swung open. Inside, on the small metal shelf, was the rosewood box with brass corners. Lily took it out and closed the safe door. She tried the lid but the box was locked, so she replaced the picture and the urn just as she'd found them. Then, with the box under an arm, she crept from the room, shutting the door behind her before locking it again.

Back in her bed, she positioned the box at her feet in the centre of the blanket and sat hugging her knees, staring at it. The keyhole of the box was made from gold, and the plate around it was shaped like a tiny heart with patterns of cogs pressed into the metal.

Lily took a hairpin from the discarded pile on her bedside table and tried one in the lock, but it didn't work. Silly to think it would. The mechanism was obviously far too complex.

She was wondering where the key could possibly be when she heard Madame's soft footsteps in the passage. She licked her fingers, doused the candle flame, then threw a blanket over herself and the box, and lay curled up against it, pretending to be asleep. Her heart thumped in her chest, blood hissing in her ears as she waited.

The door rattled and creaked as if someone was opening it and peering in. Then it shut softly, and there was a quiet click as a key turned in the lock.

Lily let out a sigh of relief, before she realized: Madame had locked her in! The housekeeper was up to something.

She got up and hid the box beneath the loose floorboard under her bed. As she replaced the board, she heard the putter of a steam-wagon creeping quietly along the drive, and the sound of Madame's feet descending the staircase.

The steam-wagon jittered to a stop outside, and there was a scraping noise as Madame dragged something heavy across the downstairs hall.

Then there was a pause, and the same scraping noise again.

Lily stepped to her window and, pressing herself against the glass, looked out along the side wall of the house towards the porch. Beyond it, the steam-wagon was parked.

Lily squinted into the gloom. Two men in long winter coats were walking up the front steps, their top halves rendered momentarily invisible to her by the corner of the house and the porch roof. One was razor-thin, like the man with the mirrored eyes on the zeppelin the other day, the other big and lumpy as a sack of bricks.

Lily crouched down lower against the glass, trying to get a better look at them, but their faces were hidden by tall stovepipe hats.

After a moment the front door creaked open and a light appeared; Madame must be standing there with a lantern talking to them. Lily wondered whether she might hear what they were saying if she opened the window, but then she realized the noise would alert them to her presence.

The two men stepped into the vestibule and, when they reappeared, she felt a chill run through her. For they were carrying the stiff unwound bodies of Mrs Rust and Captain Springer.

Madame followed them carrying a small lamp as they dragged the two still mechanicals over to their vehicle. Lily's heart leaped to her throat as she watched all three open the doors to the baggage compartment and thrust the mechs inside. She wished dearly that she could run downstairs and stop them, but her legs had frozen, and anyway, her bedroom door was locked.

She glanced across the garden, searching for the shapes of the other two mechanicals, Miss Tock and Mr Wingnut, hidden under the snow, but they had disappeared. Only a line of footprints and a long white trench remained, and Lily realized they'd been collected too and thrust inside the steam-wagon.

When she looked back the vehicle was already pulling away, making new tracks down the snowy drive. She searched the wagon's high sides for the insignia of the cog-and-bone men, but it wasn't there. So who was taking Papa's mechanicals away and why? Lily watched Madame brush her hands across the front of her long black dress as she turned and walked slowly back through the ankle-deep powder towards the house.

Lily woke with a start the next morning. She got up and found her door unlocked and thought she might have dreamed the whole mech-napping affair. But when she went down to the kitchen she found it cold and bare, the fire unlit. She opened the back door and stared out. A cold blast of sadness assailed her. The falling snow had covered the night's tracks, leaving no traces. And yet the empty kitchen was all the proof she needed: Mrs Rust was truly gone, as were the others. Madame had given them away, sold them on to two strangers, and Lily wasn't even sure why, or how she could be so cruel. They may have only been machines to Madame but, to Lily, they were real people, true friends.

She slammed the door and stumbled back to her room to find Madame riffling through her things. Every desk drawer had been pulled out and her entire collection of gothic novels and penny dreadfuls had been thrown from their shelves. The wardrobe doors were open, and the linen had been turned out of the laundry basket and flung across the bed.

"What are you doing?" Lily shouted.

Madame looked hot and flustered, but then she regained control. "*Rien, chérie*, only tidying, I don't know how you can leave things in such a mess."

"Where's Mrs Rust," Lily demanded, "and the others?"

Madame folded some clothes she'd obviously just searched through. "Help me tidy, please. I had the cog-and-bone men come and take them away."

Lily folded her arms across her chest. "Why?"

"Because they didn't work properly. They'll be rebuilt, and if they're irreparable they'll be stripped for salvage."

"But Papa made them. They were part of the family."

"Mechanicals have no feelings, Lily, they're just things. They can't be part of anyone's family." Madame pretended to fold some of her blouses. "Besides, I've had a *bien* offer from someone who wanted the parts. Brain-cogs mostly, I think."

"You should've asked."

"*Ce n'est pas nécessaire*. I'm your guardian. What I say goes." Madame placed a few books back on the bookshelf.

"Now, *s'il vous plaît,* clear the rest of this up." She waved her hands at the mess. "And try not to spend the whole day skulking in here. Come take the morning sun in the drawing room with me."

"I won't clear anything up!" Lily shouted. "And if you think I'm going anywhere with you, Madame – the drawing room, hell, or otherwise – then you are sorely mistaken!" She gritted her teeth and launched herself at Madame, fists flailing.

"*Ça suffit!*" Madame grabbed her arms and pressed them against her chest. Her long nails dug into Lily's wrists and her teardrop earrings swung wildly as she dragged Lily away from the door and threw her down on the bed.

"On second thoughts…" The housekeeper's breathing was ragged. "…you shall stay here. I can't have you wandering around the house willy-nilly, investigating my actions." She walked to the door. "Perhaps you might see fit to find this perpetual motion thing amongst this mess. I know you've been in your father's office. The urn was moved, and the dial on the safe is in a different position. If that's what you've taken, Lily, then you must know—"

"I haven't taken anything," Lily shouted, her eyes hot with tears.

"*Très bien* – have it your way." Madame slammed the door and Lily heard the key turn in the lock. This time the woman didn't even try to do it quietly. Then her heavy heeled shoes clacked away down the length of the landing.

Lily threw her head down onto her pillow and screamed. A prisoner in her own home – how would she find the key to the box now? She stood and punched the yellow wallpaper, but that only made her fists ache and her fingers feel numb.

She pulled a few hairpins from her head and tried them in the door. Every one bent or snapped, and she threw them down angrily on the floor.

Even if she got out of here, where would she go? There was no one left to help her. She crossed to the window, opened it, and stood staring at the empty gates, the tracks of the men's steam-wagon had vanished under the white landscape. She hoped Mrs Rust and the rest of the mechanicals, or Papa and Malkin, might suddenly return, but there was only a dreadful silence. And when no one came for her, she leaned her head on the windowsill and cried.

Then, after a long while, a figure did appear. A boy dressed in patched grey trousers and a thick winter jacket, which his gloved hands pulled tight around his skinny frame. Underneath his cap sat a mop of unruly black hair and heavy frowning brows, and his face looked rather anxious. Lily had no idea who he was, or whether he would help her. But she was certainly going to find out. She took a deep breath, put her fingers in her mouth, and whistled.

CHAPTER 11

Robert had walked the length of the snowy driveway and was stopped a good eight feet from the house, gazing up at it, and wondering whether to try the servants' entrance or the front door, when he heard a loud whistle from above.

He blinked and stared up at a tearful-looking red-headed girl gazing out of a high window. The girl took her fingers from her mouth and called down to him, her voice carrying over the soft silent landscape: "Friend or foe?"

Robert considered this. "Friend, I think."

"Who are you looking for?"

"For Miss Hartman."

The girl smiled wearily. "That's me."

He felt a twinge of relief. "May we speak?" he asked. "I've a message for you."

"If you wait there," she said, "I shall endeavour to come down."

He watched her push open the casement window and climb out. She edged along a shelf of bricks, clinging carefully to the window frame. As she jumped down onto the corner of the porch roof, her feet slipped on the frozen tiles, but she managed to right herself before she dropped over the roof's edge and shimmied down a drainpipe. When her feet reached the handrail, she grabbed an upright post covered in dead creepers and jumped down, tumbling into a drift of snow.

"Blimey, Miss Hartman," Robert said, "you're a good mountaineer."

"Call me Lily, please." Lily picked herself up and dusted off the snowflakes, shivering as she did so, for she was wearing only a thin dress. "Climbing's fine," she said. "It's the falling I'm not used to. Normally I'd use the stairs, but I was imprisoned and my hairpins broke when I tried to pick the lock."

Robert opened his mouth to attempt a reply, but could think of nothing.

"Who are you?" Lily asked. "And what's this about?"

She folded her goose-pimpled arms. Now that he saw her up close Robert felt unaccountably nervous. She'd a friendly face, with cheeks rosy from the cold, and her upturned nose was lightly dusted with freckles. Beneath her fringe of wavy copper hair, her green eyes looked filled with sadness, and Robert wished with all his heart he could find something to say to make it vanish.

"I'm Robert Townsend," he mumbled. "Apprentice clockmaker in the village up the way..." His gloved hands twisted together, and he found himself staring. He'd planned his words carefully as he walked up the drive, but now, somehow, he'd forgotten them all. "Da used to wind the clocks here" – it was the only thing he could think of – "for your father."

"Did you want to speak to me about that?" Lily asked.

Robert fiddled with the brim of his cap. He felt the tips of his ears burn. How could he be so stupid? Her father was missing. That's why the mech-fox had wanted him to come in the first place. "No," he said at last. "It's... I think I've something belongs to you, at least, he claims he does."

"Oh. Is it Captain Springer, or one of the others?"

"He's called Malkin."

"Malkin's alive!" Lily exclaimed. A glimmer of hope sparked inside her. "Does he have news of Papa?"

144

"Not exactly," Robert murmured. "He said I had to give you a message. He would've come himself, only he was shot…"

"Shot?" Her eyes widened in alarm.

"Don't worry, he's fine. Ticking over. Me and Da fixed his leg – the damaged part, I mean – and he's going to be right as rain. He's got a strong constitution, that one. Insides of steel… How d'you own such an amazing mech anyway?"

"My father made him for me. I wish I could've taken him to school, but there were no pets allowed." Lily jiggled from foot to foot with impatience, or was it the cold? "Please," she said, "tell me what it is."

He nodded. "When Malkin came round he told me to tell you: the secret's in the safe."

Lily clapped her hands together. "The box – I knew it! He wants me to bring the box. Perhaps he has the key?"

She took Robert by the hand. "Come on," she said. "We'll go get it."

They were walking towards the front door when a black steam-wagon pulled in through the gates at the far end of the drive. Puffs of acrid smoke drifted from its chimney stack as it drove towards them.

Lily gasped and clasped his hand tighter.

"What is it?" he asked.

"That vehicle was here last night." She dragged him behind a snow-covered fir tree. "You mustn't let them see me."

They watched through the branches as the steam-wagon stopped in front of the main entrance. Two men got out of the driver's compartment. Their mirrored eyes glinted as they climbed the porch steps. One rapped on the front door with the handle of his walking stick, then they waited.

"Those men were in the village chasing Malkin," Robert said. "They're hybrids – part-human, part-mech. All bad news."

"I know," Lily said. She pointed a shaking finger at Roach. "The thin one, Mr Roach, he was on the commuter zep with us and, last night, I think they took Mrs Rust and Papa's mechanicals away."

Robert gave a shudder. "I know him too. He came into the shop. He's dangerous. And the other one too – Mr Mould. You oughtn't to go in there."

"I've got to get the box." Lily brushed back her fringe and a fierce look came over her face. "I'm sure that's what they're after. So we can't leave without it."

They crept round the side of the house, the snow

crunching beneath their feet. Through a window, Robert glimpsed a drawing room. Then the door opened and a woman dressed in black showed Roach and Mould in.

"That's my guardian, Madame Verdigris," Lily whispered. "She's in on whatever they're up to." And indeed, even at this distance, Robert could tell from the woman's posture that she wasn't at all surprised to see the two men. It was as if they were old friends.

Robert and Lily ducked away from the window and peered around a corner of an ivy-encrusted trellis. The back door looked clear.

They dashed towards it and Lily tried the handle. "Locked." She prised open an adjacent window and climbed through, beckoning him to follow.

They were in a narrow corridor. Lily grasped a brass doorknob set into a papered wall and opened a disguised door to reveal a narrow servants' staircase.

"This way," she said.

Robert followed her up to a first floor and past several rooms along a dark landing, before she paused outside a door.

"Ah-ha!" she said. "That witch left the key in it. Probably why I couldn't get out this way." She unlocked the door and stepped into a room filled with a mess of clothes and books. Robert crowded in behind her, peering over her shoulder at the rows of gruesome penny dreadful covers, pinned to yellow wallpaper. A few had been hand-tinted with watercolours: *Varney the Vampyre*, in particular, featured a lot of hand-painted red.

"Wait here," Lily said, and she crawled under her bed and prised up a loose floorboard. Then she reached into the gap beneath it and pulled out a square rosewood box.

She placed the box on a blanket in the centre of the bed. "There," she said, folding the corners of the blanket over the box's lid and knotting them tightly together. "That'll do."

Robert flinched. He'd heard the *tap-tap-tap* of a cane, and the creak of heavy boots. He peered round the door jamb. Three shadowy figures were ascending what must've been the main staircase, to the landing. "They're coming," he whispered.

Lily stepped towards the open window. "We have to climb down."

"I can't." The words felt dry in his throat.

"Why not?"

"I'm afraid of heights."

"Oh." She opened the wardrobe and stuffed her bundle inside. "Then we'll have to hide."

"I shouldn't get in there either. I have an allergy to dust."

"Never mind that now." Lily pushed back a row of dresses on hangers, and an old tattered parasol, and crammed him into the wardrobe. Then she took a last look around the room.

"Professor Silverfish's card!" she exclaimed, and she snatched a square of paper from her bedside table, then jumped in beside him, pulling the wardrobe door shut just as Madame, Roach and Mould arrived.

"Where is she?" Mr Roach glanced about, the room swooshing past in his reflective lenses.

Robert peered over Lily's shoulder through the crack in the door. The dust in the wardrobe was making his eyes run and his nose itch; he dearly wanted to sneeze.

He covered his mouth with a hand and watched as Lily's guardian stepped over to the open door.

"But, I can't understand it." Madame's reply was strained. "I locked her in."

Mr Roach leaned on his cane and crouched to examine the broken hairpins on the floor. "She must've used these to pick the lock," he said. "She hasn't got far. I'd say she's still in the house." He gathered the broken pins in his hand. "You knew we were coming, Madame Hortense. I warned you not to let Lily out of your sight."

"I've been busy."

"Not busy enough, by the looks of things. Pack a case

for her. We'll search the rest of the house. Mr Mould, come with me." The two men marched off down the passage.

Lily and Robert kept as still as they could, hiding behind the row of clothes. But when Madame opened the wardrobe, dust seemed to whoosh up Robert's nose with the sudden light and—

AAATCHOOOOOOOOOOOoooooooooooo!

"*Mon Dieu!*" Madame screamed, grabbing at them. "She's here."

His eyes streaming, Robert pulled the old parasol from the back of the cupboard and hit the woman with it, tipping her into the wardrobe. Lily wrested herself free, dragging the bundle along with her.

"Come on!" she cried, and they scrambled through the door and shut it behind them. Robert turned the key in the lock, trapping Madame inside. They ran along the landing towards the main stairs, but Roach and Mould were rushing upwards to meet them, their mirrored eyes gleaming. Lily hugged her bundle to her chest and darted the other way. Robert scrambled to follow.

When they reached the far end of the mezzanine they clattered through another disguised door and back down the narrow servants' staircase to the ground floor.

The hall was empty.

As they slipped out the same window they'd come in by, they heard the men running around upstairs, searching for the hidden door.

They ran across the garden, Lily throwing glances behind her.

Skirting the edge of the lawn, they ducked behind a snow-covered pile of compost and stopped. Lily caught her breath, and adjusted the bundle under her arm.

"We'll be safe here for a minute," she said, brushing her fringe from her face. "I'm going to have to trust you. I hope you're telling me the truth?"

Robert nodded. The smell of rotting food was making him queasy, or was it the running? "You can trust me," he said.

"Good." She gave a sniff. "This isn't the way I wanted to leave, with so much undone. But I can't go back now, not when everyone wants to cause me harm."

They set off again, heading down the incline of the garden. They were halfway down some stone steps when they caught sight of a third man, waiting in the bare rose garden at the bottom.

Lily turned and took Robert back along the balustrade, down an icy slope, through a flower bed filled with thorny stems, between a pair of trees, and along the drive towards the manor's entrance.

"Damn it!"

The steam-wagon had been moved across the driveway, blocking the gates.

She grasped Robert's hand and they sprinted along the base of the boundary wall. Lily found a broken planter, which had fallen from atop a pillar, and clambered onto it; she rested the bundle on top of the snowy wall and climbed up beside it.

Robert gulped. "I hate heights, remember?"

"It's only a few feet." Lily pushed the bundle over the top to land safely in the snow on the other side, before jumping down beside it.

Shakily, Robert pulled himself up. The icy flakes wet his gloves, and made them slippery as he climbed up onto the parapet and hung from the far side.

"Now let go," Lily said. He let his feet dangle, kicking against the frozen bricks, before he dropped and rolled to the ground. He picked himself up and dusted the snow from his breeches.

Lily swung the bundle over her shoulder.

"Come on," she said, and ran off through the deep drifts.

"Er, if you want the village," he called after her, "it's more to the west. That way."

As they stole across the countryside towards Townsend's Horologist's, the sky darkened and a heavy snowfall began, the flakes settling on their clothes and soaking through to their skin.

Robert led the way, taking Lily round the edge of the village to come in via the North Lanes, all the time keeping an eye out for the men.

He'd a horrible feeling they were watching everything he did and at any moment might jump out from behind a hedge and grab Lily and her bundle before he'd time to stop them.

When they'd crossed the green and passed the village chapel, he allowed himself the briefest flicker of a smile. "Everything's going to work out fine, Miss," he said, keeping his voice bright. "Not long now and we'll be safe at my shop." They reached the top of Bridge Road and he sighed with relief at the familiar snow-covered street. They'd made it without encountering anyone. But when they crossed the brow of the hill, things seemed distinctly less rosy.

Fifteen feet ahead, leaning against his parked steam-wagon, his face hidden under the dark canopy of a batlike umbrella, was the orang-utang shape of Mr Mould. And with him, leaning on his walking cane, was the knife-thin silhouette of Mr Roach. The pair were huddled in conversation.

Lily's face paled. She shivered and clutched the bundle to her chest. "They're here," she said.

Robert's breath caught in his throat.

Just then Mould's cigar went out. He took out a lucifer, turned away and, striking it, held the flickering flame to the cigar's tip. His fat cheeks glowed with its fiery red sheen. Roach watched, his mirrored eyes shining orange in the shadowy sockets of his face. He was waiting to finish whatever it was he had been saying, and both men were so intent on Mould's task that they failed to notice Robert and Lily at the far end of the street.

"Quick," Robert spluttered. "This way." He grasped Lily's hand and pulled her down a side alley.

They stopped behind a whitewashed gable wall. Meltwater dripped onto Robert's cap from the snow-frosted eaves of the cottage.

Lily dropped her bundle between her feet and hugged her arms. "I thought we'd lost them," she said. "What are we going to do?"

"Give me a moment," Robert replied. "I'll think of something." He tried, but he could not, and the red glowing vision of the men hung about in the dark, filling him with a feeling of despair.

"Is there any other way into the shop?" Lily asked.

"If you go to the end here," he said, "there's a path

leads back onto the road further down; from there you can cross over and sneak through the gate into the backyard."

"Then let's do that," Lily said.

"You can't, not without… I mean… They'd see us." Robert stepped away from her and headed back towards the mouth of the alley.

"What are you doing?" Lily asked.

He gulped and gestured at the street. "I'm going to go out there and distract them so you can get past. When I'm shot of them both, I'll go in the shop and let you in the back door."

Lily nodded. "Very well, but be careful."

"And you," he said brusquely, trying not to let the fear show in his voice.

His mouth dry and heart beating hard in his chest, Robert strolled out onto Bridge Road. He took off his flat cap and stuffed it into his pocket. When he glanced back, Lily was edging towards the far end of the alley. He sauntered along the street, approaching the men, listening to the crunch of the melting snow underfoot, and trying to seem as calm as possible.

When he was sure they'd seen him, he did a double take, and turned smartly on his heels; and, as he'd hoped, they rushed to follow.

Mr Mould grabbed Robert's shoulder and spun him round. "Master Townsend, so glad we've bumped into you. I was having a word with my colleague, Mr Roach, about our encounter the other day, where you sent me off on a wild goose chase."

Robert shrugged. "Don't know what you mean."

"Oh I think you do." Mr Mould frowned and leaned towards him, and Robert's face grew big and distorted in his mirrored sockets. "Tell you what, son. Mr Roach and I are on important business, looking for a lost soul, and your little 'misdirection' prank cost us."

"And didn't we see you at the big house earlier?" Mr Roach added. "You were wearing a cap."

Robert shook his head. "House? What house? And what would you characters want with a runaway girl?"

Mr Roach pounced on this. "I don't believe he mentioned we were looking for a girl."

Robert gulped. "Er, your colleague did a moment ago."

"I find that unlikely," Mr Roach said, but he wasn't sure, he turned to his mutton-chopped companion. "Mr Mould, did you say a girl?"

Mr Mould scratched his head. "I said soul."

"Oh," Robert said. "I must've misheard." In the corner of his vision, he noticed his da watching from the shop

156

window. Then he caught a fleeting glimpse of Lily, with her bundle, running across the road to head down the alley beside the shop; and under his breath, he let out a sigh of relief.

"What are you looking at?" Mr Roach asked suddenly.

"My da," Robert said. "He's watching you, so you'd best let go of my arm."

Mr Mould released his iron grip and made a pretence of brushing some dust off Robert's jacket.

"Remember, son, we've got our eyes on you." Mr Roach tapped the bare metal in his raw eye socket with one finger. "All four of them." He prodded his companion on the shoulder with the handle of his stick, and the two of them walked back to their vehicle. The engine growled and, as they got in, a sputter of steam spurted from the chimney.

They didn't drive off straight away, and Robert wondered if they were watching him through the tinted glass windscreen. He tried to ignore the panic that rose inside, telling him to run, and instead walked calmly back to the shop.

When he opened the door he found his da standing by the window, twisting the thin frames of his glasses between his fingers. "Where were you, Robert?" he asked. "You've been gone hours."

"I went for a wander," Robert explained. Distractedly, he watched the men's vehicle drive off down the street. When all that was left of it was thin wheel tracks in the snow, he bolted the shop door and locked it with the key.

"Who were those fellows?" Thaddeus asked. "The large one came in to ask after you."

"Never mind that," Robert said. "There's someone out back I want you to meet."

"Who the devil have you brought now?" Thaddeus demanded.

Robert led his da through the rag curtain. At the end of the passage he slipped the deadbolt on the back door and pulled it open.

Lily waited nervously on the steps outside, clasping her bundle in her shivering arms, her red hair filled with melting snowflakes.

"This", said Robert, "is Miss Lily Hartman, and she needs our help."

CHAPTER 12

Lily dried her hair with the warm woollen towel Robert had found her, and when she was finally done, Thaddeus beckoned her through to the workshop.

The room was dimly lit, the skylight in the ceiling frosted with snow. She looked around the walls, hung with brass tools and clock bodies. Something stirred in a box full of blankets in the corner making a low ticking sound. It pricked up its ears and raised a foxy head.

"Lily!" Malkin jumped up and hobbled over shakily.

Lily was so relieved to see Malkin alive, she put down her bundle and fell to her knees, throwing her arms around his neck and hugging him close. "Malkin! You're here. I was certain you'd been destroyed by that terrible air crash." Lily stroked Malkin's scruffy fur until his tongue lolled out the side of his black-lipped mouth, and his bushy tail swept back and forth. It was good to see him. If he'd found help, surely Papa could have too, couldn't he?

She was almost afraid to ask, but she had to know the truth. "What happened that night, Malkin?" she whispered.

Malkin's ears drooped, and he shook her hand away, hanging his head sheepishly. "So John did not return?" he asked. "I had hoped he might've escaped the attack. A silver airship harpooned *Dragonfly* and tried to board, but I thought they might... I thought John maybe survived." He stopped and pawed at his snout with one black forepaw.

Lily felt a pang of despair. It was true then – what everyone said about Papa. He was probably dead. Her hope faded.

Malkin must have sensed it, for he tilted his head and gave her a foxy smile. "By all the cogs in Christendom, Lily, it's marvellous to see you! I would jump for joy if it wasn't for my injured leg."

"Was it the men with silver eyes?" Lily asked, though she'd an inkling it must've been. "Roach and Mould?"

The fox gave a mechanical growl. "So those are their names. The clanking vagabonds chased me from the crash site. They're after something of John's, I'll warrant. They must suppose I have some tick-tock of its whereabouts. The truth is, I know nothing."

Lily sighed. Her gaze strayed to the bundle on the floor. Was all this because of some invention hidden inside that box? Was that why those men had attacked Malkin and Papa? And, if so, what could she do to stop them? She wasn't strong or clever. She hadn't even managed to find the key yet.

"They came to our house," she told Malkin. "Roach followed me from school on the commuter zep. Then they took Mrs Rust and the rest of the mechanicals away; Madame even helped them. But I think what they're after is in here – in Papa's old box. Do you have the key?"

Malkin snuffled at the box under the blanket, prodding at it with his nose. "'Fraid not," he said. "But perhaps you might clock some clue in John's correspondence?"

Lily looked up. "Correspondence?"

"Yes. Did this gangly pup not tell you?" Malkin bared his teeth at Robert and gave a stern growl. "Your father left you a letter. I have it here, in my pouch."

"Oh," said Lily. And then she didn't know what to say. Because there was a finality to it somehow. Whatever the words were in that letter, they were very possibly Papa's last goodbye. She gave a sniff and wiped a hand across her face. Then, steeling herself, she reached out and stroked Malkin's chin, while she untied the pouch from around his neck with her other hand.

The leather felt soft and damp, but when she smoothed out the folds she was dismayed to find the centre of the pouch was singed with a small hole; evident on both sides.

Malkin's dark eyes rounded at the sight of it. "Crankshafts!" he said. "It must be from that clanking bullet that got me."

Fingers shaking, Lily fumbled with the drawstring and pulled an envelope from within the pouch.

Her name was written in its centre in Papa's hand. To her relief she found the bullet hole had only passed through the corner of the envelope. Perhaps the contents were still readable?

She turned it over and on the other side, covering the flap, she found her papa's scrawled hieroglyph, intact.

She opened the envelope and unfolded the single-page letter, but it was not as she'd hoped – the bullet had singed a hole in the folds of paper, burning straight through the heart of Papa's words and, though she peered closely, many were unreadable.

"What's it say?" Malkin's ears flicked forward and he waited expectantly.

"Yes, what does it say?" Robert asked.

Lily looked at them both and at Robert's father, standing in the doorway, his eyes filled with the desire to help.

She took a deep breath, and read Papa's words aloud. At least, the ones she could make out, round the big black hole…

My Darling Lily,

Your life is more precious than anything, not just because of what I'm about to tell you, but because you are my only beloved daughter, the heart of my life. And these secrets are things I meant to divulge long ago…

Dragonfly is ⬛⬛⬛ from my past that is about to catch up ⬛⬛⬛ u were born. Professor Silverfish ⬛⬛⬛ perpetual motion machine. The plan wa⬛⬛⬛ ng, replace their heart with clock⬛⬛⬛ I hid the machine, but bad peopl⬛⬛⬛ They killed Mama and injured yo⬛⬛⬛ teful day I had to use the device to ⬛⬛⬛ Afterwards we found a new home. A pla⬛⬛⬛ long to tell you this. It was all becaus⬛⬛⬛ Silverfish, your godfather – he was a good friend, ⬛⬛⬛ be trusted.

Find somewhere safe, my darling, and never reveal the truth to anyone, for it will put you in grave danger.

Your loving Papa x

Dark images whirled in Lily's head as she finished reading the letter. The crash, her injuries, Mama's death – they'd all been deliberate. A planned attacked.

Roach and Mould, or men like them, had murdered Mama trying to get hold of Papa's machine. That's why he'd changed their name and moved them to the countryside, and that's why he never spoke of the past – not to try and forget the horrible things that had happened, but to hide from them.

But if Papa's enemies were capable of murder, then they were capable of anything. They'd made Papa disappear, and now they were coming after her. They were more dangerous than she could've possibly imagined.

Lily felt a dizzying fear. She took a deep breath. When she finally looked up, the others were watching her with silent concern. She glanced once more at the letter and three strange words jumped out at her:

"Perpetual motion machine. What does it mean?" she asked, looking around, hoping one of them might know.

"It's a device which requires no power," Thaddeus explained. "It runs on its own momentum for ever without stopping. But, as far as I know, such a thing is only an idea, it hasn't actually been invented. Unless your father created one." He glanced down at the box in its bundle. "If there truly is one in there, then it's certainly a compact machine. And probably the most valuable thing that currently exists in this world." He laughed nervously.

"Valuable enough to kill Mama for," Lily said, grief heavy in her chest. "It's true. Papa had that box with him on the night she died. I remember. I saw it in my dream."

She glanced at their faces, full of horror.

"He always told me it was an accident," she mumbled, "but it was something much worse. And now it's happening again." She laid down her letter and stared at Malkin.

"You must tell me what occurred on that airship," she said. "And I want the truth this time, not the rubbish Madame Verdigris told me."

Malkin eyed Robert and his father suspiciously. "I don't know whether I can speak frankly in front of them."

"Us? But we saved your life!" Robert blurted.

Thaddeus shushed him. "Do you want us to leave, Miss Hartman?"

"No, it's fine."

"It's not a pleasant story," the fox said. "In fact, it's positively tocking awful."

Lily took a deep breath. "Tell me anyway," she said. "I have to know the truth."

"All right," Malkin said, "but I imagine no good will come of it." He sat up and shook his head from side to side, rattling the loose parts in his skull. It was as if he was trying to get what he wanted to say clear in his mind before he spoke.

"We were flying home to Brackenbridge, John and I." Malkin gave a sniff. "We'd been on a secret trip to buy mechanical parts. Upon our return journey we were attacked by a silver airship with a pointed hull. I remember jumping up at the window to look back at it. It was bristling with spikes like some weaponized—"

"I saw that ship," Robert interrupted, "it flew over the village the night you first came here."

Malkin gave him a pointed look. Lily knew this was because he didn't like to be interrupted. "Go on," she prompted.

"Well," the fox continued, "*Dragonfly* couldn't fight such air power. She's not a warship, after all. Our only option was to try and outrun them. Unfortunately, we failed. John was able to get me into the escape pod, but he stayed with the ship. I tried to argue with him but he wanted to get it down safely. He released the pod and as I fell, I saw the other airship drag *Dragonfly* in, as if they intended to board her.

"In a crunching explosion, I hit the ground. The pod was bouncing and twisting, turning and spinning, shaking me up like a stone in a tin can, until I thought every cog inside me would be crushed. Then, with a jolt, I came to a stop.

"The pod's door had burst open on impact, and hung loose on the inside wall. Gyros spinning in my head, I crawled towards the door. My hackles raised, I peered over the rubber seal, and out of the opening.

"A deep groove stretched away from the pod, cutting across frosted fields, leaving a trail of broken branches and debris. I heard the screech of clashing metal, and glanced up. The two airships were locked tight together.

"Suddenly, *Dragonfly* was cut loose and drifted, in a fluttering tailspin.

"When she reached a distance of three ship-lengths, the other zep fired, and I saw *Dragonfly* explode in a whoosh of flames. My heart-cogs skipped as I watched her burning fragments fall.

"Whether they took John prisoner, I cannot say. But either way, it didn't look good. And from what he says about your mother in the letter..." Malkin paused and gave a snuffling cough.

"I was winding down fast, couldn't hang around any longer. The moment I crashed, I knew they'd send a ground crew out looking for me.

"Quickly, I stepped over the door seal and darted into the foggy night. And then I ran. I knew I couldn't stop until I found you." Malkin shuddered. "But it seems my journey's been as futile as a broken cam-spring. For I have no real solutions, Lily, and my arrival's put you in even more danger as I have led the enemy to you." He tipped his head apologetically at her.

Lily reached out and stroked his chin once more. She felt Papa's absence more keenly than ever. He would've known what to do. "Roach and Mould would've found me eventually," she said. "I think Madame Verdigris is working with them. She told them our real name and where we live."

"That gear-grinding woman," Malkin growled. "I always knew she was a bad lot."

Lily put the letter in her pocket, and stared in despair at the bundle on the floor. "We may have learned the truth about Mama, but we've still no concrete answers about Papa or this machine," she said. "And, in a way, things are worse than before. I can't go home because those men and Madame are there and I can't stay here either, because they have their suspicions about Robert already. What on earth am I to do?"

"We'll think of something," Robert said.

Thaddeus put a hand on her shoulder. "And perhaps," he said, "while we do, a little tea and toast would not go amiss?"

It was a funny little kitchen, on the first floor above the shop, tucked under the eaves and full of odd angles. Lily watched Thaddeus fill the copper kettle at the sink in the corner, while Robert stoked the fire in the large blackened range, bringing it back to life.

"Do you want any help, Mr Townsend?" she asked.

The clockmaker shook his head. "No thanks, young lady. And please, call me Thaddeus. You must take it easy, you've had a trying few days." He handed the kettle to Robert, who put it on top of the range to boil.

With a sense of relief, Lily settled herself at the kitchen table. Malkin, who had been on edge since their discussion, crawled under her chair and sat by her heels, with one black-tipped ear pricked up, listening to the conversation.

"Get the things for tea, Robert," Thaddeus said and Robert fetched three mugs from the dresser, took some bread and cheese from the larder, and laid everything out higgledy-piggledy on the table.

Thaddeus eased himself into a seat opposite Lily and got out his tobacco to prepare a pipe.

"May I have a look at your father's box?" he asked, when he had his pipe lit and was puffing away.

Lily undid the blanket and placed the box on the table in front of him.

Thaddeus pushed his glasses down to the end of his nose and picked up the box, turning it around in his hands. "This is a well-made thing," he said, "not designed to be opened without the key. Even its hinges are on the inside."

As Thaddeus peered closely at the lock, Lily looked at its back and saw he was right – she hadn't noticed before, but there *were* no hinges outside.

"So these men think this contains a perpetual motion machine?" Thaddeus asked. "And do they have the key?"

"I don't know." Lily swallowed, and her stomach gave a grumble. She reached across the table and took some bread and cheese. "Perhaps," she said, "they thought Malkin or I would know where it was, or how to open it for them."

"When this snowstorm is over," Thaddeus said, "we should take the matter to the police."

Lily was too busy eating to reply, but Robert answered for her.

"Those men said they *were* the police, Da. A secret police."

"Of course they did." Thaddeus nodded. "But, do we believe them?"

"It seems unlikely," Lily said, through mouthfuls of bread. "But, if not, how would they have so many resources at their disposal?"

"Hmm." Thaddeus put the box down. "A tricky situation." He puffed on his pipe, and when it went out, relit it with a match. "Perhaps…"

He reached into the pocket of his trousers and took out a small keyring full of different sized keys. Lily swallowed her mouthful and held her breath as he flicked through them and tried a few in the lock.

He shook his head. "Nope. No good. What about your penknife, Robert?"

Robert handed it to him. From the folding elements within the casing, Thaddeus opened out a small sturdy screwdriver. He tried to force it under the rim of the lid, but that didn't work either. "The clanking thing's on too tight," he muttered.

"We could smash it open," Robert suggested.

"But then we might damage what's inside," Thaddeus said.

Everyone moved in closer to peer at the lid, and when the kettle whistled Lily nearly jumped out of her skin.

Robert took it from the stove and poured three mugs of tea with milk and sugar, then handed them around. Thaddeus, a little agitated now, brushed his aside. "May

I see the letter as well?" he asked, handing Robert back his penknife.

Lily took the letter from her pocket and passed it to him. As he read, Thaddeus glanced up every now and then, frowning at the box. When he'd finally finished, he folded the page and placed it back in the envelope. "What about this fellow John mentions, Professor Silverfish?" he asked. "Who is he?"

"He's my godfather," Lily said. "When I was small he was always coming to visit Papa. They had a business together – a big factory creating mechanicals – but Papa sold up his share after they had some sort of falling out."

"That's right." Thaddeus nodded. "I remember, John told me a little about it: I think there was a difference of opinion over the type of mechs they wanted to create. Your father was interested in machines with feelings, while Professor Silverfish wanted to make ones that ran longer. Seemed the business did very well, but then Professor Silverfish left the country for some reason, after your mother died."

"It was his heart." Lily took a sip from her cup of milky tea, cupping her hands around the warm china to absorb its heat. "He came to see me when he heard of Papa's disappearance. I think he wanted to apologize.

Make everything right again." She drank the last sugary mouthfuls of tea from her mug.

"If he knew your da well," Robert said, "perhaps he'll have some clue about this box." He nodded at it.

"That's right," Thaddeus said. "It might have been part of their work together."

"And any clue could help lead us to Papa," Lily added. For she still so wanted to believe he was alive. "Perhaps he's a prisoner somewhere?"

"Maybe." Thaddeus didn't sound convinced about that part.

"If only you had an idea where this Silverfish character lived, then we could go ask for his advice," Malkin muttered from under her chair.

"But I do know where he lives!" Lily cried. She took out Professor Silverfish's card and placed it on the table. "He gave this to me, and told me if I was ever in trouble he would help."

Thaddeus took the card and whistled. "Riverside Walk, Chelsea. This is a smart London address. He must be an important well-to-do man." He pushed back his chair. "We shall go see him at once."

"We?" Lily said.

"Yes. Robert and I will escort you."

"Thank you, but I couldn't ask you to take such a risk."

"Nonsense, those Roach-men, or whatever they're called, are obviously dangerous. We will accompany you until you arrive safely at your destination. First thing in the morning we shall shut up shop and take you on the train to visit this fellow."

"Couldn't we go by zep?" Robert asked.

Thaddeus shook his head. "They'll be expecting that. Besides, we can't afford it. No, a train's better, and there are more passengers so it will be easier to blend in." Thaddeus smiled at them both. "Why don't you go and get Miss Hartman some of your old clothes to wear tomorrow, Robert? It's best if she travels incognito. Besides, she'd freeze to death in just that dress."

Robert sighed. He stood and went out into the hall. Lily heard him open a door, further off, and he returned a moment later with a patched jacket, corduroy trousers and a grey felt cap.

"They should be about your size. Used to be mine a year ago, before I grew too tall for them. Should make a decent disguise."

"Thank you." Lily put the card and the letter in the pockets of his jacket, and tried it on. The jacket was warm and comfortable and smelled slightly of mothballs and of him.

"Not a bad fit," Thaddeus said and even Malkin

perked up, scrambling from under the seat to peer at her.

"Is there a looking glass?" Lily asked.

"Over on the wall." Robert pointed behind her.

She stood and examined herself in the mirror. The jacket sloped off her shoulders and the sleeves came nearly to her fingertips, but she actually quite liked it. She folded the cuffs back over each wrist, exposing the moth-eaten silken lining. Then she ran a hand through her hair, so matted and clumped. "It looks an awful muddle," she said.

"That's what caps are for," Robert told her.

She wedged the cap on over her hair and tipped the brim down to hide her eyes a little. "What do you think, Malkin?" she asked the fox.

He angled his head, and his black eyes narrowed, taking her in. "You look like a vagabond."

"I rather like it." She peered closer at herself, and smiled. How horrified the Kraken or Madame would be if they saw her now. Suddenly, she felt a little better. Thanks to Malkin and Papa's letter, she had some clues as to what was going on. And, thanks to Robert and his father, she had a disguise and a plan. Perhaps, together, they'd solve this mystery and find Papa, after all?

"It's a funny thing," she said, talking to her reflection,

"but I always felt something of a tomboy inside. This way my outside matches that better, wouldn't you say?"

"True." Malkin gave a wide, pink-mouthed yawn.

Thaddeus glanced at his wristwatch. "Heavens! Look at the time – we'd best get some sleep if we're to catch the first train."

As soon as he said this, Lily realized how tired she was. She glanced over at Robert and saw his eyes drooping too.

"We'll make up the daybed in the corner for you," Thaddeus said. "It's beside the range, so it's the warmest place in the house."

He and Robert went out into the hall once more and returned moments later with a pile of blankets. When they'd finished making the bed for her, they retired to their rooms.

Lily lay down on the daybed and found it rather soft. She pulled the blankets over herself and plumped the cushions. She could not sleep at first. Tears itched at her eyes, and black thoughts of all she'd learned crowded her mind.

Roach and Mould were dangerous men to be up against, and things were far worse than she could've possibly imagined a few days ago, but at least she had help now.

She touched the scar on her chest, remembering Mama, long gone; killed for a secret – a perpetual motion machine in a locked box. And then Papa, who'd tried to hide that truth from her. Now he'd gone too. She missed him most of all. The hurt felt keen and sharp, as if a new cut had been made deep in her chest. But, beside that, sat a soft glimmer of hope that he might still be alive somewhere. If she could only open the box, she was sure she'd discover a clue that would help find him.

Malkin padded over and licked her face with his rough tongue. Then he climbed across her lap, and soon the ticking of his little heart helped her drift off to sleep.

CHAPTER 13

Robert woke to find someone shaking him. He sat up and groggily scratched his head. Lily stood by his bedside, twisting his cap in her hands. She was wearing the old clothes he'd given her and her face was flushed with worry.

"What time is it?" he asked, yawning.

"One o'clock." Lily rubbed a hand across her face. "You've got to come. Those men are outside the shop."

"You're certain?"

"Yes, Roach is standing at the end of the street and Mould's out there too, hidden in the dark – I'm sure of it."

"I'd better have a look." He jumped out of bed and twitched a gap in the curtains.

Melting snowflakes spattered the windowpane. Mr Roach stood bold as brass under the single naphtha street lamp, his mirrored eyes glinting like quicksilver. He raised his skull stick and beckoned, and two men appeared from the shadows: Mould and someone else – a rough-looking type.

Robert stepped back from the window as they glanced up at the shop.

"Did they spot you?" Lily asked.

"I don't think so. There's someone else with them as well – another big bloke. He looks like one from the hunt when they were after Malkin."

Lily fidgeted with the lining of the cap. "I knew they'd find me."

Robert reached for the candle stub, and she leaped at him.

"Don't light that – they'll see!" Her voice was tinged with hysteria.

"It might scare them off," Robert said. "Besides, they won't get in. Not with Da's locks. They're unbreakable. We're safe as mice in a mill here."

Her eyes darted about the room. "I doubt that. Anyway, I can't stay, not with them watching the house. You'll have to help me get away."

"How?"

"I don't know." She frowned. "Could we ask your da?"

"I'll go wake him." Robert pulled his trousers on over the top of his nightshirt and threw on his shoes and a warm jacket.

Lily hurried to the doorway. "I'll wind Malkin."

Two minutes later, they all met at the foot of the stairs. Lily had her bundle wedged under an arm, while Malkin stood at her feet, his ears alert, listening for the slightest noise.

Thaddeus took charge. "Robert's told me what's going on," he said.

Lily smiled at him, but she seemed on edge. "I'm afraid, Sir, I haven't thanked you or Robert properly for everything you've done for Malkin and me."

"It was nothing, Miss Hartman," Thaddeus said. "But listen, we don't think you should go, not yet. It's not safe."

Malkin agreed. "You should listen to them, Lily—"

"No," Lily shook her head. "We've put you in enough danger already."

Robert interrupted. "We want you to stay, Lily... I mean, I want you to. You can hide till tomorrow, Da knows a place—"

"We're going."

"As you wish," Thaddeus told her, "but, in that case, we're coming too. You need protection." He turned to his son. "The back door's probably our best bet. Robert, check the yard."

Robert crept to the end of the corridor and peered through the frosted panes at the white footprint-less surface. "Looks clear," he said.

Thaddeus searched through the keys on his chain. "D'you need a warmer jacket, Miss Hartman?" he asked.

"There isn't time," she said.

"Here have this." He reached up and took a long woollen coat from a peg on the wall, which he helped her put on, his nimble fingers buttoning up the mismatched buttons. "It's a little big, I'm afraid, but it'll keep you warm on your journey."

"Thank you," she said.

Thaddeus beckoned his son. "Robert, come, we'll get some money from the till."

The four of them peered through the rag curtain into the shop.

The street outside was dark and empty, and yet something wasn't right. It took Robert a moment to realize what... Then his da spoke his thoughts aloud: "How queer; the clocks have stopped."

"You must've forgotten to wind them," Malkin said.

"It's a bad omen," Robert whispered. "When the clocks go silent, death is near."

"Oh tush." Thaddeus stepped through the curtain. Unlocking the till, he counted out a handful of coins from the drawer into his hand.

Suddenly, behind his head, two figures wrapped in long coats sidled into the frame of the window outside. It was Roach and Mould – their eyes flashed in the moonlight.

"Da!" Robert hissed.

Thaddeus looked up, just as Roach raised his stick and smashed the silver skull-handle through the window. Glass shattered and fell like sheets of water, scattering across the shop floor.

Mould pushed past his companion and reached a meaty paw in through the jagged hole to unbolt the door.

"Quick," Thaddeus shouted, "out the back way, I'll hold them off!"

Robert pushed through the rag curtain, hustling Lily and Malkin down the passage ahead of him. They stopped short of the back door – a shadow lurked outside, visible through the glass – the third man. He rattled the handle.

At the far end of the passage, Roach and Mould pushed past Thaddeus and raced towards Lily and Malkin.

"The workshop!" Robert yelled, but he barely had time to bundle the other two through the doorway and turn the key in the lock behind him, before the two men barrelled against the door.

It shook as a barrage of fists and swear words were thrown against it.

"They'll break the door down!" Robert screamed. And then he realized... "Da's still on the other side!"

"Oh no! It's me they want. He'll be fine." Lily searched the workshop for an extra obstruction and her eyes alighted on the old wardrobe with mirrored doors. "Help me move that."

They wedged themselves into the gap between the cupboard and the wall, and pushed the groaning thing into movement, inching it partway across the door.

Lily moved round to the front of the cupboard. "Push it back hard."

They heaved the cupboard against the door and its mirrored front juddered.

Thud!

"What are you doing in there?"

Thud!

"Removals?"

Thud!

"Don't think that'll stop us, Miss Hartman, because it won't."

The thudding turned into a heavy hammering. A riot

of blows rained down on the door panels. The men were using a blunt instrument against it.

Then lamplight flickered up through the crack on the still-exposed side of the door and Thaddeus's voice rang out: "I warn you, Sir, if you and your associates don't leave—"

"Be quiet, you!" Mr Roach yelled.

"Da!" Robert called, but Thaddeus couldn't hear him.

A loud explosion, sharp as a gunshot, ripped through the hall. There was a horrible ringing echo like a high bell, and the thud of something hitting the floor. Then, in a flash, the light went out and smoke filtered round the edge of the door.

Lily gave a strangled gasp and Malkin let out a horrified yelp.

Robert stared at the floor. A line of blood was trickling under the corner of the door.

"Robert?" his da croaked, his voice a phlegmy gurgle. "Are you in there? For the love of heaven, son, get away—"

The door handle rattled.

Mr Roach spoke again. "No way out I'm afraid, boy. Your father's had rather a nasty accident, but if you open the door maybe we can help him."

Robert gasped.

"Boy, are you there?" Mr Roach shouted. "Answer me."

"What have you done to him?"

"Come out and see. I'll give you to the count of three. One…"

Hot tears streamed down Robert's face.

"Two…"

How had things come to this? He should never have let his da face those men alone. He desperately tried to move the wardrobe back, while Lily stumbled about behind him, frantically yanking open drawers in the workbench, searching for a weapon.

"Three…"

Lily grabbed a hacksaw and a screwdriver and tucked them into her belt. She tried to hand him something but he brushed it aside. He felt dizzy, spinning with sickness. He never would've believed the men could take things this far.

"Time's up," Mr Roach said. "No more negotiations. If you won't come of your own accord, then we'll have to smoke you out."

There was a fizzing hiss and an orange glow flickered under the door.

Fire!

In less than a minute it would start to lick round the edges of the cupboard. Then it would engulf the room.

Malkin scurried in frantic circles, whining and

yapping at them both. Jumping onto the workbench, he pointed up with his nose at the only way out.

"The skylight!" Lily seized Malkin by the scruff, and climbed onto the bench.

Robert couldn't move. He stared at the dazed boy in the mirror, framed by the bubbling veneer of the cupboard.

Behind him, Lily hammered on the skylight with her palms. Stiff with age, it refused to open.

Out in the corridor the crackle of flames exploded into an inferno, and beneath the noise he heard the men's bickering.

"Out of control…"

"Idiot, you let it run wild."

The back door banged. They'd left. With a roar of air, and a blast of intense heat, the flames broke through the wood panelling and began licking across the room.

Smoke swirled around Robert's feet. He glanced once more at the boy in the mirror, so far back it seemed he was in the corridor.

He should've been there. It should've been him, not his da.

"Help me with this, would you?" Lily hacked away at the skylight with her screwdriver.

The paint was softening in the heat and she hit the

frame with her palm until it grumbled open, letting in a tiny chink of the night.

She forced the screwdriver into the gap, pushing until it widened.

Robert watched her shove her bundle and then a yelping Malkin through the opening. He thought she was going to climb up behind the fox, but she didn't.

Instead, she put her face to the gap and sucked in a mouthful of fresh air; then she jumped down and put a hand on his shoulder.

"Robert, please." Her voice was strained and fierce. "I'm so sorry about your father. But you must come with us now."

Robert's eyes smarted and his chest ached. His guts and lungs and head and heart were filled with burning fire, and an intense shocked sadness.

"Why?" he asked finally.

Lily wiped the smears of soot and tears from her face. "Because he told you to. He told you to get away."

The smoke had risen above his nose. It drifted between them, fogging his view, confusing him. He fumbled with the buttons of his jacket, and took one last look at the workshop as it melted around him. Lily stood waiting until he was ready. "I'm coming," he choked, the words spiky in his throat.

She nodded, and they climbed onto the bench together.

Now the smoke had reached the roof. It rolled along the blackening ceiling, engulfing everything in dense clouds.

"Where's the skylight?" Lily's voice cracked with panic.

Robert shook his head; he couldn't make it out in the choking haze.

Then, from somewhere above, a little red snout appeared, snuffling at them.

"Thank God! Out of the way, Malkin." Lily pushed the skylight wide.

"You first," she said, and shoved Robert out into the night.

The roof tiles steamed and meltwater rushed along the lead-lined gully, streaming over their shoes. Malkin whined softly, and Lily gulped in great gasps of air. They were at the base of a slope with eight feet of roof above them and a row of adjoining terraces on the other side of the summit.

Robert leaned forward and coughed up wads of black mucus. Watery flakes were settling on his head, dripping through his hair, and running down his cheeks in rivulets.

Da was gone. He felt empty. A numb mess of skin and bone. As if his insides had been scooped out with a spoon. He grabbed a handful of mush and rubbed it roughly across his face.

"We have to keep going," Lily said, picking up her bundle.

With Malkin at her heels, she started to climb. When she reached the apex of the roof she leaned against a chimney stack and glanced back at him.

Robert wiped a sleeve across his face, brushing away snow and tears.

He had no choice but to follow. He set off after her, numb fingers searching through the steam and cold for holds among the broken slates. His leather shoes slipped as he clawed his way forward. When he was within reach of the chimney, Lily clasped his hand and pulled him up.

Wind and snow whistled round the stacks, knifing and cold in Robert's throat. Another wave of sickness washed over him. He caught his breath and stared down into the street at a fiery orange glow. Neighbours, wrapped in cloaks and coats, scurried from their houses with tin baths and buckets, shovelling snow and throwing it on the fire. A knot of men, their clothes and hair steaming with black smoke, wrestled his da's body through the melted shop window.

Robert slumped forward, tumbling into the slush. His fists met the tiles, and his mouth fell open, letting out a shrill cry that joined in the roar of the wind and fire. There was nothing he could do any more. His life here was over.

Robert's scream cut Lily to her bones; it was as if it were coming from somewhere inside her. She shuddered and slid down next to him; reached out a hand to take his, but he brushed her away.

"Please," she whispered, "I know what it's like, that hurt, but we've got to go—"

"Why?"

"Because," Malkin interrupted, "if we don't, those men will kill us."

"This is your fault!" Robert aimed a kick at him. "Get away from me, both of you."

"I'm sorry," Lily said. "We should've helped. I…I didn't realize how far they'd go to try and get what they wanted." She glanced at Robert. His face was puffy with pain and his numb gaze had turned inwards. He had scraped at the tiles until his fingers bled, but was barely aware of it.

Lily hugged her bundled box tight under her arm. "My family," she said, "I mean, I…I'm involved in this.

But you, and your da, Robert… He's innocent. He saved us. If it weren't for him, we wouldn't be here."

Robert let out a loud sob. "And if it weren't for you, he *would* be. This", he hissed, "is all because of you. Look after number one: that's what you're about."

"No," she sputtered, "it's not true."

But *maybe* it was? She had brought the box here, and Malkin had come. She'd decided it was safe to stay with them, despite all she now knew. That thought made her queasy. She tried to think of something else to say, something comforting, but the words dried in her throat. So instead, she took off his da's coat and draped it over Robert's shoulders. "There," she said. She felt the cold now, in only her thin jacket, yet she knew Robert needed the coat much more than she did.

Malkin shouldered his way between them and licked Robert's bleeding fingers with his rough pink tongue.

A minute passed, and though Lily dearly wanted to let him sit, to comfort him, they couldn't afford to stop. Not now. There was still so much danger.

"Robert?" she said quietly.

He glanced up and seemed to finally see her, for he wiped away an angry tear. "Should we go back?" he asked them.

"I don't think so," Malkin said softly. "What would we be going back for?"

And Lily knew in her heart of hearts he was right. They couldn't really, not as things stood. What had Mrs Rust said? *Life can be painful. And if you can't change what's happened today, bide your time, until you're strong enough to fight tomorrow.*

Over the roof's edge she glimpsed a row of searchlights in the lane. Mould and Roach's harsh voices echoed up to her. Malkin's black-tipped ears pricked up – he'd heard them too. "Time to move on," he said.

"Yes." Lily nodded. She shifted her hold on the box and put an arm around Robert. Malkin tugged at his sleeve, while she nudged him to his feet. As he leaned against her, she felt the ragged sobs on his breath.

They slid down the far side of the rooftop and, in the next dip, Robert stumbled forward into a crawl. Lily and Malkin crawled beside him.

Robert moved carelessly, barely taking in what he was doing. He was about to put his palm on a protruding nail, when Malkin yapped him a warning, and he shook his head and seemed to come around.

They crossed three more summits this way before they found a place to descend – a yard piled high with packing cases, where a low outhouse, ending in an overhanging roof, met a high brick parapet, covered with a thick layer of snow like icing.

Her heart racing, Lily stepped forward and peered down. The white ground seemed to spill away beneath her in the dark. She lowered herself over the edge, and when she felt the tips of her toes graze the snowy parapet, she closed her eyes and let go.

The wall met her body with a mushy thud; Malkin jumped down beside her as she steadied herself. "Now you," Lily shouted to Robert.

He stared down at her. "I can't do it," he mumbled. "It's too high."

"Come on," she said. "You've got to."

She took his hand and he eased himself over the roof's edge, collapsing into her arms. When she looked down, Malkin was already in the yard, standing at the gate, his head cocked, listening.

Lily held on to Robert and they scrambled down a mountain of damp boxes to join him.

"It's clear," the fox yipped as soon as they arrived.

Cautiously Lily opened the gate and the three of them tumbled across the road and ducked into the hedgerow opposite. They brushed through the snowy branches and into the dark field beyond, and Lily let out a sigh of relief. They'd escaped – or three of them had. And at least for now, they were safe.

CHAPTER 14

They ran with stealth; not stumbling or stopping, just fleeing into the night. Dark as the Devil's mouth it was, and the wind was sharp as vinegar. Lily could not see her hands in front of her face and was forced to listen out for the ticking of Malkin's limbs as he made his way along the snow-covered path.

The blizzard of flakes eased, and they were halfway up Brackenbridge Hill when the clouds parted and a milk-faced moon, one day's wax from full, appeared. The wind battered the frosted tips of nearby gorses and whipped cold air in through their clothes as they pushed their way up a slope of deep drifts.

They ran up the bank until a tangle of thick thorny

underbrush stuck up from the smooth white surface of the snow, blocking their path. Malkin led them around it, bounding through the white dust that came practically to his chin.

Robert was fading fast, stumbling in and out of drifts, kicking at fallen branches until they showered snow. Lily could sense the anguish flooding off him. Water had soaked through the toes of her shoes, and her feet had started to numb; worse still, her gloveless fingers were beginning to seize up with the cold. She stopped for a moment, and pushed back her cap to look around.

"We should rest," she said. "The trouble is, I don't know where."

Malkin shook a flurry of flakes from his snout, and licked his whiskers.

"I came this way before. It looks different under all this white stuff, but I think I can find a place for us to stop." With that, he slipped off ahead, into the undergrowth.

Lily and Robert stood leaning against each other, waiting for his return. Lily realized Robert hadn't spoken since they'd been on the roof.

"That was a narrow escape," she said suddenly, "back there at the shop… Look, Robert, I'm sorry for what happened. If I'd've known—"

"It's not your fault," he muttered. "Not really." He glanced at her, as if he wanted to say more. Lily felt her weariness lift for a moment, but when his face fell, it seeped back in with the cold.

Another few minutes passed in shivering silence, then Malkin returned with news of an empty building ahead, where they might bed down for the night.

"Fine," Lily said. "Let's go there."

Hidden behind a copse of tall larch trees, the derelict mill straddled one end of a frozen pond. Its upper half was clad in moss-covered planks of wood that ended halfway down its height, like a skirt. Under this, fat red legs of brick, banked with snow, waded in the ice-cracked pond. An outhouse arched over a waterwheel, whose uppermost lattices were covered in dripping stalactites.

Malkin slunk across an iron-railed bridge and approached the building. He slipped between two planks of wood nailed over the entrance, and through a rotten gap in the base of the door itself, his tail flicking as it disappeared into the dark.

They stood at the end of the small bridge, waiting for him to return. Lily jigged, and clapped her hands to keep them warm, and Robert brushed a shower of snow off the length of handrail.

Malkin's nose poked back out through the hole. "It's clear," he barked. "I don't think anyone lives here any more."

"Well, now we do," Lily said cheerfully, trying to give them hope.

It was almost as cold inside the old watermill as it was outside. As her eyes grew accustomed to the dark, Lily saw a space filled with gigantic cogs. Wooden workings spanned the room, connecting to a grindstone at the far end. A chain led up and up to a wooden trapdoor set into the roof above. In between the planks of the ceiling, weeds grew like a blackened upside-down garden.

"It's like crawling inside the chest of some gigantic broken mechanical," Lily whispered to Robert.

"Or the heart of a clock tower," Robert said.

"My papa would probably know how it worked. Be able to explain it all."

"Mine too." Robert patted a cog, connected to a shaft of wood. "These must've all turned once to grind the corn, driven by that waterwheel outside."

She nodded. In the corner, against the driest wall, she spotted a pile of empty flour sacks, and they settled down on them to make a camp for the night.

Lily dropped her bundle and watched Robert slump to the foot of the wall. Then she collapsed down next to him. She leaned back against a rough post, shivering in her shirt sleeves, and loosened the laces of her shoes.

"Do you want the coat back?" Robert asked her suddenly.

She shook her head. "No. You keep it. I'll use my blanket." She unknotted it from around the box, and opened it out, spreading it across her legs.

"We could share them both," Robert said, and he shuffled towards her and tucked the coat around their shoulders. Lily dragged the box between her feet, and threw the blanket across his legs too.

The silk lining of the coat gave off a sharp whiff that reminded her of Thaddeus's tobacco and the blanket smelled of Papa and her home. Lily missed him, and her mama too. Tiredness seeped through her bones. She took off her cap and put it against the wall behind her head to make a pillow, then shut her eyes and waited for sleep to take her.

But, instead, only a sickly feeling of emptiness came, and a slow nagging despair. She tried to concentrate on the night noises – she ought to listen out anyway, just in case.

The wind was up and she could hear the creaking of

the old mill...the strange distant squawking of birds...
Malkin's cogs gradually ticking to a standstill as he
wound down for the night...and Robert's breathing soft
and steady... Soon the sounds fell away, and she drifted
into a deep sleep.

She dreamed once more of the accident. The snow
falling. The stone in her hand. Mama's laughter. The box
at Papa's feet. The two vehicles colliding with an earth-
shattering crash that split the night in two. Her mother's
body tipping forward, flying through the carriage
windscreen, and her own tiny frame tumbling after it.

City lights smudged the sky. Blood and water smeared
across her face as her body broke against the kerbside,
crumpling into the white drifts; inches from her mother's
frozen form.

Snowflakes coated her hair. Cuts seared across her
scalp; pain bloomed in her chest. Unstoppable.

Then, another new part of the dream: she seemed to
leave her body, and she watched from on high, floating
above her static six-year-old self as Papa clambered out
from under the overturned steam-wagon, still clasping
the box. She heard his hoarse screams whipped away by
the blizzard.

Another man appeared, limping through the fog, and he wrestled with her papa, trying to take the box. Lily recognized his red sideburns, his fat cheeks, and his silver shining eyes – it was Mr Mould.

Papa fought him, screaming and shouting into his face, never letting go of the box, until Mr Mould seemed to take fright and ran off. Then Papa battled towards the bodies of his loved ones: Mama and Lily, lying side by side like rag dolls on the road.

Tears melted the snowflakes on Papa's face. He threw down the box and dropped to his knees in the snow. Then he scooped up his two girls in his arms; cradling them against his chest.

Lily wanted to stay, watch more, but she felt herself waking, detaching from the dream, as if an umbilical-line of mooring had loosened inside her, and she floated off. She tried to call to Papa, but no words came. Tried to swim back, but a blizzard of snow pushed against her, spiralling her upwards; melting the accident into a flurry of flakes. A cold blank whiteness seeped into her bones and she heard the thud of her pulse, ringing in her ears...

Lily woke with a cold gritty taste in her mouth. The interior of the mill had grown lighter. A rising sun split the slatted boards of the wall with orange stripes. Lily's thoughts flashed straight from her dream to the burning shop. She glanced at Robert and was shocked to find him awake and watching her.

He sat a little way off, with his back against the curve of a large wooden wheel, his chin on his knees and his arms hugged around his legs. His cheeks were streaked with sooty tears, and his dark curled hair was tangled with leaves and dust. "Nightmares?" he asked.

She nodded.

He leaned towards her. "I didn't sleep much either. It's all so different. I miss the ticking of our clocks. When I did sleep, I dreamed of Da and the fire. I don't want to think of how it must've hurt." He took his penknife from his pocket and turned it over in his palm. "This is the last thing of his I have. He gave it to me for my thirteenth birthday."

A wave of sadness flooded Lily, and she wondered what she'd done to bring such misery down upon them.

"Your dream was about your parents too, wasn't it?" Robert asked, putting the pocketknife aside.

"Yes." She fiddled with the blanket. Damp had soaked through into the wool. "How did you know that?"

"I heard you cry out their names." He took a deep

breath. "What happened to your mama? You said she was killed?"

Lily nodded. His words floated sharp between them. "What happened to yours?" She asked, trying to change the subject.

Robert shrugged. "She left when I was very small. I don't really know where she is now. All I know is her name: Selena." He swung the coat around and put it on. "You said you were in a steam-wagon crash?"

Lily shifted uncomfortably under the blanket. "I dream about it. The details are coming back to me. I used to think it was an accident – at least, Papa talked of it that way. Now, because of his letter, and the things I'm remembering in my dreams, I know that was a lie." She scratched at her chest through her damp shirt. Her scar felt unaccountably itchy. She never liked to speak of the past, and no one had asked her about it in a long time. No one except Robert. He sat there, expectantly. Staring at her, waiting for her to elaborate on her suspicions.

She rubbed her hands together and massaged the stiffness from her neck. She should tell him the truth – at least what she knew of it. She owed him that much.

"The crash was terrible," she said. "The other steam-wagon hit us on purpose. Mama was killed instantly, and I was injured…but Papa, Papa was fine. He was the one who saved me… In fact, in my dream, he had the box. Someone was trying to wrestle it from him. I think it was Mr Mould." Robert gasped. Lily glanced down at the box. "After the crash, Papa nursed me back to health, healed my injuries. But, with Mama gone, and all the awful things that had happened, he didn't want to stay in London."

"So you moved here?"

"Yes." She brushed her hair back from her forehead and wedged it away under the cap. "We came to hide in the country. But it was hard to live without Mama. He was so lonely, we both were. So he made Malkin, to keep us company."

Lily stood and crouched beside Malkin. She took his silver winder from her pocket, stroked his head softly, put the key in the hole in his neck and wound it, feeling the fox's springs tighten. "Then Papa got me a governess, because he said we needed a woman around."

"She was the one at the house?" Robert prompted.

"No – the first three didn't seem to like being shut up in the house. They left. Then Madame Verdigris arrived. She and I never really got on. Papa ended up sending me to Miss Scrimshaw's Academy, on her recommendation, and she stayed on at home as our housekeeper."

"I didn't know you went to some fancy academy," Robert said.

"Fancy's not the word for it." Lily finished winding Malkin, and watched as he blinked awake.

The mech-fox yawned, smacked his lips together, and stretched like a cat. "I'll go and check ahead," he said, "get the lay of the land." Then he stood and shook out his four black paws, and before Robert or Lily could answer, he'd leaped through the hole in the door and trotted off.

Robert scratched his cheek as he watched the red shape disappear into the white outside. "I never went to school," he said finally. "Da taught me everything I needed to know – about clocks and chronometers, the business, and whatnot. 'Course it's useless to me now."

Lily didn't disagree. "He seemed a good man, your father."

"He was. I only wish I'd been a better son. A better apprentice."

She patted his shoulder. "Robert," she said, "I reckon you were the finest son and apprentice he could ever have wished for."

"Thank you." He gave her a nervous smile, and glanced at the box at her feet. "What on earth are we going to do now?"

"I'm not sure." Lily stood and paced about between the broken cogs of the old mill. "But I think we should carry on with your da's plan. We'll walk to the next town and catch a train to London. Then we'll go and see my godfather, ask for his help." She kneeled down and pulled the blanket around the box once more, then she stowed the hacksaw and the screwdriver in beside it.

Robert watched her. "Have we got enough money for tickets?" he asked.

"If we don't we'll have to hide in a compartment somewhere. That might be a better plan anyway." Lily knotted the top of the blanket tightly around her few possessions.

Then they sat in silence for a while, listening to the steady drip of water melting somewhere, which sounded like the tick of a clock. Finally, Malkin's snow-covered snout poked through the doorway.

"The path ahead's clear," he yipped. "But there's something else you should know – I think we're going to pass by the place where *Dragonfly* crashed."

Robert jolted forward. "Are the police there?" he asked. "Or Roach and Mould?"

Malkin shook his head. "Neither. The whole site looks mysteriously empty. Untouched even."

"Oh." Lily bit her lip. "In that case," she said queasily, "perhaps we should take the opportunity to go and investigate."

CHAPTER 15

For the rest of the morning they followed the river southwards from the old mill. As the day warmed, shards of ice broke apart and melted into the free-flowing water. Soon the crunch of the snow under their feet became a soft slush and rays of dappled sunlight drifted through the bare branches above. Otherwise, things were ominously quiet; Robert heard no sign of their pursuers, nor saw any evidence of them.

They took turns carrying the box, bundled in its damp blanket. It wasn't particularly heavy, but it gnawed at Robert's mind, along with the loss of his da, and all their other troubles.

He worried they wouldn't find evidence of Lily's papa

in the wreckage of the airship. Or, worse still, that they would. Another body would be too much to take at this point, and he could not help but think, after everything they'd been through, that the crash site was not the safest place to be heading.

Late in the afternoon, Malkin's ears pricked up and he stopped further up the track. "This is it," he called, pointing with his nose through the trees.

Robert and Lily stepped through a gap in the foliage into a blackened clearing, eerily dead of sound.

To one side, smashed into the trunk of an old oak, they saw the dented shape of *Dragonfly*'s escape pod. Thirty feet away, further fragments of the ship lay scattered on the ground, as if an explosion had strewn them across the landscape.

"Oh, Papa," Lily whispered.

Robert tried to take her hand, but she flinched and pulled away, running through the melting drifts towards the clusters of burned metal. When he caught up with her, she was searching through the fragments for any sign of her father.

"Lily, stop," Malkin barked. "There's no one here, and if there was they left days ago."

Lily shook her head. "There must be something. Some clue to what became of Papa after the silver airship locked together with *Dragonfly*."

Robert shifted the bundle across his back. "Perhaps the flight recorder," he said. "All airships have them."

"What does it look like?" she asked.

"It's a grooved silver cylinder covered in markings, like the metal roller of a music box. It records sound – it will have recorded the last few minutes on the ship. After the pod ejects it kicks in automatically so it would tell us what happened after Malkin's escape, before the crash. If it's here, it would be somewhere in the cockpit wreckage."

Lily bent low over the remains of the pilot's chair, which lay hump-backed on the ground. Beside it, twisted metal tubes exploded from the cracked front panel of a control console. She pulled the panel away and focused on the tangle of wires.

"It's meant to look as if it was an accident," she said, "just like with Mama, or your da, Robert. They want people to think he crashed, but that's not the case. We know they destroyed the ship for whatever's in this stupid box." Her voice, loud with rage, echoed around the clearing.

"This isn't a safe place for us to be," Robert said. "Roach and Mould might guess we'd come here. I don't think we should stop too long."

Lily ignored him and rooted through the rest of the wreckage. "I've found it," she shouted, pulling a silver cylinder from within the interior casing of another mangled console box. "This'll tell us what happened to Papa."

Robert furrowed his brow. "It's no good yet. We've nothing to play it on."

"We'll find something when we get to London – listen, we just need to—"

Her breath caught. There was a crunch of feet across the snow.

"Hush," Malkin snapped. "Be quiet. I think someone's coming."

"It might be Papa!" Lily felt a rush of hope, and made to run towards the noise, but Robert grabbed her arm and held it tight.

"It might not be," he said.

"He's right," Malkin growled. "The footsteps are not John's, they're too heavy."

They ducked behind the broken ribs of *Dragonfly*'s hull and waited. On the far side of the clearing, they heard a clang. And another...followed by a ripping noise. Someone was rummaging through the rest of the wreckage. Lily peered around a burned-out section of fuselage.

Half hidden behind the broken shape of a hydraulic pump, a figure in an aviator helmet examined a littering of flywheels and exhaust rods. Its stout body, wrapped in a bulky leather flying jacket, resembled a half-filled flour sack, Lily thought. "Who is that?" she whispered.

The figure stopped and scratched its forehead with one fingerless-gloved hand, muttering to itself.

Malkin peered at it. "I've no idea," he said. "But they're taking parts from *Dragonfly*."

There was a loud screech of metal as the figure wrenched an exhaust pipe from a row of clips. It turned and threw the piece with a clatter onto a pile of scrap, then wiped its hands on the front of the leather jacket and, in one deft movement, pulled a gun from a holster strapped to its back.

"I know you're over there," the figure said, stepping between the broken pieces of the stern. "I can hear you. And, whoever you are, know this: there may be only one of me, and perhaps you think the three of you could take me easy in a fight, but I've got a pistol full of big exploding mechanical-piercing bullets. So, why don't you come out and we can talk about splitting this salvage fifty-fifty – or sixty-forty since, by salvagers' law, I was here first. Then we can all be on our way."

Lily and Robert shuffled out from behind the fuselage with their hands in the air. Malkin slunk sheepishly behind them, head bowed.

When the figure pushed the scarf and goggles from its face, Robert saw it was a woman. Her cheeks were round and ruddy from the cold. Her blue eyes looked them up and down, pausing on the tube in Lily's hand. "A recording cylinder," she said, "now that *is* an interesting find."

Lily didn't reply, just pulled her jacket tighter around her.

"Lost your tongue, have you, young man?" the woman asked.

Robert shifted the bundle to hide it behind his back.

"And what've you got?" the woman asked him.

"Nothing," he said.

"It doesn't look like nothing to me." The woman pointed the gun at him. "Looks like you two boys have found the catch of the day. Now, hand it over."

"No," Lily blurted out. She stepped forward. "We're not going to give you the cylinder, or this box, or anything else. Not after what we've been through. If you want them so badly, you're going to have to take them from us."

The woman laughed. "I see. It's like that, is it?" She holstered her weapon. "I think you'd better both come with me. Maybe I can help you."

The three of them marched through a nearby field, the woman, walking a few steps behind, carried an armful of various mangled engine parts. Robert clutched the bundle containing the box against his chest. "Do you think we can trust her?" he whispered.

Lily shrugged. "What choice have we got?"

"Let's keep on our guard," Malkin advised.

The woman ushered them downhill and into a small clearing behind a line of frosty trees. A bulging patchwork balloon, tethered to the ground by an iron anchor, bobbed jauntily in the breeze. Rigged to the hull of its weathered wooden gondola were scraps of rusted wreckage – pots, pans, buckets, boxes, baskets and bundles of wood – that clanked and clattered together in a syncopated rhythm, like a motley wind chime. One word was stencilled on the airship's prow in white paint: *Ladybird*.

"What is all this stuff?" Lily asked.

"Scrap," the woman said. She deposited her gleanings in the various boxes and bags scattered around the snowy clearing, and tended to a blackened cauldron that hung on a trivet over a smoking campfire. As she lifted the lid on the cauldron the hearty smell of stew wafted out, making Robert's mouth water.

"Can we have some food?" he begged. "We're starving."

"You look it," the woman said. "Go on then, fill yourselves up." She doled out two bowlfuls for them, and scooped a mugful out of the cauldron for herself. Then she handed them each a spoon. "Lunch is served."

After a night and a morning of walking on an empty stomach, it was a pleasure for Robert and Lily to have hot food, and bread to soak in it. They set to eating as quickly as they could. The stew tasted spicy and delicious, and the warmth of it suffused their bellies.

"What are your names, boys?" the woman asked.

"I'm Robert and this is L—"

"Lenny," Lily said, interrupting. "We're Robert and Lenny."

"I'm Anna Quinn: scrapper and aeronaut."

After they'd finished eating, and cleaned their plates with the crusts of bread, Anna offered them a second plateful. She even had some scraps for Malkin, but he turned his nose up at them, and lay with his head on his paws, facing in the other direction.

"He's not hungry?" Anna asked, tipping her head to the fox.

"He doesn't eat," Lily explained, "he's a mechanimal."

"Really?" Her eyes widened. "I've never seen one that looks so lifelike before. Or acts it. How'd you get hold of him?"

213

"My da repairs clocks." Robert spoke with his mouth full. "He's a horologist. The fox was left with us when his owner never came to pick him up."

Lily gave him a smile for such a quick-thinking lie.

"Does he speak too?" Anna wondered.

Malkin's ears pricked up. "Only when spoken to," he muttered, glancing at her over his knitted shoulders. "And by the way, it's very clanking rude to discuss a person as if they're not there."

Anna guffawed, and slapped her knees with a hand. "Blimey, he does! Has he got a moniker?"

Lily looked up, spoon halfway to her mouth. "A what?"

"A handle, a denomination, an appellation, a name."

"His name's Malkin," Robert explained.

"And what were the three of you doing at that crash site?"

"Nothing," Lily said. "Just scavenging, like yourself."

"Somehow I doubt that," Anna said. She leaned forward in her seat. "Let me tell you who I think you are: you're Lily Hartman, and this mechanimal belongs to your father, Professor John Hartman, whose airship, *Dragonfly*, crashed here."

Lily felt her eyes widen with shock. "How do you know all that? Who are you really?"

The woman smiled. "I told you, my name's Anna Quinn. I'm a scrapper of metal. And sometimes I do a bit of investigating and writing on the side."

"You're the reporter who wrote the newspaper article about Papa," Lily said.

Anna nodded. "That's right. I've been looking into his disappearance for a couple of days. The whole thing seemed fishy to me – the scant coverage in the other papers, the lack of a proper police investigation. So I thought I would come up here and find out more, and do a bit of salvage work while I was about it."

"But why didn't you contact me?" Lily asked.

"I tried to," Anna said. "But I don't think your guardian passed on my telegram. It's lucky we found each other though."

"Lucky how?" Robert asked.

"As I said, I can help you." Anna poked at the fire with the tip of her boot. "And then you can both do an interview for me. An exclusive."

"We don't know any more about this business than you do," Robert told her. "The people chasing us, they—"

Anna grasped his arm. "You're being chased? This does puts an exciting new spin on things! Tell me more about that."

"Papa told me not to talk to strangers about myself."

Lily clasped the cylinder to her chest. "Look, we need to find out what's on this. Do you know how we can play it back?"

Anna held out a palm. After a moment's consideration, Lily passed her the cylinder. The woman turned it over, examining the dents and grooves on its surface.

"You need to plug it into the workings of another airship," she said. "That's the only way you'll get anything out of it."

She stood and kicked over the traces of the fire. "Help me pack all this away," she said, handing the cylinder back to Lily, "then we can go up into my airship *Ladybird*, and take a listen."

Halfway up the chain ladder that dangled from *Ladybird*'s gondola Robert felt queasy. This was the highest he'd ever climbed. They were higher now than when they'd stood on the roof of his house.

Above him, Lily had the cylinder tucked into her coat pocket. Malkin was curled up and buttoned inside her jacket, and she was following Anna who'd nearly reached the top of the ladder.

Robert slowed behind her, and tried not to look down at the chains, twisting and creaking in the wind. The box, in its bundle strapped across his back, suddenly felt very heavy. He glanced up at the swaying ship still thirty feet in the air above his head. "It's too far," he muttered. "I can't."

Lily looked between her feet at him. "Please, Robert. You have to try."

He gritted his teeth. At least if he fell, the last of the snow might cushion his fall. No, he mustn't think about falling. When he used to go walking in the woods with his da and climbed trees, it wasn't the up that scared him, but the down – that dreadful drop you had to navigate to get back on solid ground. Whenever his vertigo got the better of him and he got stuck, Thaddeus would clamber up and help him descend. His da had a lesson prepared for such moments, as he always did. It was similar to the thing he'd said the other day...what was it again?

No one conquers fear easily, Robert. It takes practice to reach true heights; a brave heart to win great battles.

Robert repeated those words to himself as he climbed higher, higher than ever before, towards the gondola of the floating airship. They gave him comfort – and soon he found he'd reached the top of the ladder.

"How do we get across?" Lily shouted through the wind.

"Just do as I do." Anna opened a door in *Ladybird*'s

hull and, grabbing a metal handrail, pulled herself inside. Climbing to her feet, she stood on the deck. "Simple."

Lily copied her movements, clambering through the doorway, and Robert, following behind her, shut his eyes tight, thinking once more of his da's advice.

When he blinked, he was onboard the airship, and Anna was winching the chain ladder onto a roll.

"Welcome to *Ladybird*," she said, as she rattled in the last few metal rungs and reached out to close the door. "It's a bit of a manoeuvre to get onboard, but in every other respect I think you'll find her a first-class dirigible, if rather on the snug side."

Lily unbuttoned her jacket and Malkin hopped out and skittered about giddily on the curved floor. "I hate these scruffy DIY airships," he complained.

"It's not so bad," Lily found herself saying.

Robert leaned dizzily against the wall. He was just glad to have something solid under his feet. The tiny plank-walled passageway they stood in was barely wide enough for the four of them to fit into. He glanced around. A big brass porthole behind them lensed a circle of light onto four mismatched curtains shielding the space opposite, each one hand-stitched and higgledy-piggledy.

"Let me give you the grand tour." Anna pulled back

the rear curtain, and Robert and Lily peered in at a small tail compartment filled with an engine. Sandwiched between this tail space and the front compartment, which Robert assumed was the bridge, were two small crawl spaces, one on top of the other. The bottom one was a foot-locker storage cupboard, stacked with a few empty wooden crates, and the compartment above turned out to be Anna's berth.

A small mattress entirely filled the floor space. Above the mattress, a smaller brass porthole lit a few trinkets on a wonky shelf – an airship in a bottle, a portable typewriter, and a large pile of dog-eared penny dreadful adventure magazines. Lily reached in and picked up one, examining the cover. *The Zep Pirates Versus The Kraken* it was called, and the engraved picture on the front was of a zeppelin being attacked by an enormous sea monster, who did look uncannily like her old teacher. "This is one I haven't read," she said.

"I'm not surprised," Anna told her. "That's the first issue. I only just finished writing it."

"You write these?" Robert asked.

"Don't say it with such disdain, boy. It's another of my sidelines. I've got to make a living somehow."

"They're brilliant, Robert," Lily told him. "You should read them sometime."

"I don't know about that," Robert said. "After all that's happened the last few days, I'm not sure I need more drama in my life."

"Of course," Lily said. She understood. For a moment she'd forgotten about the box and the men chasing them. She glanced down at the cylinder, tucked into the pocket of her coat. "Perhaps we should listen to this recording now?"

Anna nodded and yanked back the largest curtain and motioned them into the room at the fore of the ship. "Through here's the flight deck."

The space was so small that if Robert or Lily had raised their arms they could have touched both walls with the tips of their fingers, but crossways there was enough room for the three of them to stand shoulder to shoulder.

Anna flicked a row of switches on the dashboard and needles on various gauges and instruments came to life. Among them Robert recognized barometers, thermometers, a compass and a chronometer clock in a mounting. At the far end of the control panel was a cradle with an adjustable arm on a needle. "This machine'll play the sound on your cylinder," Anna said, and she plugged the cylinder into the cradle and put the needle down across the groove along the end. Then she pressed the button on the dash, and the cylinder began to whirl in its mounting. There was a crackling, like someone scrunching up paper, from a speaker embedded in the wall, and Robert and Lily held their breath.

CHAPTER 16

The recording was blurry at first but soon words could be heard: a sharp skewering voice, barely audible over a soft silver thrum.

"Professor Hartman?" the voice said. "Are you conscious?"

"That's Mould," Robert whispered, but Lily shushed him.

"Starting to come round, are we?" said another voice – which sounded distinctly like Roach. "I suppose that means we're ready to begin."

Lily's papa spoke then. "My name's Grantham," he stuttered. "Grantham. Not Hartman. You've got the wrong person. How did you get onboard?"

"Grantham – G Hartman – Grace Hartman," Roach said. "It's not the best of anagram aliases, considering we were the ones who killed your wife in the first place. When we'd worked out your false identity, it wasn't hard to discover the real registration papers for your mechanicals and get your address. It's been seven years, Professor. You have been rather a slippery fish to get hold of, but we have you in our sights now, so to speak."

There was a distinct tapping then that Lily knew with certainty was Roach hitting one of his mirrored eyes with a finger. A shudder ran through her as his broken face surfaced in her memory, like a corpse floating from the depths of a glinting pond.

"I warn you," Papa was saying – his voice sounded assertive, but Lily could tell he was frightened – "boarding another airship without permission is illegal."

Roach spoke again. "And what you did was illegal too, Sir. Very illegal."

"What on earth are you talking about?"

"The theft of our master's perpetual motion machine, Professor Hartman. Where is it?"

There was a crackle on the cylinder.

"I can't," Papa said. "It's hidden."

"Come, come," Mr Roach said. "No games."

Another crackle; and then a scream.

223

Lily cringed.

There was a pause, filled with ragged breath.

"I...will...tell...you...nothing," Papa cried. "You may do as you see fit."

Mr Roach chuckled, and the laugh rippled through Lily, as if the vile man stood right beside her.

"Well, isn't this a pleasant surprise," his voice oozed. "I'd quite hoped our conversation might take this turn. I was authorized to offer money, but I see now such action would be fruitless. You're an ethical man, Sir, far too ethical for me, but perhaps you will respond better to this?"

Another scream and a horrible intense whining filled the recording... And then the needle reached the end of the cylinder; with a clunk-click, it raised up and the sound stopped.

Lily slumped against the wall. Suddenly the wave of emotion she'd been holding in for so long rushed over her. It was as if the last glimmer of hope she possessed had been pulled from her chest.

She gazed out of *Ladybird*'s slanted window, over her snub-nosed prow. In the distance she could see *Dragonfly*'s parts messily strewn across the glade.

She knew now for certain it was Roach and Mould

who'd caused that destruction. They'd tortured her papa and taken everything: Mama's life, and Robert's da's too, Mrs Rust, the other mechanicals, her home. And all for this box; this perpetual motion machine. They'd done so much damage to possess it. They'd kill her and Robert too, if they had the chance, and nothing she could say or do, no help she could call on, would ever stop them.

"Papa's dead," she said suddenly. "This whole time I hoped he might be alive, might still come back, but he's not going to, is he? We should just give them the box – the machine – before they kill us too."

Robert took a deep breath, his mouth dry. "If we give in now," he said, "then everyone who's tried to protect it would've died in vain, and we'll never discover its secret – the truth of what it can do."

"He's right, Lily." Malkin narrowed his black eyes. "There could be dangerous things inside, and clank knows what chaos Roach and Mould could cause with them."

"I realize the odds don't look good," Robert added. "They know everything about us, and we don't have a clue about them, so how can we ever win? But we *have* to win, Lil. We have to. Because of them, I've got no one. They're evil, but we can't give up. We've got the one thing they want – the one thing that'll draw them to us.

We can make them suffer. We mustn't let them get away with what they did. And we must never give in. Not ever."

Malkin nodded in agreement. "This box is the only thing we have against them," he said. "The only clue left. When we get to London we'll ask your godfather to alert the proper police, then use the promise of the perpetual motion machine to draw Roach and Mould into some kind of trap."

"What do you know, Malkin?" Lily yelled. "You didn't know anything before we read Papa's letter." She kicked at the box, bundled in its blanket. "If only we had the key."

Malkin said nothing, just narrowed his eyes and tipped back his ears, staring at her with that foxy superiority of his.

"If you're going to London," Anna said, "I can take you. I have to go back anyway. File my copy and check in with my editor at *The Daily Cog*. I could play him this recording, and see if we can help you find out anything more about this Roach and Mould or the perpetual motion machine. There must be information about it somewhere, don't you think?"

Lily didn't answer; she felt as if they were all drifting far away from her, and at any moment she might fall into a comatose state.

She could hear Robert speaking a long way off. "Thank you, Anna. A ride to London and anything else you can do, would be greatly appreciated."

"Let's put her to bed for a while in my berth, young man. Robbie, was it?"

Lily let them carry her into the passageway. Anna drew back the curtain of the narrow berth, and she and Robert laid Lily carefully on the bed. Then Anna tucked a blanket around her and she drew the curtain, before Lily heard her and Robert step away.

"Come on, Robbie," the aeronaut said, "I've a few more questions, and a job for you in the engine room."

Lily woke some time later with the odd sensation of moving sideways. The wooden wall of the berth juddered with the thrum of the engine; outside the sky had darkened, and the brass porthole framed a few stars.

She felt around for Malkin, but he wasn't there, and when she sat up she hit her head on the shelf above the bed. The pile of penny dreadfuls and the airship in its bottle slid from the shelf and landed on the mattress around her, and the typewriter rocked on its nail. Cursing softly, she pulled back the curtain and jumped down from the berth.

Except for the soft chug of a motor, *Ladybird*'s passage was quiet. The cabin rocked back and forth under her feet, buffeted by the light winds. Lily wandered towards the sound of the engine, rubbing the bump on her head.

She found Robert wedged in the stern of the ship. Standing beside the hissing furnace, which connected to a greasy propeller shaft, he was frying eggs in a pan on the furnace top. Malkin lay curled up at his feet, and something about the two of them together reminded Lily of her papa.

"Hello, sleepyhead, feeling better?" Robert asked. The eggs spattered and hissed in a pan in the belly of the open furnace and toast browned on a fork.

"Look at you," Lily said. "You're a proper little cabin boy and no mistake."

"Anna's let me take charge of the cooking, and the engines." Robert opened another door on the front of the furnace with a stick of wood, then he threw in a shovelful of coal. "Keeps me busy, stops me thinking too much…about Da."

Lily glanced away and pretended to examine the engine. Eight spidery piston legs emerged from the rear of the furnace and turned the prop shaft and various other mechanisms that were crammed into *Ladybird*'s tapered wooden tail. "This is an amazing device."

"Isn't it?" Robert wiped his brow with a sleeve. "Anna built it herself. I've been shovelling coal into it for the last few hours. I told her everything while you were asleep, about what's happened to us. I mean the things she didn't know – she knew a lot of it anyway. And she promised to help us."

He flipped the eggs in the pan to cook the runny yolks, then slipped one egg onto each slice of toast. "She even gave me this grub from her belly box."

"Her what?"

Robert made a face. "It's what she calls that small box, where she keeps the food, in the footlocker under her berth."

"Oh." Lily laughed. "She's an odd one, isn't she?"

"But nice. I think we *can* trust her." Robert handed Lily a slice of eggy bread and she bit into it ravenously, savouring the warm, soft taste.

When they'd both finished eating, he closed the furnace door and walked with her and Malkin along the passage to the flight deck.

"Ah, she's awake." Anna was standing at the helm, steering. She consulted a chronometer on the dash. "You've both had a spot of midnight-breakfast, I hope?"

Lily nodded. "It was a feast."

"Jolly good. Jolly good."

"Have we made much progress?" Robert asked, brushing away a yolky mark he'd made on his jacket.

"See for yourself." Anna pointed at a map of Great Britain pinned to the back wall of the cabin. "We've passed three push pins, that long piece of thread, and the marmalade stain over the Midlands."

"How long will it take us to get to London, do you think?" Lily asked. She watched Malkin sniffing away at the four corners of the cabin.

"We're doing better than I thought." Anna lined up the sextant. "See the dot there? Means we're not far off. If this tailwind keeps up we should make it by first light. In a few hours we might get a glimpse of street lamps on the horizon – hundreds there are, like the stars, and when it's dawn you see them disappear as the lamplighters go round and snuff 'em out."

"Where are we going to land?" Robert wondered.

Anna consulted the compass. "Depends. Gypsy balloons like *Ladybird* aren't welcome in a lot of places and I haven't paid my air-dues. But there's atchings out east we could make for."

"Atchings?" Lily tried out the strange word.

"That's traveller polari – traveller speak – for a place to weigh anchor."

Anna turned the ship's wheel and the thick ropes that

looped through the metal eyelets on the wall shifted.

"What are those for?" Lily asked.

"They run along the insides of the balloon to connect the steering column to the port, starboard, and tail rudders," Anna explained. "One of them breaks and the entire airship goes off course, could hit anything."

"Strange they're not outside the gondola," Lily mused.

"Not so strange," Anna said. "Your delicate parts are all inside. If not it would hurt a darn sight more when you got hit."

Robert was examining some of the controls on the dash. "They're also on the inside so they don't freeze and break at high altitude," he explained.

Anna lit up. "He knows!"

"Oh. I see," Lily said, though she didn't quite. She examined an odd looking rifle-like gun in a mount on the wall, beside the flight controls.

"And what's this?"

Anna slapped her fingers away. "Don't touch that! It's dangerous. It's an emergency harpoon – in case of sky pirates."

"But where's the harpoon?"

"I don't have one. There was an emergency..." Anna blinked sleepily. "With sky pirates." She yawned. "Tell you what, Robbie, why don't you take the wheel? I think

I'll go grab forty winks. You can steer for a while. You'll be good for an hour or two, at least, both of you. You can keep each other awake."

"We'll manage," Robert said.

"Reckoned you would." Anna pointed out a group of stars through the cabin window. "Those constellations are going to move across the sky, but keep the middle star centre of the glass and the compass needle on the S of south and you'll be heading in the right direction. Wake me when you see those street lamps on the horizon."

With that she left, and they heard her climbing into the berth behind. Soon there was the sharp tap of typewriter keys, but that drifted off into silence after a while, and Lily assumed the aeronaut had fallen asleep.

Robert furrowed his brow and turned the wheel, keeping *Ladybird* on a straight bearing, pushing her onwards. The gentle thrumming of the engine filtered through the walls and the heat from the pipes made the cabin pleasantly toasty. Malkin had stretched out in a corner, his body against a warm pipe, and fallen asleep.

Lily gazed out at the stars, hung about the night sky like freckles. In the distance a tiny speck of light slipped across the firmament. "Do you think that one's a shooting star?" she asked.

Robert studied it. "I'm not sure. I reckon it's moving too slow."

"A comet, then?"

"Comets only appear once a century, we'd be lucky to see one in our lifetime. It's probably another ship moving along the airways."

"How do you know so much about airships and astronomy, Robert?"

"My da knew a fair bit about both – from the chronometers he fixed, and from books."

"I'm so very sorry about your da," Lily said. "Really I am. I never thought such terrible things would happen to him because of me."

"Let's not talk about it," Robert said. "I don't think I can bear to." He wiped the condensation from the windscreen and the cold water made droplets in his palm. "Da told me people used to think the stars were gods and goddesses," he said finally. "That they'd some magic in them – and it's true, 'cause they're part of the past. Their light's travelled whole galaxies, glittering hundreds of thousands of years, just to reach us. But you know what the oddest thing is?"

"No, what?"

"Each star's light takes a different amount of time to get here. There's stars out tonight shining from every moment in history. It's why they each shine different."

Lily turned and stared out at the night. It was true what he said – some stars shone brighter and stronger than their compatriots, while others were hazy, or dim. But all were a sight to behold.

"A few folks reckon the whole of time's happening at once," Robert said softly. "And no one's ever born, nor ever dies, and everyone's with us always, right here." He put a hand over his heart and looked out at the sky. "It's a queer thought."

"A queer thought, indeed." Lily grasped the steering wheel and her fingers brushed against his. Suddenly, despite all she'd lost, she felt lucky to be here with him. Two friends flying among stars. "Did your da teach you those things too?" she asked.

"Some of them," Robert said, tilting his head. "Some of them I read for myself in his books. He'd a lot of books on stars, and time as well, of course. Time and the stars are related, see? Stars are how people knew the time and navigated in the old days. He taught me to read from those star books, taught me the names of the constellations. I wish I could remember more of them, but I can't." He paused. "Some people think everything's made of stardust."

"Even us?" Lily asked.

Robert nodded. "Even us."

They stood in silence together and took in the great expanse of sky.

The infinity of it.

Lily peered out the windscreen. "Robert, that light – I think it might be coming closer."

In the time that they had been talking, the luminous ball of white on the horizon had grown to the size of a second moon. It swooped and became a searchlight, which settled across *Ladybird*'s bow, filling the cabin with brilliance.

Lily saw her reflection and Robert's in the dark glass, and heard the crackle of gunfire. Robert ducked, dragging her down behind the ship's wheel, as the windscreen shattered and broken glass rained over their heads.

Malkin woke with a jolt and let out a loud, screaming yelp.

Robert scrambled across sharp shards towards him.

Lily grabbed the communication tube from its hook on the wall and shouted into the receiver. "Emergency! We're under attack!"

There was a loud *thunk* – like someone bumping their head – then Anna pulled back the curtain and rushed in. Rubbing her brow and swearing profusely, she flicked various switches on the console.

The attacking airship let loose another volley of gunfire. In the brief flash of powder, Lily glimpsed the name written on its side. Her voice shook as she read it aloud: "*Behemoth.*"

"That's Roach and Mould's ship," Malkin barked.

"So they've found us," Robert said, quietly.

"Yes," Lily nodded. A dreadful knot of terror tore at her insides as the silver airship approached. Its fierce, spiked prow was heading straight towards them.

CHAPTER 17

"They mean to bring us down," Lily yelled. "Take evasive action! Turn the ship around!"

Anna grabbed the helm from Robert, spinning the wheel three-sixty degrees, and, slowly, *Ladybird* began to pivot to face the opposite direction.

Robert examined the instrument panel on the binnacle. The pressure gauge needle was tipping towards the zero mark. "We've got no steam to outrun them," he told Anna.

"Then go stoke the boiler, both of you." She glanced at Lily. "Throw in everything you can!"

"Stay with Anna, Malkin," Lily cried, and she and Robert rushed down the corridor.

In the engine room Robert threw open the door of the

furnace and started hastily heaping in coal. Lily grabbed a spare shovel to help. The dark shape of *Behemoth* loomed outside the starboard portholes, its spiked hull heading straight for the heart of their ship.

Ladybird had almost turned three-sixty when—

Thud!

She was hit by a harpoon.

The cabin rocked back and forth, and there was a long, low scraping as *Behemoth* began winching her in.

Lily and Robert steadied themselves and threw spadefuls of coal into the furnace; the engine's piston sped up, pumping frantically, but, still, *Behemoth* tightened her winch rope.

Malkin dashed through, and ran back and forth between them in a crazed skittering loop. "This is what happened with John's ship," he yapped. "And it's happening again!"

Lily felt sick. If they didn't escape now, well…

Anna's voice crackled from the communications tube. "Stoke the boiler, they're trying to board us!"

Lily looked around. Robert was scraping up the last of the coal dust and throwing it into the furnace. Soon there would be nothing left to burn.

"We're out of fuel!" she cried down the communications tube.

"Chuck in the empty crates from the footlocker compartment," came Anna's curt and echoing reply.

Lily rushed into the corridor and heaved out a pile of boxes, handing them in to Robert, who smashed them against the side of the furnace and threw the fragments into the flames.

The engine began pumping double time, the mechanical motor turning at full tilt, clanking its crazed spidery arms.

"Did we break free?" Robert asked.

Lily glanced out the port-side porthole and was met with a blast of bright light. "No!" she cried.

Behemoth was getting closer, pulling them in. The noise of her humming engines filled the cabin, rattling the fittings and shaking Lily's teeth and bones.

She had to do something, and quick. She left Robert and a mewling Malkin, raced the few steps down the corridor, and burst onto the bridge.

Anna glanced round from the wheel. "What is it?"

Lily grasped the wall. "I have to go out there, cut their line."

"Are you sure?" Anna asked. "It's dangerous."

Lily nodded. "It's the only way now, I think – our engine power isn't strong enough."

Anna nodded. "Fine. Do it. And cut loose all the scrap,

239

everything tied to the hull: it's holding us back. But be safe – don't leave the ladder. Have you got something to break the lines?"

Lily undid her bundle and pulled the hacksaw and screwdriver from where they were stuffed in beside the box. "Will these do?"

"Aye, they will."

Lily tucked them into her belt. Back in the passage, she struggled to open the cabin door. A blast of cold air battered her against the wall as she pulled the lever to lower the ladder.

Outside the wind whipped by. While she climbed out onto the highest rung, *Behemoth* loomed at her elbow, preparing to fire more harpoons, and *Ladybird* bucked on her line, shuddering like a dying whale.

Lily yanked the hacksaw from her belt and swung about on the ladder. Pulled taut across the narrowing airspace, the towline crackled and groaned, brittle with frost, but the opposing pull of the two airships kept the line steady as Lily hacked at it, again and again. The wind battered hard against her, trying to stop her efforts, until her face stung with the cold, and her arm felt weary, ready to drop. Just a few more cuts and—

keerrrRRACK!

The rope snapped and *Ladybird* bucked free, jerking

forward, her propellers spiralling with a sudden burst of speed. *Behemoth* readied another harpoon; they weren't going to make it out of range unless Lily could lighten the load.

Quickly, she began hacking at the hanging ballast. With every line she cut, tangles of scrap dropped away, and *Ladybird*'s props turned faster and faster. Soon, Anna's airship was jigging and zigging across the sky, rising above *Behemoth*'s hull, so that the harpooner in his hatch could not take aim at her.

There was one more rope of scrap-ballast.

Lily leaned forwards and hacked at it.

The rope frayed, but refused to break. The sharp-toothed pieces of jagged metal tied to its end clanked together, twirling in space.

Lily leaned out further, slashing at the knot, the hacksaw loose in her slippery hand, cold sweat pouring down her back.

Finally the rope broke, and the last of the scrap plummeted and fell, bouncing off *Behemoth*'s prow, and scattering across the sky.

Ladybird jolted, rising fast. Lily dropped the hacksaw and grasped with her free hand for the ladder, but she had stretched too far. She flailed, slipping on the icy metal...and fell...

The clouds streamed past…

A mess of flailing ropes whipped at her face…

Thunk!

She juddered to a stop with a tooth-smacking, spine-wrenching yank.

Her foot had caught on the ladder's last rung, and she swung about like some mad metronome; the melting white patchworked landscape wheeling around and around beneath her.

Her stomach fluttered in her mouth and her heart beat a tattoo in her chest in time with the howling wind. She needed to think, catch her breath, get herself out of this. Her brain clattered against the inside of her skull as *Ladybird* spun in dizzying circles above her head.

She screwed her eyes shut and made a grab for the rung above her.

It took every ounce of her strength to pull herself upright, and when she blinked her eyes open, the world, though still spinning, was once again the right way up.

She took a deep breath and began to climb, looping her elbow over each crossbar. Arm over arm she clambered upwards, while *Ladybird* rose steadily like a bubble, and the roar of *Behemoth*'s engines receded. Soon it became a small silhouette, and then, finally, it looked no bigger than a tin toy.

Lily climbed into the shadow of *Ladybird*'s gondola and crawled through the opening in the hull.

They were breaking through the clouds when she wound the ladder in and slammed the hatch shut behind her, cutting out the roar of the sky.

"Bravo!" Anna called from the bridge. "You've given us enough pep to outrun them."

But *Ladybird* didn't quite agree – her wooden frame juddered and shook, complaining.

"Crunking useless machine!" Anna hit her palm against the dash.

"What is it?" Lily hurried to the flight deck.

"We're going too high." Anna's white knuckles gripped the wheel. All about her, needles in their dials fluttered and pulsed, and *Ladybird* rattled as she rose. "She's going to break up if we carry on like this!" Anna shouted. "We've shed too much ballast. We need to release gas from the balloon – equalize and bring her down." She pulled a lever at the side of the cabin, but nothing happened. "Clank it!" she cursed again.

Robert appeared in the doorway. "What's wrong?" he asked.

"The gas vent release is jammed." Anna tried a few

different buttons on the dash, but the ship didn't respond. Another brass dial twitched into the danger zone. Anna glared at it.

"That's the oxygen warning – ten minutes and we'll run out of air. Take over, would you, Lil?"

Lily took the wheel from Anna and felt the ship buck and twist under her hand, like an angry animal.

Malkin jumped up and leaned against her. "I don't like this," he whined. "I don't like this at all! We'll end up smashed to smithereens, or worse."

"Don't worry her," Anna yelled at him. "Lily, you keep our course." She took Robert's arm. "You, come with me."

Anna ushered Robert into the passage.

She pulled back the curtain on the berth and pushed open a panel in the gondola's ceiling.

"There's a rope opens the gas vent – it runs through the inside of the zep just like with the steering cables. It must've snapped or jammed somewhere. You're going to have to climb into the balloon and fix it."

"It looks dark up there," Robert said. "Can't I take a light?"

Anna shook her head. "Not unless you want to blow

us up. You'll have to feel for the break. The rope starts just above this ceiling hatch, and runs through a series of loops. Pull yourself along it until you find where it's broken. I would go myself but I need to check on the clanking engine!"

She pushed him through the hatch.

Robert stared down at her, framed in the square hole. "What do I do when I find the break?"

"Tie the two halves together again, and paint some tar over them so they stick." She reached down and pulled a short length of rope, a pot of gloopy tar and a brush from the footlocker, and handed them to Robert. "If there's any chance the knot might snag on an eyelet, make a join on either side with this spare length."

"What happens if I can't fix it?"

"Then we'll keep rising and we're dead in ten minutes when the oxygen runs out. You got all that, Robbie?"

"Yes, Ma'am."

Robert ducked away from the hatch and scrambled into the dark interior of the balloon. Carrying the pot of tar and the rope and brush, he couldn't even cover his mouth against the particles of dust that the juddering ship was kicking up. He blinked them away, and sneezed.

Helium gas filled the empty vault above his head. It dizzied him at first and he had to take slow deep breaths to get enough air. Soon his eyes adjusted to the lack of light, and he could see a little. The space inside the balloon must've been three times as tall as he, or more.

He put one hand out and felt for the end of the rope. It ran along the roof of the gondola. He inched himself down its length in the dark, before he finally found the break in the rope.

Clinging on tight, he hooked the brush and bucket over the inside of his elbow and put his hand out, feeling for the other length of broken rope. It was loose and flapping, hitting the interior of the silks on the far side of an eyelet.

He'd have to tie the two lengths of rope together with the spare section.

He threaded it through the eyelet and knotted each end to the existing rope, using reef knots, and cut the frayed lumps off with his penknife. Then he painted tar-bitumen over the joins to seal them, and tugged the nearside rope to check it didn't catch.

It didn't.

Relieved, he picked up his pot. Fixing airships was easier than fixing clocks, that was for sure. Climbing back towards the opening in the floor, he realized that he'd been so busy with the task that he'd forgotten all his nagging fears. Once more he remembered Da's advice about being brave, and it was almost as if Da was there with him.

"It's done," he called out, jumping down from the crawl space into the berth.

"Great!" Anna cried, emerging from the engine room.

"Has it worked? Are we losing height?" he asked. He coughed. His voice appeared to have gone a little squeaky all of a sudden.

"I think so." Anna hustled him towards the bridge.

Lily, at the wheel, had already pulled the vent rope. The balloon hissed, releasing gas.

"Nice job both of you," Anna told them. She took back the controls and evened out their path. "One good thing's come of this: we appear to have lost our pursuers."

Gradually, as they dropped to a lower altitude, the cabin filled with fresh air, and *Ladybird*'s wooden frame stopped shivering. Soon, she grazed the cloud tops again and, one by one, the needles in her instrument panels tipped from their red danger zones into black.

They flew on. Robert and Lily stoked the dying boiler, feeding it with the last scraps of the wood and coal dust. Malkin even ripped a few damaged boards from the deck with his teeth and threw them in.

After an hour, Lily's shirt clung to her back, and the sweat dripped off her in fat globules. She felt like she could barely go on, but then the communications tube came to life with a crackle, and Anna's voice boomed out from its brass trumpet: "London ahoy – dead ahead!"

Lily, Robert and Malkin ran up to the flight deck. The three of them stared out the shattered windscreen, Malkin craning his neck to see over the broken glass.

In the distance, the pre-dawn light was coming up over the curve of the Earth, and *Behemoth* was nowhere in sight. Anna pushed on the throttle and took the airship south, towards the great city of London, but it was barely visible through the fog. When she saw the looks of disappointment on their faces, she spoke up. "Tell you what, I'll take her down a touch. If this pea-souper clears, you might catch a glimpse of the famous skyline."

She flicked some switches on the dash and tugged the vent lever, releasing more gas. *Ladybird* dropped through the smog and bobbed above the maze of frosty rooftops that suddenly spread out before them.

In the east, a red winter sunrise washed over the city. Along the lanes beneath them, pocket-sized lamplighters extinguished street lights, and tiny knocker-uppers banged on condensation-covered windows with their long sticks, tapping out alarm calls to get people up for work.

"Where to now?" Anna asked.

"To Professor Silverfish's house," Lily said, handing her the professor's card.

Anna read the address and shook her head. "I can't drop you here. I'm not allowed to land unauthorized in these posh parts of town. Tell you what, though, I'll get you as close as I can."

Anna turned the wheel, swooping *Ladybird* past a row of building-block houses, and over the vaulted steel ribcage of St Pancras airdock.

She steered their tiny craft past King's Cross Station, where a maze of tracks led early-morning locomotives to platforms. Out front, steam-wagons and horse-drawn carriages waited to collect arriving passengers, while pin-sized pedestrians and hawkers streamed across miniature cobbles.

Anna squeezed *Ladybird* between two fat aerostats which marked the gateway to the city's airways, and jostled her through the lines of airships that filled the soot-stained sky.

Soon, the bulbous dome of St Paul's Cathedral, topped with its golden cross, loomed out of the fog. Anna turned *Ladybird* hard starboard, taking the east–west airway, which she told them followed a direct path along the Thames to the professor's house. Beneath the other airship traffic, Lily could make out coal barges and steam tugs navigating the watery blue snake of the river as it cut through the heart of the city.

A single red aerostat, floating over the north bank on a long chain, marked the turn-off for Kensington and Chelsea. Anna pulled out of the air traffic, and flew over an expanse of large houses that stood beside the river.

Lily's heart leaped when she saw them, for something about the streets spoke of home. Even though the professor had only just moved back to London, he had obviously returned to the area where they had all once lived.

She felt as if she knew the landmarks from before – the piers, and bridges, and streets, the park on the south side – they all looked remarkably familiar. She was sure she'd be safe here, with the professor, and, most importantly, he would be able to give her some answers about Papa and the perpetual motion machine at last.

But Anna didn't stop. Just floated on past the rows of tree-lined houses, and finally, ten minutes later, jerked to a halt over a derelict stretch of dockland between the waterfront and a railway siding crowded with engines. Below, on the port side, was a wharf filled with boats. A few steamers chugged in and out of a narrow canal that led to the river.

"Sorry about the detour," Anna said, as she lowered *Ladybird*'s anchor.

"Where are we?" Robert asked.

"Counter's Creek – an airship mooring – and as near as I can get to your fancy address. I don't want to get fined for weighing anchor in Chelsea. I've got a whole slew of unpaid air-tickets as it is."

She scribbled down a map on a scrap of paper and handed it to Lily. "This is how you get back to where you want to be. I'll be moored right here if you need me. Tomorrow I'll take a trip to Fleet Street, visit the offices of *The Daily Cog*, and then I promise to stop by and see you and your godfather, let you know what I've found out about your father and those men, Roach and Mould." She smiled at them.

"Thank you, Anna." Lily kissed her cheek.

"Not at all," Anna said. "I hope I can drum up something useful." She turned to Robert and gave him a big hug. "Robert, I'm so sorry for your loss. I hope you find safe harbour and good advice with Lily's godfather." Finally, she leaned down and scratched Malkin's ears. "Take care of them both, Malkin. Goodbye and good luck. I shall see you all soon."

They unwound the ship's metal ladder and Lily fastened Malkin in her coat once more before beginning her descent. Robert followed behind, with the box and their few other possessions strapped to his back in the blanket sling.

He was getting used to the up and down of air travel much more now. He still felt a little vertigo, but his da had been right – with practice, the panic did subside. He wondered if his deep sense of loss would fade the same way over time, or whether it would be with him always? And what was he going to do if Lily's godfather couldn't take him in? Then he'd be alone in the vast grey city.

They reached the bottom rung of the ladder, and jumped the last few feet to the ground. Anna stood in the aperture of the doorway above waving at them. They smiled and waved back, and Malkin poked his head from Lily's jacket and gave her a loud yipping howl of thanks.

As Anna pulled up the ladder, and closed *Ladybird*'s door, Lily undid her jacket and let Malkin jump out. Robert decided he would miss the aeronaut. "I'm afraid we're on our own again," he sighed.

"Not quite," Lily said. "Help is at hand and, in the meantime, the three of us still make a team." She took his arm and, with Malkin trotting beside them, they stepped from the mouth of the alleyway and set forth into the bustling streets of London.

The search for the professor's house proved to be more complex than they had imagined and took most of the morning. It was easy to get lost in the hubbub of Chelsea. Away from the smarter suburban streets, the main roads were like mechanical rivers. An endless stream of carts and wagons, trams and double-decker omnibuses, steam-drays and clockwork carriages chugged along, spitting out smoke. Clamour and shouting emerged from every alley, while hawkers with handcarts wove about the pavement, and the stench of oil, gas and manure filled the air, suffusing everything.

Malkin led the way, claiming he'd memorized the route after a quick glance at Anna's map. Despite his bravado, his dithering gait did not inspire much confidence.

Very few of the streets were signposted and, after they'd been walking for a good twenty minutes, Robert wondered if the mechanimal knew where he was going at all. So he began stopping passers-by to ask for directions.

That got Malkin rather huffy. "Tell him, Lily," the fox grumbled, "how John's mechanicals never get lost."

"Tell him yourself," Lily said. "I'm busy." She consulted a squiggle on the map. "I wonder if we have this up the right way?"

When they finally found it, the street – Riverside Walk – turned out to be a tree-lined avenue, filled with detached houses with long drives, tall iron railings, and large gardens that backed onto the north side of the Thames, all the way along to Battersea Bridge.

Lily found number nine and pushed open the gate. But, as they walked up the drive and approached the house, she stopped and said something so quiet Robert almost didn't hear.

"We used to live here."

CHAPTER 18

"Are you sure you lived here?" Robert gazed up at the facade of the professor's house. It didn't look much like a family home. The front was so encrusted in ironwork, a demented architect might've stuck the fireguards on the outside by mistake. At the corner of the roof, a fat grey chimney, with four stubby pot-shaped fingers, reached out, grabbing at the iron sky.

"I think so." Lily seemed uncertain now. "All that decoration wasn't here, admittedly, but it feels the same."

They climbed the marble steps to the front door and Lily banged the silver knocker, shaped like a leaping salmon. "That wasn't here either," she whispered.

"It's easy to change things," Robert said – her

confusion had made him slightly uneasy. "But you could be mistaken."

They waited.

Eventually footsteps approached. The door opened a crack and a smart mechanical butler, all spit-polished brass and oily gold hair, peered out. "Yes, may I help you?" he asked.

"We're here to see the professor," Lily told him.

The butler gave a steely sniff. "I'm afraid Professor Silverfish is not in the habit of entertaining each passing ragamuffin who darkens his door."

"I am *not* a ragamuffin." Lily squared her shoulders and stood up straight. "I'm Miss Hartman. Professor Silverfish's god-daughter. He told me if I was ever in trouble I could call on him."

"Miss Hartman?" The butler looked her up and down, examining her barrow-boy apparel.

"I'm in a sort of disguise," she explained.

"I see," he said, though he clearly didn't. "Do you have a visitor's card?"

"Do I look like I have a visitor's card?" Lily snapped.

Robert could feel her growing frustration. He nudged her on the arm. "Lil, you have *his* card, remember."

"Of course!" Lily fumbled through her pockets and produced Professor Silverfish's card.

The butler took it distastefully in his white gloved hands, turned it over and examined it. "I will tell him you're here, Miss Hartman. And Master…"

"Townsend. Robert Townsend."

"Very good." The butler stepped aside. "You can wait in the hall. Not your mechanical dog though. I can't have mechanimals in the house. You'll have to leave him outside."

"I'm not a dog, I'm a fox," Malkin growled, baring his teeth. "And I'm perfectly house-trained if that's what you're worried about. I won't be dropping any cogs on your carpet."

Lily bent down and whispered to him. "Please, Malkin, do as he says, we won't be long, I promise."

The fox nodded. "Don't be," he said and slunk off to sit under a holly bush in the flower bed.

The butler watched him with distaste. He held the door open for Robert and Lily, who stepped across the threshold and found themselves in a grand atrium.

"This way," the butler said, turning on his casters and ushering them across a chequerboard marble floor. It was lit from above by a bright glowing chandelier – that made Robert think of a thousand glass stalactites – each one burning with a flameless light that must've been electricity.

257

The butler jerked to a stop at the foot of a grand staircase. "Wait here a moment," he said and disappeared down the hall.

Lily gazed past the chandelier at the ornate ceiling, where a fresco depicted a map of seas and continents, ripped away to reveal the world's internal clockwork mechanism. "I don't remember any of this," she whispered. "The hallway was different."

Robert shifted the bundle on his back. "The thing is—" he said, but he never had time to complete his thought, because he was interrupted by a big expansive voice echoing along the corridor.

"Show them in, you foolish mech...oh never mind, I shall do it!"

Professor Silverfish appeared from around the corner. He greeted Lily with a warm hug and Robert with an enthusiastic handshake. "Master Townsend, a pleasure to meet you, and, Lily, so good to see you. I was worried sick after our last meeting: leaving you in the hands of your dour guardian. I felt terrible. I'm sorry I didn't return and check on you. I meant to, but I've been so unwell." He tapped the centre of his chest, which gave a metal ring; when he leaned forward Robert saw he had a complex machine attached to his body, under his jacket.

"How is your heart, Sir?" Lily asked.

Professor Silverfish laughed. "Much better now I see you, dear child. But, tell me, what on earth has been happening?"

"All sorts of things." Lily shook her head wearily. "I still haven't found out what happened to Papa, and I need your help more than ever."

Professor Silverfish scratched his head. "It's quite the conundrum. Does anyone know where you are? Your guardian?"

"No one," Lily said. "Men were chasing us and we had to run. Awful things have happened, and we're in the most terrible trouble, aren't we, Robert?"

"Come, come." Professor Silverfish put a hand on each of their shoulders. "It can't be that bad, surely? I feel certain we can solve your problems. Why don't you join me for a spot of lunch? Nothing seems so bad after a hearty bite to eat!" He looked them up and down. "But perhaps you want time to recuperate from your journey first, hmm? We can eat a little later, if you desire? In the meantime, you can have a wash, and a rest, and my mechs will find you some clean clothes. What do you think of that plan?"

Robert nodded. He suddenly felt he would very much like a moment to himself, and perhaps a little sleep.

The unfriendly butler led them along the polished parquet of the first-floor landing and showed them to two adjoining rooms. "You may relax here for a time," he said. "Luncheon will be served in an hour."

Lily nodded her thanks. Taking her bundle from Robert, she flashed him a reassuring look and disappeared inside her chamber.

Robert waited on the landing for a moment, glancing about. The house was overwhelmingly grand. A corridor ran along three sides of the mezzanine, above the massive atrium. Behind the hanging chandelier there was another set of stairs at the far end of the hallway that led up to a second floor. It had looked like there was a basement too, for he'd noticed stairs on the ground floor leading down. Momentarily he wondered if he should go and explore, but there'd be time for that later, after a rest. He could hear Lily wandering about in her room, and he turned and stepped through the door into his own.

It was the most opulent chamber he'd ever set foot in. The walls, panelled in green velvet, matched the curtains that surrounded a floor-to-ceiling bay window, and against the near side wall stood a comfortable-looking four-poster bed.

There was even an adjoining bathroom with a sink but no bath – instead there was a strange glass-sided cubicle, with two gold taps set into a marble-tiled wall, and a brass pipe that looped down from the ceiling and ended in a head that looked like a petal-less sunflower.

Robert stepped into the cubicle and tried the taps and then jumped back in shock, for a sudden shower of hot water rained down upon his head. He barely had time to undress before his clothes were soaking wet. Then, in a wall-sunk marble shell, he noticed a bar of soap.

When he stepped out of the cubicle after washing himself, he saw a thick white towelling dressing gown hanging on the back of the door. He put it on and, picking up his wet clothes, wandered back into the room.

The mechanical butler had left a smart-looking suit on the corner of the bed. He tried it, and found that the trousers, pristine white shirt and jacket were an exact fit.

He looked a new man in the mirror, and he wished his da was there to see him. But Da would never have been able to afford such clothes, Robert thought sadly, and when he looked again he barely recognized himself. It was like he'd left too much of his past behind already.

He took off the clothes and put his own damp things back on again. Then he lay down on the bed. There was a lump digging painfully into his chest. He fished the object out of his pocket. His penknife, the one Da had given him – he'd almost forgotten about that. He tucked it into his sock – a far better place for it. Then he curled up into a ball, shut his eyes, took a sharp, deep, sob-filled breath, and fell asleep.

He was woken by the tinkle of a bell somewhere far off, and for a second, as he lay with his eyes closed, he thought it might be his da opening up the shop for the day. But then the tinkle went on for too long and he realized it was not.

There was a knock at the bedroom door, and he opened his eyes and sat up, remembering where he was.

Lily peered in. She wore a beautiful silk dress, her hair was pinned back and her face looked clean, scrubbed of the road dirt. She pushed the door open wide and he saw that she carried the box under one arm. It was no longer wrapped in its blanket.

"You look different," he said, as he stood and stretched his tired legs. "Is that a new dress? It looks…I mean, you look…pretty."

She smiled. "You mean I didn't look pretty before?"

"No… I… Don't you think it's odd here?" he asked, changing the subject. "Almost too quiet."

She shrugged.

"Did you remember anything else about this house, from the old days?"

"Not really," she said. "It does seem familiar somehow, but all of that was so long ago. Maybe I was wrong? Maybe, it's just this week, everything from the past being dredged up... Who knows... Still, it's a relief to get out of those dirty clothes, though this is possibly not what I would've chosen." She straightened the front of her dress, then stepped towards him and leaned in. Robert thought she was going to give him a peck on the cheek, but she raised a hand, conspiratorially. "The mechanical maid told me she was sent out to get this from the haberdasher's down the road as soon as we arrived. A little too formal, don't you think?"

He didn't know what to think; his face felt hot. He brushed the dry sleep from his eyes. "Was that the bell for lunch?" he asked. "I'm starving."

It took the whole meal for Lily to explain to Professor Silverfish what had happened to her and Robert, and while she talked the professor listened attentively, making little sounds of encouragement and shock.

Meanwhile the shiny mechanical butler whirred softly across the ornately patterned carpet, bringing in endless courses under silver domes and placing them down on the long mahogany table.

Robert sipped from a crystal glass full of lemonade. He was only half-listening to the conversation. He had enjoyed the starter of cold tomato soup, and then a meltingly light Dover sole, which came with butter sauce and mashed potatoes. But now they were onto the main course, a massive haunch of roasted venison, he was beginning to feel rather ill. He had trouble working out which of the remaining cutlery he was supposed to be using. He was accustomed to simple meals at home with Da; here he didn't have a clue. And despite all the delicious things he'd eaten, he still could not shake the feeling that there was something odd about the house. Time drifted past too quietly. If any work took place, he wasn't sure what it could be. There were no clocks, he realized suddenly – that's what it was, and the only ticking in the room came from the professor's strange heart.

The pudding arrived: a wobbling, jellified rich chocolate cream, served on a silver platter. Robert took a small slice, and when he'd finished eating, he looked up to find Lily had reached the end of her tale.

Professor Silverfish sat back and lit a cigar, then he examined John's letter. "My dears," he said, "you've been through the most terrible strife. If only you'd telegrammed, I feel sure I could've helped sooner."

Lily leaned towards him. "So you know something more about Papa's disappearance, about this perpetual motion machine?"

The professor frowned, twisting the cigar in his hand slowly. "Dear child, of course I know something about it. Thinking about it has taken up thirteen years of my life." He waited while his mechanical butler cleared away the last of the dishes and left. Then the professor dragged a marble ashtray across the table and tapped the ash from the end of his cigar into its bowl.

"Seven years ago," he began, "your father and I were working together on hybrid machines. Your father was designing mechanicals with new feeling-engines, and I was studying bionics, making repairs to soldiers who'd been injured in combat.

"Unfortunately I was only able to save a few men before my own health problems worsened. Every day I found myself losing breath, and forgetting pieces of vital knowledge needed for the work. On more than one occasion, I lost consciousness for a time. The doctors assisting me did lots of tests. They discovered I was mortally ill – my heart was failing.

"Your father offered to help; he had been making a

copy of a human heart from clockwork, and he thought if he could finish it, and implant the thing, it might save my life. I agreed and paid him handsomely to start right away."

"Well, it looks like he did a good job," Robert said. He couldn't stop himself staring at the bulky device connected to the professor's chest. He hoped he wasn't being rude.

"What, this?" Professor Silverfish tapped his device again. "Oh no – this primitive monstrosity has to be wound daily, and constantly repaired. Makes me feel like one of those blasted useless mechs!"

Lily baulked at this outburst, but she said nothing, just let the professor continue; she needed him to get to the end of what he wanted to say.

"No." The professor thumped the chest plate of his machine. "John didn't create *this* heart. His device was much more sophisticated. Far more compact. A genius piece of engineering." He brushed some ash from his white shirt cuff.

"Even before it was finished, I begged to see the device, but John was always so secretive. He refused. Hid the thing in his safe each day.

"Only when it was nearly finished did he change his mind. Showed me to his office in this very house."

Lily gave a start. The professor gave a little nod of acknowledgement, then continued. "John removed a painting from above the fireplace, uncovering a safe, which he opened to reveal a small rosewood box."

Robert saw Lily glance down at the box by the foot of her chair.

Professor Silverfish hadn't noticed – he was deep inside the memory. "John placed the box on the workbench in front of me. From inside came a quiet ticking. He turned a key in the lock and opened the lid, and the tick got louder.

"I peered into the padded velvet interior. Nestling inside was the completed device: the Cogheart."

"The Cogheart," Lily whispered.

"What did it look like?" Robert asked.

"It was different in appearance from any piece of clockwork I'd ever seen," Professor Silverfish said. "Organic and lumpy, like the organs one finds in a butcher's shop, and its surface was pocked with indents and metal vessels.

"I reached out and took the Cogheart in my hands. It felt cold and heavy, and yet the shape was not uncomfortable. In fact, it fitted perfectly into my palms. Almost as if the thing was moulding to my skin; wanting to become part of me.

"When I touched a catch on the front of the device, a panel flicked open and I saw that the heart contained four glass chambers and hundreds of tiny metal cogs turning in unison. At the centre, a glowing red stone emitted a pulsing light.

"I stared at it in amazement. It was the perfect piece of hybrid technology, an impossible device made real. Better than anything I could've come up with myself. I had so many questions, but your father waved them away.

"'When can I have it?' I asked. 'When will it be mine?'

"'Soon,' he said. But, when I saw him the next day, his face had hardened.

"'What is it?' I asked. 'Problems with the device?'

"'No,' he said. 'It's something else. I'm afraid, Simon, I've changed my mind. I cannot give you the Cogheart.'

"'Why not?'

"John shook his head. 'I did some tests and discovered something amazing: this device runs on perpetual motion. It's a perpetual motion machine. I've created the most powerful machine in existence. It will not slow or break or stop. It will not die. I could never put that inside someone.' He scratched his beard and looked at me, and his eyes were deadly serious. 'You see, Simon, I believe I've discovered a way to keep humans alive for ever.

And that's not something which should make its way into the world.'

"'But you made a promise,' I said. 'Surely you'll reconsider?'

"And it did seem for a moment that he was thinking about it. But then he turned his back on me and I knew he'd made his decision. 'The proper thing to do', he said, 'is to destroy the device. You can ask me tomorrow, but I don't think I'll have changed my mind.'"

Professor Silverfish ground out his cigar in the ashtray. "Neither of us knew *that* tomorrow was not to be. Events took a rather different course, what with your mother's accident, and your illness, Lily. And then your father went into hiding. I could only assume he did so because he had stolen the Cogheart. In all honesty, I don't think he ever intended to destroy it. In my opinion he planned to study the thing, to learn more of the secrets of the impossible energy it possessed."

There was a long silence and Robert waited for Lily to speak, but she seemed lost for words.

"So that's what everyone's after?" he asked finally. "What they want from Lily and Malkin and her papa? What they wanted when they came to my da's shop and killed him."

"Yes." Professor Silverfish nodded. "There had been

rumours in certain circles of what John was working on at the time. Even his disappearance didn't stop people looking for the Cogheart. But he always kept himself very well hidden. As for myself, I never saw or heard from him again. I was forced to go south, to the continent, for my health, and there I began designing a primitive machine which would help me to survive.

"When I returned to England last year, I found this old house of yours up for sale. The broker was your father's ex-lawyer, Mr Sunder. At first he refused to tell me where John had gone, wouldn't let me contact my old friend directly. But after John's airship crashed, I managed to persuade him – and it's a good thing I did, because I see you've brought me the Cogheart."

Lily gulped and her face drained of colour as she glanced down at the box. Her godfather was smiling like a cat who'd caught a bird. Finally Robert understood why the professor had invited her here.

Professor Silverfish stood and took a small key from his pocket. "Your father entrusted this to me when I last saw him," he explained. "It's for the lock."

Lily reached under her chair for the box and put it on the table in front of him. "If I give you this, will you help me find him?"

He nodded.

"Then you can have it," she said. "It's caused my family, and Robert's, nothing but pain and trouble."

Professor Silverfish took a deep breath, put the key in the lock, turned it…and opening the lid, stared at what was inside the box.

Then his face fell and he let out a strange cry. He tipped out the contents and they scattered across the table. A handful of photographs, a thick braid of hair, a piece of old lace, a wedding ring, and a stone. Pictures and memories.

"Where is it?" he cried.

Lily let out a gasp. She picked up one of the photographs. It showed her and her parents, standing together outside this very house.

"These things belonged to Mama," she said, examining the stone. She turned it over in her hand, so that Robert caught a glint of a gold swirling creature embedded at its centre. "This is one of her fossils," she said softly. "She collected them. And here's her wedding ring and a braid of her hair, and part of her favourite dress…"

"Worthless," Professor Silverfish said, staring at the stuff. "All of it." He brushed the box aside. "Just like you."

Robert felt suddenly sick. Tears were forming in Lily's eyes; she grabbed at her mama's things, snatching them across the table towards her. "But Papa's letter…" she said.

"He wrote that we could trust you; you promised help… promised to find him."

"And what are promises worth?" Professor Silverfish said angrily. "No. You're mistaken, Lily. The letter was a warning *not* to trust me. Ever." He turned and gave her a strange look. "But because you at least brought me the box, I will do you one last favour. I will allow the meeting your heart desires."

He took a miniature bell from the centre of the table and rang it. A clump of heavy boots and the *tap-tap-tap* of a cane came echoing down the hall, and the door swung open to reveal a grinning Roach and Mould, their mirrored eyes gleaming. Slumped between them, his head bowed, was Lily's father.

CHAPTER 19

"Papa!" cried Lily, but the relief that flooded over her was quickly followed by a growing sense of horror. Papa looked awful, his body twisted, his arms limp. Her heart went out to him. "What've you done?" she cried.

"Nothing he didn't deserve." Mould's mirrored eyes shimmered with glee.

"Say hello," Roach told Papa, and the pair of them let him go, so that he slumped to the floor, collapsing in a tangled heap like a stringless marionette.

Professor Silverfish regarded his old friend with bare disdain. "I'm afraid my men performed a few experiments on John to jog his memory." He stepped back as if

Papa's despair might tarnish his shoes.

Papa raised his head and stared at Lily. "My darling… my dear one." His words sounded fractured and choked with tears, but he gritted his teeth and continued. "Why did you come?"

Lily gulped down the pain in her chest. "To find you."

"I sent a letter…with Malkin, warning you not to. You're supposed to hide. Where is he? He should be taking care of you."

Professor Silverfish laughed and waved the singed letter at him. "Oh, she got your letter all right. Thought it said I would help. Imagine – your own words brought her right here! Along with my encouragement, of course.

"And now, John, you will tell us where the Cogheart is, or resume work on your new prototype. Otherwise I shall be doing a little surgery myself." He took Lily's chin between his strong fingers, and turned her face towards Papa's.

"First I shall cut off her ears, then her toes, then fingers and then when I've finished with those, I shall cut off every other piece of her, until there's nothing left."

He let her go and Papa gave an anguished cry, but Professor Silverfish ignored him and consulted his pocket watch. "I'll give you an hour to accept my offer." He glanced at Robert. "Meantime, while we wait, perhaps

I'll chop a few digits off this boy. I hear he's not a particularly good clockmaker." He waved a hand at Mould. "Take John back to his lab."

Mould bent down and grasped Papa round the neck.

"You let go of him!" Lily screamed. She grabbed a glass from the table and threw it at them.

It missed, smashing against the wall.

Mould laughed as he dragged Papa from the room.

Professor Silverfish stood in the doorway and lit another cigar as he watched Mr Roach creep round the table towards Lily.

"No, you don't," Robert said. He picked up a china plate and threw it at Roach, but Roach batted it away harmlessly with his stick, and it clattered onto the floor.

Robert took Lily's hand and pulled her round the far side of the table, then realized there was no escape: the pretty frescos on the walls, the plants on their stands and tables of bright objects all disguised the fact that the room had no windows.

"This way," Lily cried, kicking over a chair. She tried to drag Robert under the table, but Roach dropped his stick and scooped them up in his arms, throwing two sweaty palms across their faces.

"I've tried to be nice." Professor Silverfish exhaled a puff of smoke. "But I can't have you wreaking havoc in my house." He stepped into the hallway. "Lock the children in the coal shed, Mr Roach. I'll attend to them later. Right now I want to see if John has had a change of heart."

Mr Roach gripped Lily's and Robert's arms and marched them across the courtyard behind the house. The coal shed was set into an exterior wall, and Lily immediately thought of the one back at school. Roach opened its door, then frisked Robert and got him to turn out his pockets.

"Now you," he said, stepping over to Lily.

"If you dare lay a hand on me," she spat, "I'll kill you."

Roach laughed. "I'm not the one who'll be dead, missy," he said, throwing them both inside. "We'll be back to collect you in a while. Something tells me Papa's going to start cooperating pretty soon."

He slammed the door and locked it, leaving them alone in the dark. Robert and Lily watched him through a barred grate in the door as he hung the key on a hook embedded in the end wall, then went back into the house.

As soon as he'd gone, Lily shook the door handle. She pressed her face against the grate and peered down at the padlock. "We have to get out of here," she whispered.

"What's the use?" Robert said. A sudden flash of jealousy flared inside him. He slumped onto a pile of coal in the corner. He'd lost everything because of her papa and that stupid Professor Silverfish's quarrel. She still had a glimmer of hope, but he had *nothing*.

"I knew something about that professor wasn't right," he snapped. "And now – after all we've been through – I'm in a coal shed waiting to die."

Lily glared at him. "So don't wait then. Look: we're not going to die in a coal shed. We're going to escape, and save Papa."

"If you say so."

Lily rolled up the sleeves of her dress and stuck her arm out through the gap between the bars. "I can almost reach the lock." She plucked a hairpin from her head with her free hand and straightened it in her teeth, then passed it out through the gap in the bars.

Lily bit her lip, concentrating. Robert held his breath. There was a *scritch* and a *scratch*, then—

Tink!

"Drat," she said. "I dropped it." She stamped her foot, and stared at him. "Well? Aren't you going to help me?"

He felt guilty then. None of this was her fault. Not really. They'd all been hurt by those men. She was right, he should at least try and do something to get them out of here. He pulled his penknife from where it was tucked inside his sock and handed it to her. "Here, try this instead."

Lily examined it. "The blades are too big. How have you still got this anyway?"

He shrugged. "I hid it earlier, in my sock. It's been pretty uncomfortable there, actually." He rubbed his ankle. "If only Malkin could get the key for us."

"Of course!" Lily twirled him around. "Malkin's still waiting! MALKIN!" she shouted through the door grate.

"He'll never hear you," Robert grumbled. "He's too far away. Besides, he's probably run down by now."

Lily ignored him. She wiped her coal-blackened fingers on her silk dress, put them in her mouth and whistled.

Robert thought it was probably the loudest wolf whistle in the world. But, instead of a wolf, they got…

Malkin. He shot across the yard in a red streak, and jumped up at the door. His red snout poked between the bars, pushing until his whole head fitted through the gap.

"Got yourself into a spot of bother?" he asked sniffily. "What's going on?"

"I'll tell you in a moment," Lily said. "But you need to get us out of here."

"I see," Malkin said. "*Now* you need my help."

"The key's on the hook, over there." She pointed across the yard.

"First you have to apologize," he told her.

"What?" she spluttered.

The fox licked at his black forepaw. "Because you said I was too scruffy to come inside. You've had a wash and brush-up, I see."

"There isn't time for this," Lily cried, exasperated. "Besides, it wasn't me who said you were scruffy, it was that butler."

"You didn't disagree with him though," Robert chimed in.

"Precisely," the fox snapped, "and now look where you are."

"Fine. I'm sorry," Lily said. "Get the keys, would you?"

"As you wish."

Malkin stepped over to the wall and jumped and snapped at the key on its nail. It was unreachable. He'd have to leap much higher to snatch it.

He looked around. Some old barrel kegs were stacked in a corner.

Malkin butted one over with his head. His tail drooped as he rolled it towards the hanging key. Then he hopped up onto the side of the barrel, and…

Jumped!

This time he managed to snap his teeth round the bottom of the key. It fell from its hook, and Malkin caught it in his mouth, before collapsing in a heap on the floor.

"Thank heaven." Lily thrust her hand through the bars of the shed. "Now, quick, bring it here!"

Malkin jumped up and dropped the key into her palm, and she reached down and undid the padlock.

As soon as she stepped from the shed, she bent down and kissed his nose, and Robert crowded in and stroked his head. "Malkin, you're a cat-burgling genius!" he whispered.

"Yes, Malkin!" Lily murmured, scratching the fox's fluffy ears. "You *are* a genius! I shall write to Jack Door of your exploits. He's bound to immortalize you in his next burglary book."

Malkin gave a protesting yap. "Enough messing. We have to go."

Lily took the winder from round his neck and wound him.

"No," she said. "You have to. Find Anna, and ask for her help. Robert and I are going back inside for Papa."

Malkin's dark eyes widened, and his whiskers twitched. "John's in the house?"

"Yes," said Lily. "And we're going to rescue him."

Lily and Robert crouched in the frosty garden and watched Malkin squeeze himself between the tall railings. He dropped his tail and kept his body low as he slunk off down the street.

When he'd finally gone, Lily wrinkled her nose, and looked up at the house. "We can get in there," she explained, pointing at a small open window over the back porch, obscured by the bare branches of a tree. "Like climbing the trellis at home." She gave Robert a searching look. "It's going to be dangerous, so if you don't want to come, you don't have to."

Robert shook his head. "I do want to. For my da. I want to help you stop them."

"Good." Lily jumped up and grabbed a low-hanging branch of the tree, then she climbed into its bare crown.

Robert took a deep breath and followed.

By the time he got up among the branches, Lily had already crept out along a bough.

She dropped down onto the porch roof above the back door, and beckoned for him to follow. As soon as he arrived, she climbed through the open window.

The room they tumbled into was dimly lit. Robert crept across the floor, opened the door, and looked out.

He was about to step into the hall, when Lily brushed his arm.

"There's someone else here," she whispered.

She was right: Robert saw the room was filled with the shadowy shapes of old mechs. One leaned stiff against the wall, another sat square in a corner with its legs sticking out. A third lay toppled on the floor. Wires sprouted from their chest panels and their arms and some of their limbs had been ripped open.

Lily stepped towards them, and started as she saw their faces.

"Why, it's Captain Springer," she said, "and Mr Wingnut, and Miss Tock – all our mechanicals from home." She stroked their faces and examined their injuries. "Madame Verdigris must've sold them to him."

Then she stopped. A funny look came over her face and she rushed into the corner where a mechanical woman stood, half-hidden in the shadows. Robert heard her sharp intake of breath.

"Robert, it's Mrs Rust!"

The old mech woman had wires sprouting from the end of one arm. Metal flanges and springs stuck out in a jagged pattern from the place where her hand should be. Lily searched round Mrs Rust's neck for her unique winder on its chain and when she found it she wound the mech-woman's springs until she flickered to life.

Mrs Rust blinked in surprise at Lily. "Clockwork and click-wheels!" she cried. "It's my tiger-Lil!" And when she realized what this meant, she burst into tears. "Those ratchet-faced villains – they captured you too."

"They did, Rusty, but what on earth are you doing here?"

"It was those men – Roach and Mould," Mrs Rust explained. "They brought us to this place. Wanted to know about one of John's inventions: the Cogheart. I'd already told Madame we knew nothing about it. I told them that too, but they kept us prisoner, tortured us, pulled our grommets and loose bits off."

"I'm sorry," Lily told her.

"It's all right," Mrs Rust said, "we'll survive. We're made of sterner stuff. Quick – wind the others."

"Of course, Rusty." Lily kissed her on the nose and then she and Robert ran around winding the other mechanicals as fast as they could. While they wound, Lily whispered their names to awaken them.

"Captain Springer, Mr Wingnut, Miss Tock – please, wake up."

And, though he didn't know them, Robert found himself joining in.

He helped Lily with a mechanical man whose beard was made from curled metal shavings and who had eyebrows of moulded steel. As soon as he was ticking, the man jumped to attention and saluted. "Captain Springer: chauffeur mechanical, first-class, at your service."

They wound a mechanical woman with a bottle-top nose, who blinked pin-light eyes behind thick round eyeglasses. "Who's there?" she spluttered.

"Miss Tock," Lily exclaimed, "it's me!"

"Lily?" Miss Tock seemed confused. "Where am I? I was in the garden, clearing leaves with Mr Wingnut. What the devil is this place?" Then she saw Mrs Rust and Captain Springer, and her bright eyes faded. "Oh," she said, "now I remember."

Lily and Robert wound the last mechanical: a fellow in a long tailcoat with ears made from wing nuts that stuck out the side of his bucket head. He woke with a jitter, and bowed low and creakily to them. "Mr Wingnut, gardening mechanical, at your service."

The four mechanicals shambled about, talking and ticking with one another.

"Thank goodness you woke us," Miss Tock said.

"Claptraptions!" cried Captain Springer. "Now my wheels are turning; I can recall everything!"

"If I can just get myself perambulating in third gear,"

Mr Wingnut spluttered, "then we shall see what we shall see…"

"By all that ticks," Springer concluded, "we're still alive, aren't we?"

"Pipes and pin-cushions, yes!" Mrs Rust hugged Robert and Lily, dusting their faces with rusty kisses. "Thanks to these two lovelies here."

"This is Robert," Lily explained. "And he's ever so brave. He helped me escape Roach and Mould when they came to Brackenbridge and he repaired Malkin's bullet wound with his da."

"Mangles and motors! You have been through the wringer." Mrs Rust gazed at Robert. "He must have the heart of a mech-lion if he helped you survive such dastardly dealings." She pinched Robert's cheek, until he turned away, blushing.

Mrs Rust took Lily aside. "Lily, your papa's alive," she whispered. "Being held in the basement."

"I know," Lily replied, her voice full of determination. "And with your help, we'll get him out."

CHAPTER 20

Lily, Robert and the rest of the mechanicals, led by Mrs Rust, crept along the halls and corridors of the professor's house, looking for the entrance to the basement. It was hard to keep the mechanicals quiet, because they rattled and jittered and clanked and ticked all the time.

"This seems crunkingly familiar," said Captain Springer.

"Yes," said Miss Tock. "I think I might've been here before, ten thousand ticks ago, though, to be fair, my memory-valves aren't what they used to be."

"Click-wheels and coat hangers!" exclaimed Mrs Rust, "I believe you're right – we lived here with John and Grace, when Lily was knee-high to a tin toy."

Just then the parquet floor gave a loud creak.

"Quiet, all of you," Robert cried. "You need to hush."

They paused, listening to see if they'd been heard. Luckily this part of the house seemed relatively still. Professor Silverfish's mechanical butler and maid were obviously busy in another wing of the building.

Lily found a staircase that led down, and Mrs Rust seemed to think it was the right way to go, so the entire group crept down into the cellar.

At the foot of the stairs, Lily stopped. "I remember this too," she whispered. "There's a workshop at the other end." She started down the long subterranean hall, lined with oak panelling. Robert followed her and so did the mechanicals, jittering and creeping along the wooden floorboards behind them.

They came around a curve in the passage, and found their route blocked by a locked metal door.

"This is it," Lily said. She was reaching for a hairpin when Mr Wingnut stepped forward and wrenched the whole door off its hinges.

"There," he said, propping the door carefully against the wall. "No point taking care with someone's locks and escutcheons when they're keeping you prisoner."

Robert wished the mechanicals had been with them earlier.

Save for the shelves of machine parts along one wall, the room they stepped into was large and clinically bare. At the centre of the space, Papa sat at a long workbench, examining a half-made device.

He stood and ran towards Lily, but was brought up short by a chain around his ankle, fixed to a metal hoop embedded in the floor.

Lily rushed towards him as he tugged wearily at the links.

"Papa," she said, "we've come to get you out."

Then Papa let go of his chains and gave her an enormous hug. Captain Springer reached down and broke the chain about Papa's ankle; and Miss Tock took his arm. John smiled at them both. Then he greeted Mrs Rust and Mr Wingnut, and Robert too, shaking his hand.

"My friends, you've escaped! But, Lily, I told you not to come back here. It's not safe. You should've run far, far away. Found help."

"Malkin's gone for help," Lily said. "I had to save you." She was close to tears. "And I need to know the truth."

Papa squeezed her hand. He was crying too. "But the truth will hurt, Lily dear… It always does. And you've been hurt so much already… As have our friends." He smiled weakly at them. "It's my fault. If I hadn't offered Simon the Cogheart in the first place… I should've told

288

you everything when Mama was killed, but you were so broken…by the accident. I thought you needed protecting. I was scared you'd think ill of me…of my choices—"

"Please," Robert interrupted. "There'll be time to talk later. We have to go."

"Of course," Papa muttered. He put his arm round Lily and kissed her on the forehead. "Lead on, Macduff."

They followed Robert and the mechanicals along the hall. Lily hugged Papa. How could he think she was broken after all she'd done to save him?

"I'm strong, you know," she said. "You can tell me anything."

"Yes," Papa agreed. "But maybe I'm the weak one. Maybe that's why I wrote you the letter in the first place – so I wouldn't have to tell you the truth face to face. You see, Lily, with the Cogheart, I never set out to create a perpetual motion machine and I hadn't realized what Silverfish would do to get hold of it. He'll stop at nothi—"

"Hush!" Robert cried. They'd reached the end of the corridor and he thought he'd heard something.

The mechanicals jittered to a stop, and everyone stood still and listened.

There was a tapping and many footsteps, and suddenly,

Roach and Mould appeared at the top of the stairs with a motley-looking crew of armed men.

"It's the kidnappers!" Miss Tock gasped.

"And the others from the hunt," Robert added.

Lily clung tight to Papa. Her stomach lurched as she recognized the face of the man who'd been in the street outside Robert's shop.

"Punchcards and pistons!" Mrs Rust wheezed. "Looks like trouble."

"We'd best beat a hasty retreat," Captain Springer muttered.

He shooed Lily, Robert and Papa back down the corridor, and he and the rest of the mechanicals followed, shambling after them. Lily's eyes darted about. If they went this way they'd be trapped for sure.

Roach and his men had reached the bottom of the stairs. "You mechanicals, step aside," he spat. "We need to recapture Professor Hartman and our prisoners."

Mrs Rust shook her head. "I don't think so," she said. "You'll have to come through us." She linked arms with Captain Springer, and then with Miss Tock and Mr Wingnut, and they all made a wall in front of Lily, Robert and Papa.

"So be it." Roach made a sharp gesture with his cane, and Mould and the rest of his men spread out across the width of the corridor, pulling pistols from within their jackets.

"They may turn us into sieves," Miss Tock whispered to Lily, "but we'll save you, if we ca—"

RATA-TATA-TATA-TATA-TAT-TAT!

The men let loose a volley of gunfire. Their bullets pinged off the mechanicals, embedding themselves in the corridor's walls and wood panelling. Then the hall filled with choking smoke, and the gunfire stopped.

There was an eerie silence, and Lily heard the click of reloading guns.

"We have to get out of here!" Robert cried. "Is there no other way out?"

Papa put a hand to his head. "There is: a secret passage! I had it installed when we lived here, in case of attack. One of these light fittings opens it." He staggered along the wall, grasping at the metal stems of the electric lamps, trying to twist them sideways. "It's none of these. We must try them all."

The firing began again; bullets exploding loudly on metal and wood.

Robert and Lily ducked and ran along the corridor, yanking the arm of each lamp bracket, trying to twist them like door handles.

"Here it is!" John shouted. He stopped beside one in

the centre of the row, whose bracket looked slightly discoloured. He reached up, and twisted the fitting.

There was a ratcheting sound, like mechanical gears moving, and a wooden panel in the wall whooshed aside, revealing a narrow dark tunnel.

"In there, quick," Papa told them, and Lily and Robert climbed in.

Papa beckoned to the wall of mechanicals. "Come on, my friends, hurry!"

Mrs Rust shook her head. "You go, John, get the children to safety. We'll hold back the men, and follow as soon as we can."

Papa nodded. "Thank you, Rusty." He climbed into the tunnel beside Lily and Robert, and pulled the panel shut.

As the three of them struggled away, the battle between the men and mechanicals raged through the wall, echoing down the dark tunnel.

Papa was having trouble walking, and had to stop and rest every few feet. After fifty paces they reached a set of steps, climbing upwards and ending in darkness. At the top, Papa pulled a lever on the wall and another panel slid away, tumbling them out into hazy afternoon light.

They stepped from an opening hidden at the back of a stone arch, and Robert saw they were standing outside a little folly at the end of the garden, its roof covered in melting snow.

An icy path, flanked by frosted topiary cut in the shapes of leaping fish, led back towards the house. In the other direction, a small jetty ran out onto the river.

Roach and Mould's airship, *Behemoth*, was tied to the jetty's mooring post. Its bobbing zep balloon cast a torpedo-shaped shadow over the busy waters of the Thames, and the spiked gondola hovered a few feet above the pontoon, its rear cargo bay open.

"We'll take that," Lily said. She grasped Papa's hand, and Robert's, and they ran along the planked jetty towards the airship.

"Should we wait for Mrs Rust and the others?" she asked, as they clambered into the cargo bay.

"No need." Professor Silverfish stepped out from behind a piece of engine housing. "My men will take care of them."

He pulled a gun from behind his back and pointed it at them. "I told you before, John, if you didn't cooperate with my plan one of these children would get hurt."

"We can discuss this, Simon." John held up his hands. His face looked calm, but his legs were shaking. "I understand – you need my help. But so does my daughter, and her friend. Surely, after all that's happened, we can still come to some arrangement?"

"It's too late for bargains," Professor Silverfish said. "I can't trust your words, or actions. These children know how serious I am, but I think only a show of force will convince you."

He pointed his gun at Robert's chest and clicked off the safety catch.

Lily felt a sickening jolt of energy.

Time seemed to slow.

She saw Professor Silverfish squeeze his finger on the trigger.

"No—" she cried.

And dived in front of Robert as the gun fired.

A sharp molten pain seared through Lily's body. The bullet cut through her skin and pierced her chest. Her teeth grated, there was a hollow ringing, and she felt the projectile bounce off something metal deep inside her.

The momentary relief was followed by a jitter, like springs unwinding, cogs catching. Her head spun with dizziness. A sickly aching arced through her, and a carnation of red blossomed on her dress front.

She clutched at her breast, pressing at the silk. It stuck to her ribs, warm blood dripping through her fingers, and she dropped to the floor.

Robert kneeled beside her and grasped her hand, cradling it in his. Papa dropped to his knees and threw his arms around her.

Lily tried to sit up, tried to stay with them, but her limbs felt heavy, her bones brittle. She sensed her will fading, her self slipping away. Her head fell forward, lolling against Papa's shoulder.

"Don't die, Lily," he whispered. "It's the heart – don't let the bullet break your heart."

Professor Silverfish's eyes widened. "The Cogheart – it's inside her. She's had it all along – of course, what a fool I've been!"

Tears rolled down Robert's cheeks. Beside him, he felt John's body shaking, wracked with sobs. "It was that terrible night…" John said. "The night of the crash…" He broke off and brushed a tear from his eye, glaring at Silverfish. "You tore my world apart that night…killed my beloved Grace. For what? Trying to steal the Cogheart… Because of you, I *had* to keep it. I had no choice – I knew it could save one of them… And I chose Lily, my only child. I took her to the hospital, and they operated, gave her the Cogheart. It saved her life. And now…and now this…" He couldn't finish; he buried his face in Lily's hair, and sobbed.

"What about me?" Professor Silverfish shouted at him. "What about our bargain?"

"You!" John didn't even look at him. "You're not important. The way you've behaved you don't deserve to live."

Robert stroked Lily's fingers. They were still twined with his, but her breath had become shallow, and her grip was loosening, going limp.

He glanced over his shoulder to see Roach and Mould running madly across the courtyard towards them. They stumbled up the loading ramp, coughing heavily.

"We had to retreat, professor," Roach mumbled, leaning on his cane. "John's mechanicals are destroying your home."

"Never mind that," Professor Silverfish said, "we have what we want." He nodded at Mould. "You, go ready us for take-off." Then he waved his gun at Robert. "And, you, Roach, get this boy off my ship. He's useless to me now."

"With pleasure." Mr Roach wiped a hand across his face, and caught his breath. Then he grabbed Robert.

"Lily!" Robert called out.

She tried to turn her head, but only her eyes would move. The floor hummed beneath her and a dull ache rippled round her chest. She watched as Roach dragged Robert by his arms to the end of the cargo ramp and threw him off. There was another figure at her side, but she could barely make out his face, it was so filled with shadows. "Papa, is that you?" she asked, squinting through the dim light, trying to see him. "You're still here. Promise me you won't leave this time."

He nodded. "I promise. I'm sorry, my love, sorry for everything. Sorry I never told you the truth about yourself. About what happened. I was so worried. Worried you'd feel guilty. Worried you wouldn't love me when you heard what I'd done. Worried about how weak you were, how the shock of all this would hurt you more." He brushed at her face. "But, most of all, worried I'd lose you to the truth: that I'd sacrificed Mama, my work, everything for you."

Lily shook her head. "It doesn't matter now, Papa. Honestly it doesn't. You haven't lost me, I'm right here." She wanted to say more, but the words dried on her lips. The breath was being pushed from her as a heavy metal weight calcified in her chest. She swallowed a lump in her throat.

"The Cogheart. It's… It's going to stop. I can feel it."

"Don't say so. It's not your time." Papa pushed a lick of sweat-soaked hair from her forehead.

She squeezed his hand. "I have to go now," she said.

"Don't go, Lily." Papa's voice wavered. "Please don't go. Not again. I'm sorry for everything I've done." His brown eyes, so close, blinked back glistening tears, and he pressed his balled fist against her bleeding chest and pushed hard.

Lily smiled up at him. His words and actions felt so distant, like it was happening a long way off. The pain had begun to envelop her. The Cogheart gave a final shudder beneath her ribs, and she opened her mouth and let out one last breath…

CHAPTER 21

Malkin raced downhill, dodging the various pedestrians who jostled along the pavements wrapped in their thick scarves and coats. Around him, hawkers and cog-and-bone men shouted from every corner and crevice of the street, selling newspapers, mittens, roast chestnuts and machine parts. He streaked past them all, slaloming between their legs.

He jumped down a brick passageway between two buildings, and came out behind a row of outhouses and a small unhealthy-looking courtyard piled high with rubbish.

Two butcher's boys in bloody aprons with rolled-up sleeves, talking shop in a sawdusted doorway, glanced up as he shot past.

Malkin leaped a pool of frozen water, snapped at a group of squabbling pigeons, and sped on across the cracked uneven paving stones of the back alleys of London.

He was getting close to Anna's mooring at Counter's Creek now, he could sense it. Finally, as he got to a block he recognized, he spotted the tip of *Ladybird*'s zep bobbing above a ruined burned-out building.

He darted through the bars of a fence onto the weed-filled empty lot and ran along, jumping piles of shingle and bricks dotted with patches of white frost.

He passed the twisted metal frame of a beached airship, and the half-built crumbling walls of an unfinished warehouse, then leaped over a pile of broken crates. Finally, he reached a row of wooden mooring posts along the river, at the far end of the lot.

Ladybird was tethered to an iron loop embedded in the ground. Her ladder swung back and forth, its lowest rung grazing the icy grass.

Malkin rushed over and yapped up at *Ladybird*'s doorway until Anna, wearing woollen fingerless gloves and her hat and flying goggles, peered out. She gazed down at him. "What the devil's wrong, Malkin?"

"Lily and Robert are in trouble," Malkin barked. "You have to come."

She nodded, and disappeared inside the gondola, then threw down a basket on a rope.

"Climb aboard," she yelled at him. "You can explain on the way."

Malkin's tail drooped, and he sniffed at the basket distastefully. Did this mean more clanking air travel?

CHAPTER 22

Robert woke with his face mushed against the frosty gravel. He tried to stand but his knees were weak. A sickening emptiness whirled in his belly and twisting dizziness filled his head. The pulsing backwash from some sort of engine had swept him off his feet.

Behemoth – it was taking off, with Lily onboard! He glanced up as, in a blur of noise, the airship pulled away from the jetty, raised its landing gears and floated out over the river.

"Robert! Lily! John!" Voices bellowed behind him, mixed in with the clattering of metal legs. Mrs Rust and the rest of John's bullet-ridden mechanicals tumbled from the arch of the secret passageway.

"What happened?" Mrs Rust asked, helping Robert to his feet.

He caught his breath, let go of Mrs Rust's arm and hobbled forward a few steps. "Lily's on that airship. I have to get her back. I think she's still alive."

A shadow passed overhead, along with the putter of engines. *Ladybird* was floating above the chimney stacks of the house. Thank goodness! Robert felt a wave of relief. Malkin had got through – and now help had arrived.

With a loud hiss, *Ladybird* descended from the sky, careening towards them. Robert gasped and ducked, and the mechanicals threw themselves to the ground and rolled against the walls of the folly, as the airship dropped, wavering over the garden.

Her patched wooden hull barely missed the house's frosted roof; she skimmed above the stone balustrades of a retaining wall, and knocked the head off a giant topiary fish. Hovering barely a foot in the air, she passed the ice-sprinkled folly, and squelched into the manicured lawn. Turning with a muddy skid mark, she bumped along the path and out off the end of the mooring pier, where she finally came to rest, her hull floating in the Thames.

Her engines puttered to a standstill, her door opened, and Anna and Malkin jumped down onto the icy slats of the pier. Malkin's ears flicked and he swayed dizzily from side to side; it had only been a ten-minute trip but, what with his journey across town through the traffic, it felt as if he had spent an hour on a fairground ride. He ran towards Robert and the mechanicals, who stood slowly and dusted themselves off, and collapsed at Robert's feet. By the time Anna had arrived he'd shaken off his jitters and jumped to attention.

Anna pulled the goggles from her eyes. "Now I remember why I stopped trying to land this thing," she shouted. "*Ladybird*'s all right at take-off and flying around, but she doesn't like landing!" Then she saw Robert's face, and her smile fell. She pulled him close, embracing him in a bear hug. "What happened to you?"

Robert winced, clutching his side, while the mechanicals twittered and chirped with each other, trying to repair their damage.

"I was thrown from the airship." Robert steadied himself against Anna's shoulder. "They've taken Lily aboard, John too. Lily's been shot. You have to help us save her."

"How?"

"We can give chase in *Ladybird* – she's faster than they are. We can board them from the air. It'll be like air piracy."

"We can't do that!" Anna cried. "I've got no fuel."

"We'll take it from over there." Robert pointed across

the garden towards the yard on its far side, where the coal shed sat.

"Quick, everyone," he shouted to the mechanicals. "Run and bring as much coal as you can carry."

Anna flew *Ladybird* above the river, following in *Behemoth*'s wake. In the engine room, Miss Tock, Captain Springer and Mr Wingnut threw great handfuls of coal into the furnace, and Robert shovelled with them. The pistons turned manically and, in between spadefuls, he peered out the open side porthole to see if they were gaining on their enemy.

Behemoth had a good ten minutes' head start; it steamed ahead, bloated with air, its spiked hull bristling. Robert watched it bob low over the suspension cables of the Albert Bridge. He closed the porthole and, leaving the mechanicals in charge of the engine, ran down the corridor to the flight deck.

Anna and Mrs Rust stood at the wheel with the wind battering against them, staring dead ahead. Malkin had his head stuck out of the broken windscreen; his tongue lolled out, and the air rippled through his fur. Beneath them, on the south side of the Thames, a park whizzed past. Tugs and night-steamers and the odd airship streamed up and down the river.

"She's crossing Chelsea Bridge and the Victoria Railway Bridge," Anna called, pointing out through the shards of glass.

Robert saw she was right – *Behemoth* had already breached the top of the next looping suspension bridge, and was wending her way over a puffing steam train on the railway viaduct beyond.

"Where do you think they're headed?" he asked.

"Who knows?" Anna said. "Maybe St Thomas's, or maybe they're going to take the north–south airway at the top of the next river bend – that would take them out of town altogether."

"If they go onto that," Robert complained, "we'll never find them in all the traffic."

"They've got to get there first." Anna waved a hand at the sky ahead – beyond the river, past the rows of houses that clustered on either bank, a mass of black storm clouds was brewing on the horizon. "They'll have to slow to avoid that squall, and if we cut across this bend here, through the city, we can catch them by hooking in on their port side, before they reach Westminster."

She pushed the throttle to full and cut out across a cluster of riverside houses, keeping *Behemoth* dead on target on their starboard side.

In front the storm was rolling in along the river, and behind, over the wilds of West London, the fat red winter sun was setting. Its light glared in the side mirrors, flashing in Robert's eyes, and he gasped.

"That's good," Anna said. "Sun behind us means we're in their blind spot – with a bit of luck, they'll be so busy with the storm, they won't clock our approach."

They were catching up fast now – *Behemoth* was barely sixty feet away, dipping low in the frame of the broken windscreen. Robert wiped his coal-dusted hands on his trousers and watched the other airship loom closer in the starboard window as they swept in towards it.

"How on earth am I to get onboard?" he asked.

Anna patted his back. "Don't you worry, Robbie. I've a plan. Take the helm, Mrs Rust, and keep your hand on the throttle. Robbie and I are going to get some rope."

"Boilers and brake levers!" the old mechanical cried. "Don't put me in charge of this contraption! I ain't even ridden a bicycle before. Malkin, you do it."

The fox spread the claws on his forepaws. "With these?" he asked. "I've no opposable thumbs, you know!"

"Just keep the wheel straight, both of you," Anna muttered. "Lock their zep in the centre of your view, and hold us steady. That's all I ask."

Anna grabbed a loaded harpoon gun and a length of rope from a hook on the cabin's back wall, and pulled Robert out into the passage.

"Lucky we were attacked last night," she explained, as she tied the end of the rope through the eye on the harpoon's flight. "I had the gun but nothing to load it with; if they hadn't shot the harpoon in *Ladybird*'s side, we wouldn't have had anything to fire." She handed him the looped lengths of rope. "Now, let's get you onboard that ship."

Turning the handle, she threw the cabin door open. Cold air rushed in, screaming in their ears and pushing them back against the wall. Far below, the waters of the Thames whipped past. Anna recovered first and began aiming the harpoon; Robert readied the loops of rope attached to it.

Behemoth's fat silver zeppelin filled the aperture of the doorway, floating below to their starboard side a little beneath them. Robert could see its port-side propeller, sat halfway up the curve of the balloon. Even though it looked like they were right up close to it, he estimated there was at least thirty feet of sky between them.

"See that prop?" Anna said, putting the harpoon gun to her shoulder. "There'll be a maintenance hatch behind it that leads into the balloon. From there you'll be able to climb down into the gondola. I'd better try not to hit the silks!" She aimed hastily through the gunsight and fired out of the doorway at a support strut beneath the propeller.

The harpoon flew straight, its silver edge cutting through the dusky sky; lengths of rope unfurling behind it.

They held their breath and watched.

The harpoon slowed and seemed to hesitate, hanging in the air, then it dropped like a stone, falling far short of *Behemoth*.

"Blast it," Anna cursed, and she and Robert quickly reeled in the rope.

It took a nervous few minutes to gather back all the length, plus recover the harpoon and reload it into the gun.

As they swooped over Vauxhall Bridge, *Ladybird* wavered and dropped back. Robert glanced over his shoulder. Mrs Rust was struggling with the wheel, but she seemed to regain control and they rallied. This time, *Ladybird* kept pace with *Behemoth*, buffeting about in the larger airship's backdraught.

Anna steadied herself and aimed once more. She took longer squinting into the gunsight, bracing her body against the cabin wall. Aiming just behind the propeller, she bent her knees to compensate for the bucking of the ship, and fired.

The harpoon flew fast, reeling out the lengths of rope.

It missed the propeller strut by inches, and pierced the zeppelin's silk with the slightest pop.

"Clank it," Anna cried. "It's gone into the balloon."

But then there was a ripple around the entry point, and a thud echoed down the line – the harpoon seemed to have hit the zep's internal frame, under the silks.

Anna yanked on the rope to check it had taken and was sturdy.

"Will the hole bring them down?" Robert asked, pulling the slack loops through a metal eyelet on the floor and tying the end off on a cleat on the wall.

"I shouldn't think so," Anna said. "For a thing their size, being hit with a harpoon's like being bitten by a gnat." From the footlocker cupboard, she produced a steel frame, like a heavy metal coat hanger with welded-on wheels, and a harness.

"What's that?" Robert asked.

"It's called a death slide," Anna said as she clipped it over the length of taut rope.

Robert bit his lip as Anna checked the harness and wheels on the death slide, testing they would run along the quivering line. He felt a knot in his guts, and a sudden sickness welled up inside him as he realized just what he'd have to do.

"We'd better hurry," Anna shouted at him through the wind. "It's like hooking a whale on a fishing wire – if we're not quick, their ship will drag us down."

As she buckled him into the harness, Robert glanced down the vertiginous slope cutting between the two airships; his belly spasmed and his head swam. "I don't think I can do this," he said, "I can't stand the height."

"Nonsense, Robbie." Anna secured various safety buckles around his waist. "At this altitude, the terror becomes abstract."

"Abstract? How can it be abstract?"

"It's a one-minute journey. Your brain won't even have time to register it."

"Until it's smashed into the ground, or *Behemoth*'s hull, or—"

A barking yip interrupted his train of thought, and Malkin jumped into his lap.

"Trying to leave without me?" the mechanimal said. "I'm coming too. I've lots of experience being thrown out of moving airships."

"Do you think it's wise," Anna asked, "adding your extra weight to the slide?"

Malkin gave a sniff. "I know Lily's scent. I'll be able to find her quicker."

"He's probably right," Robert admitted.

"Fair enough." Anna tightened the last few chest-buckles around them both. "Oh, I almost forgot; when you need to stop, squeeze the brakes – here." She reached above Robert's head and tapped a silver lever on the frame that looked like the brakes on a bicycle. "Once you've found Lily and her father, get to *Behemoth*'s escape capsule. Lower it down on its rope and I'll fly past and grab you. Oh, and you'll need this." She took off her flying helmet and stuck it onto Robert's head, strapping it round his chin and pinging the goggles down over his eyes. "Ready?" she asked.

Robert nodded, and gave her a half-hearted salute. Tucking his head down, he clutched Malkin against his chest. With his other hand, he grabbed the crossbar of the death slide, and shuffled his feet to the edge of the doorway.

"No going back now," Malkin muttered.

And, for a second, as Robert dangled half over the deck, half over the river, a fragment from his da came back to him: *No one conquers fear easily, Robert.*

Outside, the curved earth and the darkening sky butted against each other.

"Time to fly!" Anna gave him an almighty push and he zipped off down the line, leaving his stomach behind.

CHAPTER 23

There was before and after.

And this was after.

A bright light flooded everything and, when it faded, Lily felt an empty aching heart-shaped stillness in her chest.

Mama was standing before Lily, holding the rosewood box. She was just as she'd looked when Lily had last seen her. "My darling," Mama said, opening the lid of the box. "These things are for you."

"What things?" Lily looked into the box. It was empty.

"You have them all already," Mama said.

Lily felt in her pocket and was surprised to find the various objects there. Her mother's ring, and her lock of hair, and the photograph, and the stone. She took out the stone and looked at the golden fossil at its centre.

"Just like you," Mama said. "You carry part of Papa and me within you. I don't mean just the Cogheart, but your lineage: who you are, your values and ideas. Everything you'll be, and more besides. You're something special, my tiger."

Lily replaced the stone, and the other things, in her pockets. "But," she asked, "what am I supposed to do?"

Mama smiled and kissed Lily's cheek. "Go back into the world and finish what you started."

"But I don't know how," Lily said.

"Trust your heart. It will make the right choices." Mama put a hand on her chest, and Lily felt a warm energy suffuse her. "And fight, Lily, fight for your life. It's what I want for you."

A wind blew up between them, and Mama's hand retreated and was gone. Lily felt herself being sucked into a golden tessellating pattern of snow. It seemed to fill her head and the world around her. Then, she heard a sound: a sound that made one persistent, precise, needle-sharp noise...

TICK.

TICK.

TICK.

The beat of the Cogheart, fighting to keep pumping, fighting through the damage done, fighting to keep its cogs turning. Fighting to keep her...

Alive!

With a hacking cough and a splutter, Lily opened her eyes and was greeted by a mist of sameness. She recognized nothing. None of the forms around her seemed familiar, and she couldn't even separate them from one another. Then, gradually, they came into focus.

Her head lolled against a pillow. She was being wheeled on a stretcher along a corridor on an airship. *Behemoth?* With Papa walking bound at her side.

"You're all right," he whispered. "The perpetual motion machine – it still works, thank heaven!"

Lily nodded woozily. She was certain now all this had occurred before. Portholes dotted the walls and through their glinting glass she could make out the blue-grey waters of the Thames, the snakelike soul of the city.

"A terrible thing happened, my dear," Professor Silverfish said, stepping alongside her and blocking her view. "I shot you in the heart. In the precious Cogheart. But the good news is it's still functioning. You're still alive. So now I'm going to take out your heart and use it to replace this one." He tapped the machine on his chest. "After all, I need my upgraded machine." Professor Silverfish laughed. "How does that sound?"

Drowsily, Lily wondered if she could run, but then she realized she wasn't even standing. Dark figures gathered, their profiles ringed by halos – or was it the setting sun flashing in the portholes behind them?

Before she could decide, their hands reached down to lift her from the stretcher, and across a threshold into darkness.

Clouds streamed past Robert in streaks of grey and pink. He clutched Malkin to his chest as he arrowed towards his target, hurtling into *Behemoth*'s shadow. The gas envelope loomed large ahead. The line was skewing too close to the propeller. His heart pumping in his throat, Robert grasped the brake lever and squeezed hard.

The brakes screeched; refused to lock.

With seconds to impact, Robert pumped them again.

In a whiff of burning, they clamped the line, jerking him to a stop a hand's-breadth from the zeppelin's whirring propeller.

WHOOM WHOOM, WHOOM WHOOM.

The sharp turning blades glanced past, inches from his head.

Malkin whined softly as Robert gulped in great gasps of air and clawed at a metal maintenance ladder. His fingers brushed against the ice-encrusted metal. If he could just stretch a little further...

A crosswind knocked him sideways, but he managed to grasp the ladder. Clipping a grappling hook onto its frame, he climbed across and looped an elbow over the prop support strut, just as the storm finally hit.

A barrage of raindrops pounded his head and jacket, and pinged off the metal motor casing and the turning blades. Robert felt in his jacket pocket, beneath the lump of the fox, for his penknife. He cut his slide-rope loose and it fell away into the grey abyss beneath, with a noise like a flailing whip.

Under the whoosh of the prop blades and the tapping of the rain, he thought he could just make out the putter of *Ladybird*'s engines. He glanced over his shoulder and glimpsed her downwind, banking away. The broken shards of her windscreen seemed to wink at him.

Robert took a deep breath and pulled himself up onto the short maintenance platform between the prop and the side of the zep. Anna was right, there was a hatch into the balloon itself. By the time he reached it he was soaked through to the skin.

Robert grabbed for the handle at the centre of the hatch and yanked. It rattled loose, but one corner jammed. He prised at it with his frozen fingers as the icy wind knifed at his face, and the rain drubbed his body. Curled up inside his dripping wet flying jacket, huddled against his chest, Malkin shivered with the cold.

Finally, the hatch fell open.

Robert climbed through the gap, and slipped down a small metal shaft, dropping into the interior of the balloon.

Lily woke in a clean and airy vaulted space at the heart of the zeppelin. She was strapped down to a cold metal table. A row of globe lights hung from the tin-plated ceiling overhead.

Professor Silverfish loomed into view, examining a tray of medical equipment on a side table; a cotton mask hung loose around his neck. He picked up a needle and plunged it into her chest. Lily felt a sharp prick of pain and then the push of a plunger and everything softened into a blur of hazy shapes once more. She gritted her teeth. A queasy black tiredness flushed through her, but she wasn't going to let herself go under. She willed herself awake, remembering Mama's words: *Fight, Lily. Fight for your life. That's what I want for you!*

The Cogheart rallied, responding to her request, and she felt its pulse beating stronger in her ears. With great difficulty, Lily raised her head. She could see Papa tied to a pipe on the far wall behind Professor Silverfish. She stared woozily at them both; it was almost as if their shapes were bleeding together. "Are there two of you?" she asked. "I can't quite tell you apart."

"What did you give her?" Papa demanded.

Lily could hear him, but it was as if his words were coated in cotton wool. She couldn't quite make them out…wake it out…wake up.

Professor Silverfish picked up a bone saw and tested it against his thumb. "Just a small sedative to make the operation easier."

"Operate?" Papa shouted. "On a moving airship? That's insane!"

Professor Silverfish laughed. "Not quite. When we land, surgeons will be ready and waiting to implant the heart into my body. That part would be far too risky to take place here. But killing Lily and taking the Cogheart, that's the easy part. And should be rather fun." He stepped over to the gurney.

"Think about what you're doing," Papa said. "You're supposed to be her godfather."

Professor Silverfish's lip curved into a contemptuous sneer. "And she's got my heart."

"Don't let him put you to sleep, Lil!" Papa shouted. "I'll get you out of this, I promise."

Professor Silverfish laughed. "You, Sir, are the one who got her into this. You should've given me my heart the first time, then she'd never have been hurt. Two pieces of advice: always honour your debts, and let the dead stay dead."

Lily tried to rally, shaking her arms and twisting her hands. Her bonds were a little loose, the leather straps around her had some give – if she could just stretch out and grab the knife on the table, she might be able to reach up and cut one of the tubes on Silverfish's heart machine when he leaned over her.

Professor Silverfish turned back and saw what she was trying to do. He whisked the tray of tools away from her and placed them on a nearby table. Then he tightened her bindings until they bit harder into her wrists.

"What were you planning?" he asked. "To cut one of my metal arteries?"

Lily turned away, gritting her teeth, her blood pounding in her ears.

"I thought so," the professor said. "The draught we gave you doesn't appear to have worked. No matter, it'll be far more interesting to do the operation this way. Don't you agree? You're an inquisitive girl. I'm sure you'd like to see how the Cogheart looks working inside you. If you can keep up, that is, once I open your chest. I'm told the pain can be quite immense. What do you think? Do you remember it from the first time?"

Lily shook her head, trying to shake off the dizziness. Then she spat at him.

Professor Silverfish wiped his face. "Come, come, my dear. You're being quite impolite." He turned to Papa. "Did Miss Scrimshaw teach your daughter nothing at her prestigious academy, Sir?"

"Don't do this, I beg you," Papa gasped.

"Too late now," Professor Silverfish told him. "You should never have reneged on our deal seven years ago when you ran off with what was mine."

"I wasn't going to use it," Papa said. "I was going to destroy it, but then when you attacked my family, killed Grace, nearly killed Lily, I had no choice but to. I never would have given you the Cogheart. Never. And nothing you could ever say would change my mind. For I saw you for what you are: an evil man. You used to help people, yes, in small ways, but it was never worth the bargain, because you used them for your own ends. Even the soldiers you helped when we worked together. You used their gratitude, their willingness to work for you, to make them into your private murderous army. If all you really care about is your life, and you bargain away those of your friends, kill the ones they love, just to save yourself, I would say that I was right about you – your life's not worth saving."

Professor Silverfish laughed. "And who are *you* to say whether my life is worth saving or not? You don't get to decide, John. No, like everything else, it's survival of the fittest – and I may not be the fittest physically, but mentally I'm strong.

"Perhaps you thought I wouldn't live long enough to make you regret your decision, but as you can see, you were wrong: life has a way of fighting through. And now it's time for you to pay the price for breaking our agreement – with your daughter's life."

Professor Silverfish gripped Lily's neck with his strong fingers. "There is one good thing about everything that's happened, my dear: you've tested the safety of my device for me. By living with it inside you for seven years, you've proved it works. And look how well you've done – you're a survivor." He stroked her face. "A veritable little perpetual motion machine. You've cheated death twice.

Thanks to my Cogheart, you're practically immortal. But now you are about to die. How does that feel?"

Lily blinked at Professor Silverfish through her confused delirium. "Nobody's immortal," she muttered. "Everyone dies. So why are you doing this?"

"Everyone except the owner of the Cogheart," Professor Silverfish corrected. "The machine I spent thousands commissioning, and more money and years searching for. Do you know what I've done to find it? I bought all of your father's property and possessions, studied every single one of his papers. Paid to have him trailed, and found, and brought back to me. Why, the expense of it nearly bankrupted me. But it was worth it, because I knew if I got my hands on the Cogheart then, with one simple operation, I could live for ever…"

The professor's chuckle transformed into a wheezing cough, which he stifled. He packed towels around Lily's chest, and picked up a surgical knife, and Lily braced herself for the cut as he prepared to make the first incision.

CHAPTER 24

Robert scrambled to his feet and glanced about. He was standing on a narrow catwalk that ran along the inside of the balloon. He fumbled to unbutton the wet harness, then his sopping jacket, freeing Malkin, who dropped to the floor on his four black paws, and pressed his nose to the metal grille of the gangway, smelling for Lily's scent.

As Robert's eyes became accustomed to the dim light, he saw more detail. Metal girders stretched across the zeppelin's insides to keep the silk skin in place; their ribbed struts criss-crossed each other, creating a giant geometric frame, like an enormous rigid spider web that tapered at each end. In the huge central space, bags of gas floated above oil and fuel tanks, and bulging leather water bags hung by straps from various girders.

Robert and Malkin set off along the catwalk. A little way away, on the starboard side, was an outcropping platform where a spiral stairwell descended to a hatch in the floor. Beneath it, Robert guessed, was the gondola and passenger compartments.

Malkin reached the platform first, and darted down the stairwell; Robert limped behind, struggling to keep pace, drips of water scattering in his wake. As he reached for the metal stair rail, he heard the fox let out a strangled yelp from below.

"Malkin?" Robert called. He waited. But there was only silence.

Then, heavy footsteps – two sets of boots, and the *tap-tap-tap* of a cane. And Roach and Mould climbed into view.

Malkin struggled and squirmed in Mould's arms, but Mould's fat fingers were clamped around his jaw to keep him from snapping, and his big arm was looped around Malkin's middle. He stepped forward, making himself as wide as possible, and blocked the gangway so Robert couldn't pass.

Roach's mirrored eyes gleamed blankly in their sockets. "We heard you clambering about, boy. Back for more, are we? Here to save your friends? Anyone would think you were the one with the metal heart." He shuffled in front of Mould and slowly unscrewed the skull tip of his walking stick, withdrawing a rapier sword from the sheath of the lacquered cane.

Robert scrambled away. Pulling his penknife from his pocket, he unfolded the longest blade and, gripping the shaft in his sweaty, damp hand, swung it firmly at Roach and Mould.

Mould laughed. "Is that all you've got?"

Roach swished his rapier sword through the air, his mirrored eyes following its path as its tip whooshed past the end of Robert's nose.

Robert stumbled back along the gangway, his eyes darting round for some means of escape. He groped behind for a weapon, anything he could use against them. And then he felt the cables.

They ran through rows of eyelets on the surface of the zep's ribs. He glanced down the length of the craft and saw them disappearing into the tapering dark of the tail.

Of course: *steering cables!* Anna had told him about those the first day on *Ladybird* – how they connected the steering column to the rear rudder.

Her words came flooding back to him:

One of them breaks and the entire airship goes off course.

That was it! He grabbed a leather strap emerging from a hanging water bag for balance, and slashed hard with his penknife at the central steering cable.

The knife blade bounced wildly away, and it was all he could do to keep hold of it. When he looked at the cable, he saw his attempt hadn't even made a dink. He tried again, slashing harder, but the corded fibres were wound strongly together.

"Stop your blasted flailing, clockmaker's apprentice!" Mr Roach jabbed at his chest with the rapier.

Robert flinched and jerked away. The sword grazed the metal frame behind him, barely missing his chest and the silk skin of the airship.

That was it: Roach would cut the cables for him!

He tightened his grip on the leather strap, letting his legs loosen under him, so his arm took his full weight.

"Time to die." Roach swished his rapier through the air.

Robert stared into his silver eyes and saw his own ragged, desperate reflection. "Come on," he said. "Give it your best shot."

Roach gave a shark-toothed leer and thrust his sword at Robert's head.

Robert ducked sideways, swinging on his strap; the sword glanced past. Missing his ear by inches, it chopped into the cables and embedded itself into the metal strut.

A terrible groan juddered along the damaged cables as the threads inside them loosened and tore. Mr Roach cursed and tried to yank his blade free, but it was stuck.

Robert flattened himself against the wall as the floor of the gangway began to tremble.

Mould, still grasping Malkin, looked about warily. "What the—"

SNAP! The cable broke, slashing Roach's cheek, and slicing across Mould's mirrored gaze, before flailing away down the length of the balloon. Mould gave a cry and dropped Malkin. Roach was still pulling at the handle of his sword, clutching at his bloody face, when, with an ear-splitting groan, the ship bucked them into the air.

Robert grabbed hold of Malkin's scruff as he tumbled past, and yanked him against his chest.

The side of the balloon ripped open as the flailing cable cut through the tail silks like a knife, and writhed out of the rear of the airship. Twisting in the wind like a snake, it wrapped itself round the rudder, jamming it into a starboard turn.

Robert heard the clang of a bell, and saw a vague silhouette through the silk of the prow – it was an approaching tower with moon-round clock faces embedded in each side.

He gripped tight to his strap and hugged Malkin close. "Lock your jaw onto something," he told the mechanimal. "I think we're going to crash!"

The point of the knife touched the mess of scars on Lily's chest. Her eyes filled with tears and she gritted her teeth. Suddenly there was a massive bucking jolt and a mad screech – that sounded like a thousand metal forks being scraped down a blackboard. It came not from the knife, or her chest, but from the zeppelin balloon above.

Professor Silverfish pulled back and glanced over his shoulder. Lily let out a breath that she hadn't even realized she'd been holding in.

Outside the porthole, a bright numbered clock face filled with roman numerals loomed large. They were about to hit Big Ben!

Behemoth's nose reared abruptly upwards, and the clock face swept from view. With a massive bang, the airship careened into the roof of the tower. The portholes fractured, exploding inwards, and glass and grey roof tiles rained through the holes, shattering against the walls and floor.

Lily grabbed her bed rail and clung on tight as the room shook. The whole world tipped sideways; lamps, bowls and tools toppled from their tables and smashed on the floor.

Professor Silverfish let go of his knife and grasped at a window rail as dust and debris bounced off the heavy ticking machine on his chest.

With an almighty crunch, the ship came to a final juddering stop, her nose buried deep in the steep roof of the clock tower.

The impact seemed to have loosened the straps round Lily. She sat up and almost toppled from the table, but managed to steady herself and looked around for Papa. He was kicking back and forth on his rope – still tied by his wrists to a pipe on the other side of the room, he swayed in mid-air, his outstretched arms dangling him from what was now the ceiling. Lily thought she might be able to help him down if she could get closer.

She pulled her straps away, the rough edges of the leather burning her skin as she struggled free. Then she slid off the table onto a flat piece of wall, stood, and pitched herself across the sloping floor.

Slowly and painfully, she reached up to loosen the bonds roped round Papa's ankles. Everything felt hazy. Was she still woozy from the gunshot, or the professor's anaesthetic? She coughed and spluttered from the smoke. Then realized: *The room was on fire!*

Suddenly something hit her in the back, throwing her off balance. It was Professor Silverfish, barrelling into her. He seized her by the waist, and pulled her towards a broken glass porthole. She barely had time to struggle before he shoved her through – and they landed with a thump on the sloping roof of Big Ben.

With an ear-splitting pop the spear-sharp steeple of Big Ben punctured the front of the balloon and air rushed in with a whoosh. In the pause that followed, it seemed to Robert that the zeppelin was taking a breath.

Then the point pushed further through the bent metal spider's web of girders and pierced the first gas envelope.

KABOOOOOM! An almighty explosion battered down the length of the gangway, throwing up burning oil and fuel from the tanks as the ship tipped onto its side.

Robert hung on to his shaking strap, and tucked his head and body round Malkin, pulling his sopping wet jacket round them both to shield them from the fire.

Mould was already alight, his eyes melting in their sockets like mercury tears. He threw his arm out and grabbed Roach's coat-tails. Roach fumbled, trying to push him away, and his thin fingers lost their grip on the handle of the embedded sword. The half-burned creatures toppled backwards, tumbling down the gangway and skidding towards the gash in the smouldering silk of the upturned airship.

"Grab something, Roach," Mould pleaded, hugging his companion.

"Let go, you fool!" Roach screamed. "You're too heavy, you'll drag us both down."

He thrashed his arms about, grasping blindly for a safety rail or a steel rib. But the metal was too hot, he couldn't hold on, and the flaming pair tumbled through the opening and were sucked away in a rain of glass and dust. Their screams echoed through the smoke from the abyss beyond.

Robert clung tight to Malkin and his strap. Pain crackled in his chest and fear poured off him in sweaty globules. His wet clothes were already almost dry from the intense heat. Fragments of burning metal toppled past. He shielded his eyes and looked around.

The blackened ribs of the airship were folding in on themselves, collapsing. Oven-hot air radiated off them, licking at his bare face with flaming tongues.

This wasn't the end, it wasn't over. He wouldn't let them finish him this way, like they did his da.

Something dripped onto his nose. He looked up. Above him hung the big bag of ballast water. Of course. He reached out with his knife and slit its side, and the water poured down over him and Malkin, soaking them once more, and tumbling along the gangway, quenching the flames in their path.

Grasping the fox against his chest, Robert swung back and forth transferring his grip to a slippery new length of pipe. Following the path of dowsed flames they were able to reach the spiral staircase. It was tipped at an angle, but Robert managed to climb down the steps. At the bottom, he threw open the hatch and tumbled into the gondola.

Together they slid down the sloped floor of the corridor, skating past burning hatches and windows, and bumped to a stop at the entrance to a central atrium.

A pair of feet were kicking to and fro above them. "Robert, Malkin!" a voice cried. And when Robert looked up, there was John Hartman, dangling from his wrists on a rope, tied to the ceiling.

Robert dropped Malkin, who darted over to John and nipped playfully at his heels. There was a metal gurney bolted to the floor, and Robert climbed onto it. Standing on tiptoes, he reached up with his knife and cut John free.

John slid down the wall towards a broken porthole. "Quick!" he bellowed at them both. "Professor Silverfish has taken Lily into the tower – we must follow!"

CHAPTER 25

Robert, Malkin and John dropped through the broken porthole and crawled out from under the airship's belly onto the roof of Big Ben, which was sleeked with rain.

The hulking frame of the zeppelin burned above them. It was fast collapsing into a smoking inferno. Gigantic Os of fire burst across its surface, and flames licked up the last flecks of silk and canvas, pulling them free to drift off across the night sky.

Only the ship's metal hull, and its forest of spikes, protected them from the falling debris. That and the fact that the wind was blowing the fire and flames away from the tower. Yet still the heat was intense; it pulsed in waves through Robert's body until he could barely think straight.

Then, through the haze, he made out Professor Silverfish and Lily halfway up the steep sloping roof. Lily screamed and kicked at the professor, but he dragged her over the balustrade of a balcony. Robert, John and Malkin clambered towards them as they disappeared through a tall gold-leafed arch into the interior of Big Ben's spire.

As they skirted a line of guttering, another roar of gas exploded from the zeppelin's envelope; a whoosh of escaping fire scalded Robert's cheeks. Rivets popped from *Behemoth*'s heated metal plates and pinged past them.

They hunkered against the tiles and Robert glanced down. On the ground beneath the tower, firemen and police rushed across Parliament Square towards the blaze.

The drop made Robert's head spin and he almost tripped over the edge of the roof, but John gripped his arm and pulled him onward.

They battled through the steaming rain, and reached the balustrade where they'd seen Lily and Silverfish disappear. Climbing over it, they ran towards the gold-leafed arches.

The inside of the roof was furnace-hot; sweat ran down Robert's back as he, John and Malkin hobbled down the spiral steps towards the belfry of the tower, following the sound of the professor's echoing footsteps. With each spiral they descended, the sloped ceiling opened out and the noise of the huge clock's mechanisms grew louder.

They passed the tip of the great tin and copper bell of Big Ben, hung in the vaulted roof alongside its four smaller brothers, and arrived on a gantry at the base of the belfry, where echoing ticks were joined by the deafening grind of cogs that floated up from somewhere beneath them.

Robert's pulse beat time with the myriad of clockwork. The noises reminded him of his da's workshop, before the fire, before everything stopped – but this was a thousand times stronger. He looked about for the professor and Lily.

Behind the skirts of the bells, four identical clock dials filled the walls, and far below the metal gantry on which they stood, four sets of mechanisms radiated out from the central timekeeper, their gargantuan cogs and springs clicking and rotating in unison.

A bullet zinged past Robert's ear. He bobbed under

the rim of the great bell, dragging John and Malkin along behind him. Four more bullets exploded off the outside of the immense dome. Then the gun was silent.

"It's empty," John said.

They scrambled out from their hiding place and a flash of red caught Robert's eye in the darkness – Lily's hair.

A few feet away, she and the professor were silhouetted against the nearest clock face, like slides in a magic lantern show. As they passed in front of its vast patterned panes, Professor Silverfish fidgeted with the empty pistol. His other hand muffled Lily's mouth. She kicked at his shins, fighting back.

Robert ran at the professor and knocked the gun from his hand. He grasped at the machine on the man's chest, pulling at the tubes, trying to loosen them, but the professor fought back. Robert stumbled; his elbow cracked against the rail of the gantry, making his teeth jitter.

John was right behind – he balled a fist and jabbed at the professor. The professor shoved Lily aside to swing at him. John stepped back and tried to weave away, but Silverfish caught him with a right hook, smacking his head against the bell with a clang. John fell, clutching at his temple, blood dripping through his fingers.

Lily swayed unsteadily, clasping a hand to her chest. As Robert reached out to her, the professor turned quickly and grabbed her again. Malkin darted forward, snapping at his heels, sinking his teeth into the man's leg.

"Get away from me, you confounded mechanimal!" Silverfish kicked Malkin aside and grappled Lily back into his grip.

Robert dived at the professor again, clinging to the lumpy device on his chest, and throwing punches around it, while Lily yanked at the pipes in an attempt to loosen them. The professor cursed and swung his arms wildly, but they clung on. He stepped back, clasping at a broken length of rail, but it gave way, and all three of them toppled off the open end of the gantry.

The impact knocked the wind from Robert's body. He lay teetering on a ledge. He gasped, clawed himself upright, and found himself standing on a narrow metal beam, barely wider than his feet, that ran from the gigantic machinery of the tower into the big centre of the clock face.

In front of him the professor rose slowly and behind him, Lily clambered up from where she'd landed. Robert was the only thing that stood between the two of them.

The professor edged towards him. "You can't win, you know. You haven't the wits."

Robert's old fears bubbled up. Perhaps the man was right. He glanced over the edge of the metal beam into the abyss below. Lily coughed, trying to catch her breath.

Robert took her hand. Far beneath them, the sharp gears of the timekeeper shifted with a click.

After all he'd been through, he didn't know if he could do this. It felt as if he still had so far to fall, but then he remembered Da's words: *No one conquers fear easily, Robert. It takes a brave heart to win great battles.*

"I've heart enough," he murmured.

"What?" the professor asked.

He spoke the words louder. "I said: I've heart enough. To win this battle."

He squared off against the professor, driving his shoulder into him, but the professor seemed to have gathered extra strength. He danced nimbly on his feet, forcing Robert and Lily down the length of the beam, until they were pressed up against the glass clock face.

"Careful," Lily said, and Robert felt her arm around his waist. Grasped against her, he could sense her heart drumming wildly through the back of his chest. The shadows of Big Ben's two gigantic hands hung above them on the exterior glass, which crackled and warped from the outside heat.

Professor Silverfish lunged, shoving Robert's head

against a triangular pane; trying to force him from the beam. But Lily clung on tight, she wouldn't let go, wouldn't let him fall.

KeRrAcK! Splinters of glass sliced into Robert's ears, as his head smashed into the pane. Blood trickled down his face and dripped onto his shoes. There was no escape. He glanced down once more and felt sick.

The drop was at least twenty feet to the VI of the clock face and another thirty to the sharp-looking mechanisms and cogs that turned below, at the heart of the tower.

Then he noticed something: the beam they stood on went out through a hole at the centre of the clock dial. An image of the inside of his da's timepieces came to him:

The movement mechanisms…the centre wheel…the rod which runs from there to move the hands on the face. Of course – they were standing on that rod, that beam! Any second now, it would turn the minute hand of the clock…

Gritting his teeth, he reached up and gripped the corner of the broken pane of glass with his fingers. "Hold on to me tight, Lily," he whispered. "Any second now…"

"Out of my way, boy." Professor Silverfish threw his full weight onto Robert. He was so close Robert could smell the stench of his breath behind his big yellow teeth. But he wasn't holding on to anything…

The minute must nearly be up. Robert grasped the

broken corner of glass tighter. Pain coursed through him until he could barely stand it.

CLICK!

The beam shifted the hands of the clock; twisting under them.

Professor Silverfish staggered back, his feet slipping, his arms waving, thrashing the air. He'd lost his balance, and the weight of his heart-machine pulled him over the edge. His eyes wide with horror, his fingertips brushed the end of Robert's arm—

And he fell.

Robert heard his echoing scream.

Then a sickening crunch; and the grinding of gears.

The tick of the clock and the clatter of movement juddered to a stop.

He and Lily stared down into the darkness beneath them, where the professor's body and his machine were mangled in the gigantic stilled cogs of the clock.

"I think he's dead." Lily shuddered, letting out a sigh of relief. She loosened her grip on his waist; and Robert found he could breathe once more. He gasped a great lungful of air and let go of the broken pane he'd been clasping.

The clock had stopped. Without the noise of its cogs turning, the room felt eerily silent. Robert took Lily's hand in his, and they stumbled along the stilled beam and up onto the safety of the gantry.

"Where's Malkin and Papa?" Lily asked as Robert helped her up beside him.

As if in answer, John scrambled to his feet behind the rim of the bell, rubbing his head. Malkin yapped, and lolloped beside him, butting him gently to his feet.

"Lily!" John exclaimed. "You're all right." And he ran over and hugged her, enveloping her in his arms. Malkin's ears pricked up and he jumped crazily in circles around them, wagging his bushy tail and aiming licks at their hands, barking happily, until Lily picked him up and hugged him too.

"Oh, my dear-heart," John said. "I'm so glad you're safe."

Lily smiled in relief, then noticed the tears as they rolled down Robert's cheek.

John and Lily pulled him into their embrace too. And Malkin, who was squashed somewhere between them, gave Robert the most enormous sandpapery lick on the end of his nose that made them all laugh.

"Thank you for everything, Robert," Lily said. "You saved us. How did you know the bar would move?"

Robert shrugged. "I remembered," he said. "Remembered everything Da taught me before he died…

Not just how clocks fit together – but how people work too. How it takes quick thinking and a brave heart to win great battles."

Tears glistened in Lily's eyes. "Well, you have those in spades," she said.

"And so did your father," John told him. "I didn't realize he was gone. He was a good man." He hugged them all once more, a proper bear hug this time, and kissed the top of Robert's head. And underneath his sobs, Robert felt a warm and tender feeling: a flickering flame of hope.

Malkin gave a loud yip. "Let's get out of here," he said, "before more trouble arrives."

"Agreed. Come, lead on, Macduff." John took their arms and they ducked under the bell and limped across the iron gantry and out of the belfry, with Malkin trotting at their feet.

Slowly, haltingly, the four of them descended the steps towards the base of the tower and the noisy chaos of New Palace Yard, and the fire crews, ambulances and steam-wagons that filled Parliament Square beyond.

CHAPTER 26

A few days later, Robert and Malkin jumped down from the number thirty-eight omnibus and made their way along the busy bustling streets of Westminster. Robert's hand was bandaged; the wound was healing well but still felt a little itchy.

Today was market day and bright shop awnings stretched across wintery blue skies, shading the pavements from the November sun. Along the centre of the cobbled street, stalls and trestle tables nestled in crooked rows, each piled high with incongruous merchandise: gas lamps next to airship anchors next to wreaths of holly and ivy; bouquets of walking sticks beside rows of watch chains hung with pocket watches ticking in unison.

Down side alleys, gangs of cog-and-bone men dealt broken mechanical parts from the back of steam-wagons.

His tail down, Malkin wove along under the carts, dodging the feet of the various stallholders, looking for rotten apples and root vegetables to sniff at and prod with his nose.

At the end of the row Robert saw a fruit stall and stopped to buy a present for Lily and her papa. He had some coins Anna had given him, for he'd been staying with her, along with Mrs Rust and the rest of their mechanical friends, while they waited for John and Lily to be discharged from the hospital.

Robert selected a few apples from the stacks of fruit, crisp and red and just about perfectly ripe. The mechanical stallholder put them in a brown paper bag for him, twirling the top shut with his big clamp-shaped fingers.

As he waited for his change, Robert heard the newspaper boy on the other side of the road shout out the headlines: "Repairs continue on Big Ben! Mystery body found mangled in the mechanism!"

Robert felt a little ill. It was a good thing they'd got out of the tower when they did, before the police and firemen had made it up there. On the ground after the crash, New Palace Yard had been in chaos and, before anything could be asked of the four of them, they'd been ushered into an ambulance and taken to St Thomas's across the river. On their journey to the hospital, Robert, John and Lily had agreed not to mention their role in the airship crash, especially not to anyone official. It would cause too much trouble and there would be too many questions to answer about Lily, Professor Silverfish and the Cogheart.

After all, no one on the ground had been hurt. Even Big Ben wasn't seriously damaged – if you didn't count the hole in the roof, or the repairs that would be needed to fix the mechanisms, and Robert tried not to count these things. It was as his da used to say: *Broken clocks can always be fixed, but broken hearts are a harder thing to save.*

Malkin's yapping brought him out of his reverie. "Come on," the fox barked, "or we'll be late to meet them."

"Just a minute," Robert said, and he bought a paper from the boy.

As they walked towards the hospital he glanced quickly over the front-page story.

Our reporter, Anna Quinn can reveal that the rogue airship *Behemoth*'s owner has been discovered. She traced the papers to a Professor Silverfish – a London resident, prominent inventor, and member of the Mechanists' Guild. It is now thought that he recently re-registered the ship in the names of two missing ex-army policemen – Misters Roach and Mould. The London Met have yet to disclose which of these three was found dead in the clock tower on the fateful day of the crash, or how the fellow fell into Big Ben's clockwork mechanism, but his body was quite mangled and unrecognizable. A further two bodies were recovered from the Thames nearby.

In the last few days, Professor Silverfish's servants and close associates have been arrested and taken in for questioning to find out more about this terrible attack on Big Ben and Parliament.

Robert stopped reading there and scanned the rest of the article because he didn't want to relive the details of that day. He'd told Anna as much when he recounted the truth to her – the whole truth – and then he'd vowed her to secrecy.

She'd kept her word. There was no mention anywhere of John's, or Lily's, or his own involvement in the air crash, or the true cause of it. Nor did Anna reveal how the professor had fallen to his death trying to kill them.

Robert knew she'd done all this on a single condition: she'd made him promise that one day, when he and Lily were older and had put everything behind them, they'd let her tell their sensational tale in a book. And Robert had agreed, for he could think of no better person to write it, and no more fitting monument to his da.

He folded the paper under his arm and followed Malkin as the fox trotted up the steps and into St Thomas's hospital.

On ward nine, they found Lily and John dressed and packing to leave. John was putting things away in a suitcase, while Lily busily transferred her mama's trinkets from her bedside into her pockets. Malkin had gone back to rescue them for her from the professor's house during the days of her recovery.

"Robert, Malkin!" Lily cried in delight as soon as she saw them. "So good to see you."

"And you too," Malkin said.

"How are you doing?" Robert asked.

"All the better for seeing you both," Lily said, and John nodded in agreement.

Robert glanced into the rosewood box and saw Lily had added the cap he'd given her and a button from his da's coat to her selection of mementos.

He stepped to the window and gazed briefly out over the river at the clock tower. Teams of men, like tiny ants, were scaling the side of the tower on hanging ropes to repair the clock faces. Robert reckoned the same was probably going on inside too, at the clock's heart, only that was invisible to anyone looking from the outside.

He turned back into the room to see Lily closing the lid of her case.

She stood it on the floor, and stepped over to give him a great big hug. "I'm so glad you're here to collect us, Robert, and you too, Malkin." She ruffled the fox's fur. "I think now I'm finally ready to go home."

Robert's face fell. He wished he could say the same. There were times in the last few days, since the adrenaline of the adventure had worn off, when he'd dearly wanted to go home to his shop and see his da again, but he knew it was not to be. There was nothing for him to go back to.

"What about me?" he asked. "Where am I to go? I have no home. I suppose I could go to my ma, if I knew where she was, but I've not heard from her in years."

John put a hand on his back. "I thought we'd discussed this, Robert? You're to come to live with us at Brackenbridge."

Robert shook his head. "Thank you, Sir," he said. "But I don't want you to help me just because you feel you have to."

Lily pressed his fingers softly between her palms. "It's not that, Robert. It's not that at all."

Then John spoke up again. "Robert, since we've been convalescing Lily has reminded me what an excellent man your da was. How brave, and how clever. He saved her life and Malkin's, and yours too. We owe him a debt of gratitude. We owe you a debt too, Robert, for *your* courage. You are your father's son and he would've been proud of what you did to help us."

John sat down on the edge of the bed so his face was level with Robert's, and looked him in the eye.

"You may not realize this, but your father and I were once friends. Seven years ago, when we first moved to Brackenbridge, he often came to the house to wind our clocks and, later, he'd order a part for me through his shop to help repair my mechanicals. On his visits we'd sit together in my workshop and talk about projects, or the clockwork things he was working on. He often told me about you: how you were getting on, learning the trade. How marvellous you were, and how proud he was to call you his son. I said to him then, if you showed promise in your craft, I'd help you learn as much as you could. Teach you how to make mechanicals, and mechanimals, as I did, and your da agreed it would be something he'd like for you. So if you decide to come live with us, I'd be pleased to teach you everything I know. What's more, I'd be proud to call you my son."

"And I'd be proud to call you my brother," Lily said.

"And I a friend," said Malkin. "Though you're still a pup," he added grudgingly.

Robert didn't know what to say. A tear came to his eye and he brushed it away with the sleeve of his coat. "Thank you. But there's Anna to think of," he added. "I've been staying with her since I was discharged. Working on *Ladybird*. She's been looking after me."

"Anna can come stay with us too, if she wants," John said. "She can moor up in the garden for as long as she likes, and if she has to go off on an adventure you can go with her, if that's where you feel your heart lies. Adventures are fun so long as you have a home to go to, and a loving family around you, when they're all over. I want you to know, Robert, you'll always have that at Brackenbridge, with us."

Robert smiled. "Then let's go home," he said.

They set off that very afternoon, Robert arranged for Anna to fly everyone back in *Ladybird*. He and Anna had been busy patching her up, installing a new quiet clockwork-propulsion engine, so it would take them much less time to fly north, even including stopping overnight to allow Lily and John to rest. They were accompanied by Mrs Rust, Captain Springer, Miss Tock and Mr Wingnut, and though Malkin said it was still a terrible way to travel, and Lily pronounced it a bit of a squeeze, Robert thought it a fun journey. With his friends around him, he found he forgot his cares for a time.

Anna and Papa got on well, and Anna told them all how pleased she was not to have to shovel coal any more, though she missed the range for cooking. "But I'm glad," she added, "that I finally got to indulge in some spectacular sky piracy, and in the skies of London, no less. Who'd have believed it?"

As darkness fell, they stopped and made camp in a field under the stars. The humans wrapped themselves in thick woollen coats, and the mechanicals pottered around collecting logs and seeing to the fire.

Lily drank in the cold air, so fresh and free from the smog of London. She and Robert were helping Anna pick up kindling, but she still felt a little lost. When she glanced up, Robert was watching her.

"What's the matter?" he asked.

She shook her head. "I'm not sure I can explain. It's as if something's still missing."

He waited.

"I wish," she said, "I wish I could be sure Papa made his choices because he loved me. Not because of a promise he made to Mama, or" – a worse thought struck her – "because he wanted to save his invention."

She shook her head to dislodge the idea. "The funny thing is," she went on, "the Cogheart could've helped so many people. Done so much good in the world. And yet he chose to keep it secret. I don't think I'll ever understand that. I mean, could it really be so dangerous?"

Robert shrugged. "Perhaps we'll never know," he said, "or perhaps you'll be the one to find out."

"I keep thinking about the choices he made," she told him. "How Mama died because of them. And I don't know if I deserve to be here. Whether I can ever be good enough to ensure her death was not in vain."

"You know, once," Robert said, "I was working in the shop, doing some repairs on a music box, and it was all going wrong. Da took me aside and told me to think of it like life: 'It looks complicated when you see all the separate pieces, but the purpose of the music box is to play joyful music. You just have to remember how to fit them together so it will. The same with life really. It's just about the living of it. That's all you have, and all you can do: live and be happy.'"

Lily smiled. "That may take a little work."

"I know," Robert told her. "Underneath, I feel the same way."

They glanced over at her papa, who was sitting on the other side of the frosted field. This man who she thought she knew, who'd saved her, but then had passed her off to various governesses and guardians, before sending her away to boarding school. She was sure he loved her, but maybe, just maybe, sometimes she wondered if he regretted his choice of saving her over Mama.

"Even after all that's happened," she told Robert, "in my heart of hearts, I'm not sure who he is, what he believes in. He's something of a stranger to me."

"So you should tell him that," Robert said. "While you still can."

Lily nodded.

Later, when they were all sitting round the fire, while Anna and Mrs Rust were busy cooking, and the rest of the mechanicals played cards on an old log, Robert and Malkin got up and went for a wander across the field, and Lily took the chance to speak to Papa alone.

"Why did you do it?" she asked, leaning closer to him. "Save me over Mama?"

He rubbed the back of his neck and looked at her thoughtfully. "I made the choice because we both loved you, Lil. She would have done the same."

Lily had her hands in her lap, but her fingers twisted against each other. "How can you be sure?" she whispered finally.

"Oh, Lily." Papa hugged her. "Before any of this, when you were very young and Mama and I were both around, we made a pact that if anything happened we'd save you first. It's a little morbid, I know, but we had to think of those things. My work – our work – was so dangerous. And there was always the chance something bad could occur."

"Mama worked with you too?" Lily asked, shocked. It was another thing he'd kept from her. "Why did you never tell me?"

"I'm sorry, Lily. Sorry I hid the past for so long, but it was so painful, and I was silly enough to think that if

355

I ignored everything that had happened eventually the pain would disappear." He shook his head. "She was a great mechanist, your mother. A great inventor. But because of what we did we had to be careful. Whenever we had to go away, and we left you with Mrs Rust, we would always travel separately just in case. Your mama always made sure to put you first, Lily. All she thought about was you. So, in that horrible moment, when you were both at death's door, and I had to make a choice, I knew who to save. Because it's what she would've chosen too. I couldn't have lived with myself if I had gone against her wishes. I loved her more than anything in this world and I feel the same way about you." He brushed a tear from his eye.

Lily smiled and kissed his cheek. "Thank you."

They watched Robert throwing a stick. He was trying to shoo Malkin into catching it for him, but each time the mechanimal shook his head and refused.

"Between the two of them," Papa said, "I don't know who's more stubborn."

"Me neither," Lily agreed.

Early next morning they flew over Brackenbridge Manor and Anna brought *Ladybird* down on the frosted surface of the south lawn in the gardens furthest from the house.

The family of friends descended from the airship. As they made their way up the steps, Lily ran ahead – she wanted to get there first, so she could greet everyone as they arrived.

She opened the front door with Papa's key, but when she stepped into the porch, she was distressed to find it filled with empty tea crates all stamped with address labels marked *Rent and Sunder*. The best furniture was clustered in the hallway, and a team of mechanical movers swarmed about, wrapping everything up in blankets and dust sheets. Madame Verdigris stood by the stairs directing the operation, while Mr Sunder dashed about, filling boxes with parcelled-up things. "Is this one for auction?" he asked as he pushed a tea crate along the hall, scratching the surface of the floor.

"I think that one's for the dump," Madame said. She was busy wrapping a vase in newspaper; when she glanced up and saw Lily, she dropped it with a crash.

"*Mon Dieu, ma chérie.* Where on earth have you been?" Madame said. "We've been worried sick. I've had to sell these things, I'm afraid. If you'd only given me your father's perpetual motion machine, we would never have had this trouble."

Lily folded her arms across her chest. "I see that," she said. "Now, before you leave here for ever, I think you'd better put everything back in its rightful place."

Madame laughed. "*Zut alors!* Don't be so ridiculous, Lily. I'm your guardian now – the last remnant of your family – and if I decide to sell these things, there's nothing you can do. Why even if your father was here—"

"You are not my family," Lily interrupted. "And you never will be. *THIS* is my family…"

She pushed aside the crates in the porch and opened the double doors to reveal Papa, Robert, Malkin, Anna and her beloved Mrs Rust standing together on the steps in front of the house. Behind them in the driveway stood the rest of the mechanicals: Mr Wingnut, Miss Tock and Captain Springer. All wound up and spoiling for a fight.

They'd been home a few weeks, and Lily sat eating her breakfast of honey and teacakes in the kitchen with Robert, Malkin, Papa and Mrs Rust. She loved this room. It was her favourite place to be.

Malkin lay curled under her feet like some furry footstool. Papa was halfway through finishing his coffee and reading yesterday's paper, and Mrs Rust bustled about behind him, whisking and frying and cooking with her various silver shining hands.

Robert had his feet on the fender, warming his toes like Lily had shown him as he busily buttered a piece of toast with his penknife. She felt glad he was here. With everything they'd been through it was good they could all be together as a family.

She snatched a teacake from the bright serving plate in the centre of the table, slathered it in butter and honey and, folding it in the palm of her hand, took the most enormous bite.

"Cog-wheels and coat hangers!" Mrs Rust clucked. "At least use a plate."

"Robert isn't," Lily complained through her mouthful.

"I am," Robert said. "I just haven't chosen one yet." He pulled an empty saucer from the table and plonked his toast onto it. "There."

Funny how everyone still complained about Lily's manners when Robert could eat anything any way he liked. But then he was a boy, and boys were always treated differently – had more freedom, got to do the good stuff – unlike Lily.

Until recently, that is. Since they'd returned, and talked more, Papa had decided not to send her back to Miss Scrimshaw's horrible academy and, instead, had been teaching her about mechanicals and engines along with Robert. Lily much preferred it to the endless book-balancing, embroidery and hair-don'ts she'd had to endure at the academy. If she could just get Papa to put Jack Door's book on lock-picking on the syllabus, she felt sure her new education would soon be complete.

"Listen to this," Papa said from behind *The Daily Cog*. "The consortium of London clockmakers who were hired to repair Big Ben have finally finished fixing the tower's clockwork…"

"What good news," Lily garbled through a mouthful of teacake. She checked the byline. It was Anna's story: perhaps that was why the aeronaut had barely visited them in the past four weeks? Or was there some other reason?

But Lily didn't have time to think about this for too long because Robert had finished his toast. "Come on, Lil," he said, standing up and brushing the crumbs from his trousers. "It's almost ten thirty. Why don't we take a walk before lessons?"

"A capital idea," Papa said. "You might be able to find a good Christmas tree we can chop down for next week. And make sure you wrap up warmly," he added. "It's colder than an icebox out there, and the forecast says it might snow again later."

"Watch springs and water buckets!" Mrs Rust muttered. "Don't you go bringing any more snow into my house. I don't want to be washing the floors again at this tocking hour of the day. I already did it once this morning."

Lily nodded and plucked her coat from the back of her chair. As she and Robert struggled into their boots, she watched Mrs Rust take down a long-handled frying pan from her selection of replaceable hands hung on the dresser, and Papa turn the page of his paper, peering at it through his glasses. Since he'd been back everything had returned to normal.

Almost: for Lily knew the truth of who she was now.

She buttoned her coat and threw open the back door. More flakes had fallen during the night and the air was sharp and cold. With Robert and Malkin at her heels, Lily dashed out into the white garden making new tracks in the pristine snow.

Her pulse quickened as she ran, and she put a hand up to her chest and felt for the Cogheart hidden beneath her many layers of clothes.

BOOM-TICK-
BOOM-TICK-
BOOM—

There it was. These last few weeks its sound had changed, become stronger and deeper; more resonant.

Until she could almost believe it might go on for ever. She still wasn't entirely sure if possessing such a heart was a gift or a burden, but she knew one thing was clear: its beat was the music of living, the rhythm of life.

And, to her, it sounded beautiful.

A dictionary of curious words

A glossary of words which may be uncommon to the reader

Automaton: a self-operating mechanical device.

Behemoth: an extremely large and powerful monster. (Which is a very fitting description for Roach and Mould's huge silver airship.)

Chronometer: a timepiece which has been specially tested to meet a certain standard of precision. ("Cogs and chronometers!")

Deportment: the way one stands or walks. At school, Lily is taught this by balancing books on her head in order to achieve the posture befitting of a young lady.

Dirigible: another word for an airship.

Harpoon: a spear-like weapon. Can be used in air combat by piercing the balloon of another zeppelin.

Horology: the art or science of studying time. An horologist is someone who makes clocks and watches.

Hybrid: someone who is half-mech, half-human (such as Roach and Mould).

The Kraken: a legendary giant sea monster. Often depicted as a squid-like creature with long and large tentacles. It is a happy coincidence, then, that Mrs McKracken's name so closely resembles this monstrous creature…

Mechanimal: a mechanical animal, such as Malkin.

Penny dreadful: exciting tales of famous criminals (such as the notorious Jack Door), detectives or supernatural mysteries, these magazines were published weekly and cost one penny (which gave them their name). They are not considered proper, but if you're sneaky, you can put one between the pages of your book.

Perpetual motion machine: a machine which will run for ever, without the need for an external source of energy.

Port side / starboard side: the nautical words for left and right. If you are standing looking towards the front of a ship or airship, the port side is the left-hand side, and starboard is the right.

Zeppelin: a type of airship. It has an oval-shaped "balloon", beneath which is a rigid metal framework filled with bags of gas to keep the ship afloat. The passenger and crew area – or gondola – is usually situated under the main balloon, and can be quite roomy. (Unless you're hitching a ride in the *Ladybird*, in which case it's a little bit cosy.)

ACKNOWLEDGEMENTS

Cogs and chronometers, this book has taken an age to write! Numerous splendid people have aided its progress. My profuse and prodigious thanks to all the following...

The tenacious early readers who gave their heartfelt wisdom, including: Richy, Danny, Sarah and Connor, the Runcible Spoons, the Blue Room Writers, the SCBWI gang, and most especially my sister Hannah.

The tremendous editorial team of Rebecca Hill and Becky Walker for their thoughtful edits and inspired characterful additions. Sarah Stewart for her capital copy editing. Katharine Millichope for her captivating cover and Becca Stadtlander for her stunning illustrations.

Sarah Cronin for her beautiful text design. Amy, Stevie and Hannah for their masterful marketing and prolific PR. Everyone at Usborne for their exceptional assistance in making it happen – you have been the perfect home for *Cogheart*.

Thanks to my super agent Jo Williamson for all her ideas and enthusiasm, and for her unwavering belief in me. To Mum and Dad for their support and inspiration throughout my many crazy artistic endeavours. And above all, to Michael for always being there with good food, great company, sensible advice and silly jokes. Finally, as promised, a big hello to my splendid nieces and nephews: Lyra, Avery, Zander and Orly; Chloe, Tiffany and Kian. I hope one day you will read this book and thoroughly enjoy it!

MOONLOCKET

by PETER BUNZL

Coming in 2017

An escaped convict.
A missing locket.
A woman from the past...

The **COGHEART** adventures
continue in **MOONLOCKET**.

And head over to
www.cogheart.com
for more magic, mechanicals
and mystery...